T0285441

Midnight Harbor

Books by Davis Bunn

Miramar Bay

Firefly Cove

Moondust Lake

Tranquility Falls

The Cottage on Lighthouse Lane

The Emerald Tide

Shell Beach

Midnight Harbor

Novellas

The Christmas Hummingbird

The Christmas Cottage

Midnight Harbor

DAVIS BUNN

www.kensingtonbooks.com

This book is a work of fiction. Names, characters, businesses, organizations, places, events, and incidents either are the product of the author's imagination or are used fictitiously. Any resemblance to actual persons, living or dead, events, or locales is entirely coincidental.

To the extent that the image or images on the cover of this book depict a person or persons, such person or persons are merely models, and are not intended to portray any character or characters featured in the book.

KENSINGTON BOOKS are published by

Kensington Publishing Corp.
900 Third Avenue
New York, NY 10022

All Kensington titles, imprints and distributed lines are available at special quantity discounts for bulk purchases for sales promotion, premiums, fund-raising, educational or institutional use. Special book excerpts or customized printings can also be created to fit specific needs. For details, write or phone the office of the Kensington Special Sales Manager: Kensington Publishing Corp., 900 Third Ave., New York, NY, 10022. Attn. Special Sales Department. Phone: 1-800-221-2647.

Library of Congress Control Number: 2023951852

ISBN: 978-1-4967-3472-3

First Kensington Hardcover Edition: May 2024

ISBN: 978-1-4967-3473-0 (ebook)

10 9 8 7 6 5 4 3 2 1

Printed in the United States of America

This book is dedicated to

The artists in my family

With love

BUNNY MATTHEWS

MARY SMITH

PAMELA EDWARDS BUNN

MACON BUNN

RILEY BUNN

DIANE BUNN

JILL BUNN

Chapter 1

Ian's overnight flight from Washington landed in Los Angeles forty-five minutes early, just in time for him to watch the pale wash of a new dawn. The same travel agent who had been handling him for years had arranged this particular trip. Which had been hugely embarrassing for them both. Flying economy. Selecting the airline and flying overnight because of the cost. Ditto for the rental car. Thankfully, no explanation had been necessary. News of Ian's recent scandals had made almost daily headlines in the local Annapolis papers. Frozen accounts. Federalist townhome going up for auction. Bankruptcy. When he'd gone by to collect his tickets, the agent had actually said it was a good time to get out of town.

Ian had become accustomed to drinking his coffee black while recording his first album. The studio had kept artificial everything—sweetener, dry milk, the works. He had soon learned only newcomers took anything in their coffee. At four o'clock in the morning, with gallons of caffeine drunk during session after session of repetitive takes, it no longer mattered what anyone put in their mug or how long the pot had been stewing. All anyone wanted by that point was the jolt. The stronger the brew, the better. Six and a half years later, Ian still took it black.

Such memories struck him at the oddest times. Like now, as he stood by the terminal's east-facing window, watching the sunrise and waiting for all his fellow passengers to grab their luggage and depart. He was fairly certain several had recognized him. Hurrying now meant running the risk of them taking selfies and, as had happened several times since the scandal broke, finding himself the latest and hottest image on Snapchat.

He took his time, drank a second cup, and waited until the sun was a completed golden globe. After all, there was no longer any reason to rush.

For the past several whirlwind years, free time had been a luxury. The first few days after his world fell apart, being liberated from his dawn-to-midnight schedule had left Ian weightless. Now, though, the hours clung like weights. Memories rose unbidden, drawing him back to the horrors that had shredded his world.

Just like now.

He remembered what it had felt like seven years earlier. The morning his former manager, his supposed friend, had called. Five fifteen, the world still dark, Ian nearly shattered with exhaustion after having just returned from concerts in Paris and Frankfurt, having flown back because he was scheduled to start rehearsals with the National Symphony Orchestra the next day. Just the same, thirty seconds after being awoken, he was dancing. Shouting into the phone, almost delirious with astonishment and joy. His album had been nominated for a Grammy. It had debuted at the top of the classical list. Number one.

Ian Hart. The classical guitarist the world had been waiting for. Handsome and gifted and possessing an almost magnetic draw. Captivating audiences wherever he went. A global star on the rise. On and on, the critics gushed. For years. Long enough for Ian to assume it was his forever.

Ian dumped his half-finished cup into the trash and started down the crowded hall. Off to begin his new life.

He was three days shy of his thirtieth birthday. Too young for the world to be carving his tombstone.

But still.

Ian collected the rental car's keys, signed the papers, and ignored the stares that followed him. The Kia had a weary four-cylinder engine and almost fifty thousand miles on the odometer. The interior smelled of old ashes and sweat, which was hardly a surprise, since the air conditioner was not up to the morning's heat. The motor moaned and coughed as he entered the freeway traffic and aimed north.

There were few things that could have forced Ian to emerge into the public eye and endure a cross-country trip. But news of his aunt's passage had come as a terrible shock. When the San Luis Obispo attorney had called and requested he fly out, Ian had instantly agreed.

From his early childhood, Amelia had played the role of loving older sister. She had brought rays of hope and a promise of better tomorrows into an era that was almost as dark and dismal as Ian's present. After his own parents had vanished from the scene, Ian had been raised by his paternal grandparents. Sort of. Ian's grandfather had considered Amelia to be a "repository of bad habits"—his exact words. Ian's grandmother had referred to her only daughter as "that wretched girl." For his tenth birthday, Amelia had tried to have herself named Ian's guardian. After Amelia lost what became a vicious court battle, Ian had been ordered never to mention the woman again.

They had, of course, remained secretly in touch. That had become much easier once Ian's star began to rise and he gained the freedom that came with money in the bank. Then Amelia's partner succumbed to leukemia, but not before they ran through almost all their joint savings in treating the illness. Six weeks after the funeral, Amelia sold their Baltimore home and moved to California. "Your star is on the rise," she told Ian when he drove her to the airport. "You won't have time to miss me."

"But why California? It's the other end of the known universe."

"That's part of the appeal. We went there from time to time. I fell in love with a quiet coastal town called Miramar. You should visit."

"I won't have any choice, with you out there." He knew he sounded disappointed, and couldn't help it.

"Everyone needs a harbor at midnight," she said. "This is mine."

When Ian asked what she meant by that, Amelia's only response was that she hoped he wouldn't need to understand for years yet. By then they were standing outside the departure gate, and she begged him to come visit. But life and success got in the way, and Ian never did. Not even when he had gigs in LA. By that point, his schedule no longer permitted side trips. Or so he claimed when they met.

Amelia never revealed her failing health. She simply continued as she had all his life. Being there for him. Just like now. He learned of her death only when the mysterious California attorney called to say he needed to come out for the reading of Amelia's will.

Just past the first Santa Barbara exit, northbound traffic on the 101 came to a complete halt. Southbound vehicles continued to thunder past. Ian followed the example of other travelers: he cut off the motor, rose from his Kia, stretched, and stood in the late afternoon heat.

He waited there for almost three hours. Long enough for exhaustion to set in. And hunger. He had been skipping meals, dining instead on worry and fears. By the time the traffic started moving again, the sunset was a faint smudge on the western ridges. Ian pushed on as far as he could, but finally admitted defeat. He took the exit for a town he had never heard of before. He avoided the Residence Inn close to the interstate and selected a strip motel that had seen better days. The manager accepted his cash payment without comment and pointed him to a diner a block farther down the street.

He took a stool at the counter and accepted the waitress's suggestion of the daily special, meat loaf. The food was hot; the serving overlarge. He walked back to the motel, showered, and slipped into bed. The walls were paper thin, which forced him to listen as two men and a woman in the next room shouted and argued in a language he did not recognize. But not even the woman's shrill voice could hold him back from falling asleep.

When he woke at two in the morning, Ian knew a moment's panic. Then he remembered the flight, the drive, the motel. His mattress had grown a lump just under his left ribs. Ian pulled the covers onto the floor and settled down once more. The darkness became crowded with terrors he could scarcely name. Going broke. Being saddled with a mountain of unpaid bills. Losing his career.

And the worst fear of all. Not caring if he ever played again.

Despite the conditions, Ian slept as well as he had since disaster struck. He woke the next morning surprisingly refreshed. He entered the lobby and paused at the sight. The adjoining breakfast room was jammed, almost every table taken. The diners all appeared to share the same surly, sullen expression. Heavy and unkempt and hungover and rough. Ian was tempted to turn away. But he was hungry, and the food was free. He loaded a plate with breakfast burritos, poured a coffee from the urn, ate hurriedly, and returned to his room. He took another shower, then carried his cases to the Kia—one suitcase of clothes and two carbon-fiber travel cases for what had formerly been his favorite guitars.

Ian then returned to the lobby. The manager had the calm manner of someone who had seen it all and found much of it hilarious. "Did you have a nice stay?"

Ian tasted several replies and settled on, "The next room spent a long time shouting."

"That would be the Armenians. They show up every week or so. Noisy, but otherwise never any trouble, I'm happy to say. They've got a relative who's a guest of the state."

Suddenly, the guests crowding the next room made sense. "There's a jail near here?"

"Prison. Jail is county. Lompoc is federal and state both." The manager smiled across the counter. "First time in California?"

Ian had actually visited the state twice before, once to perform at the Hollywood Bowl, the other time to record an album with the San Francisco Symphony. But it seemed safer to reply, "Sort of."

"Lompoc's the state's largest prison. Most of these other guests have somebody doing time." He handed Ian the bill. "A lot of hard-luck tales in that room, if you have a mind to listen. Which I don't."

Ian rejoined the highway and continued north. By the time he entered San Luis Obispo, the sweltering heat had again defeated the Kia's AC. He parked in a multistory garage and headed out on foot.

The lawyer's office was done in warm desert tones, with attractive artwork and comfortable seating and a smiling receptionist, who introduced herself as Regina and asked if she could get him anything. Three minutes later, a tall, attractive woman in her early thirties strode confidently into the reception area.

"Mr. Hart? Megan Pierce. I'm afraid I have only a few minutes. I'm between conference calls with clients." She inspected his rumpled, sweaty appearance. "I was expecting you yesterday afternoon."

"I was caught behind an accident near Santa Barbara."

"Told you," the receptionist said. Regina was a cheerful, heavyset Latina with skin the color of warm caramel. To Ian, "I saw it on the news. The tailback was over twenty miles long."

"I waited there for almost three hours," he said. "When I finally started moving, I was so tired I gave up and spent the night in Lompoc."

Both women were aghast.

Megan demanded, "Why on earth did you stop there?"

"Because I didn't know any better. I heard about the prison only this morning."

Megan addressed the receptionist. "Call the inn. See if the room is still available." She inspected him again, then asked, "Why didn't you call and let us know you'd been detained?"

He shrugged. "No phone. They cut off my service."

"Who did?"

"The lawyers forcing me into bankruptcy. They froze my accounts. Which canceled my credit cards." He watched a different light enter her dark gaze. "I thought you knew."

"Of course, we'd heard about the scandal." Megan inspected him. "Let me make sure I understand. Attorneys representing groups who were defrauded by your manager—"

"Ex-manager."

"Seek to hold *you* accountable for *his* debts."

"That pretty much sums up my life these days."

Her words took on a sharper edge as she told Regina, "Call the clients. See if they'll let me reschedule our conference for an hour later. Is Sol in?"

"Working on motions. Not to be disturbed under any circumstances. By anyone. No exceptions."

"We'll see about that."

Regina smiled. "Should I tell him you're on your way?"

"Don't bother." To Ian, she said, "Make yourself comfortable. This may take a few minutes." Megan started down the side corridor, then turned back. "When I called and you said the movers had just arrived . . ."

"They're kicking me out. I was putting everything in storage. My home is going on the block next week."

"That's what they think." She walked down to the corner office, knocked, and opened the door.

A male voice shouted, "Go away!"

"This can't wait, Sol."

"I don't have time for you!"

"Tough. You just have to make time."

"Megan, not today!"

"Sol, you want to hear this. And it has to happen now."

When the door closed behind her, the receptionist told Ian, "I love it when Megan gets mad." She lifted the phone, punched in a number, then went on, "Things were getting a little stale around here. Now you'll see the sparks fly."

When Megan emerged from the office, she entered the reception area and informed Ian, "We need to put off anything further until tomorrow. Would eleven o'clock work for you?"

"I don't have anything else to do."

"You look like you could use an afternoon off. Any luck, Regina?"

The receptionist handed Ian a typed page. "You're all set. The inn is a straight shot six blocks west."

"Their restaurant is first rate." Megan must have seen his sudden discomfort, for she added, "The expenses are taken care of."

"And Amelia's will . . . ?" he asked.

"Tomorrow," Megan replied, already heading toward her next legal fire.

Ian managed to retrieve his rental car and find the inn

without getting lost. The hotel was pleasant indeed, a sprawling old house with two arms encircling a central courtyard. His room overlooked a sparkling fountain. Star jasmine filled his room with a fragrance that passed as hope. The difference between this place and the Lompoc motel was good for a smile.

He ate a solitary meal, remembering other hotels. Huge suites filled with flowers and people and phones and chatter. Ian had always moved at warp speed, arriving late and leaving early. There had never been time to appreciate his surroundings. The complimentary bottle of champagne had usually remained unopened, sweating in a bucket filled with melting ice. Just another part of the life he had worked so hard to claim.

The sun had scarcely set when he went to bed.

It felt as though he had just fallen asleep when the whispers woke him. But the clock said it was half past one. Ian sighed his way from the bed. The vague murmurs had become an unwelcome part of far too many nights. He slipped into his trousers and left the room. The night was dry and warm; the courtyard silent except for the fountain's steady tune. He sat in a cast-iron chair and watched the moonlit water. Helpless.

These ghosts had become part of his dark and lonely hours. It was impossible to ignore the whispered truth now. The real reason why he had insisted his manager arrange for Ian to take a year off. The raging argument that had followed, the bitter incriminations, the threats which Ian had thought were bogus. Until his manager had vanished, stripping Ian's bank accounts and stealing the advances from three contracts Ian had not known even existed.

Exhaustion was the only reason he had given his manager for demanding the year off. And that was true enough. But it was also just a small part of the whole picture, the one portion he had been able to confess aloud.

Now, though, the specter of truth loomed so large, it blocked out the moon and threatened to cut off his air.

The fire had gone out.

The music that had filled his world, the ceaseless flame that had carried him through so much, it was no more.

Ian sat and listened to the fountain's melody and tasted the cold ashes of everything he had lost. His last four performances, the most recent album, the live concert aired on PBS—they had been soulless exercises. He had played with mechanical precision. Had gone through the motions, had smiled as he endured the applause and ovations. The audiences had cheered; the critics had gushed. But it was all a sham. Before each of those gigs, he vomited from the dread of enduring another hours-long lie.

So he had demanded a year off. And they had fought, he and the man who had steered him to global acclaim. And on that very first free day, when he should have been readying himself to star in Miami's annual music festival, a gig he had never agreed to do, Ian learned of the man's treachery.

And now the empty days stretched out before him, a litany of lost hours.

CHAPTER 2

The gallery was on Cañon, several blocks off Rodeo Drive. The front glass wall was framed by Brazilian granite, ivory veined with palest blue, which also covered the floor in the two main rooms. Kari stood by the front windows, examining the first painting that adorned the left-hand wall. When she reached out to adjust the frame, one of the gallery owners rushed up, flapping his arms like a wounded stork. "Kari, dear, please, I beg you. It was perfect."

She took a step away. Wrapped her arms around her trembling middle. "What time is it?"

"Precisely ninety seconds since the last time you asked." Tall and impossibly slender and incredibly well groomed, Raphael was born to rule the California art trade. Graham, his partner in life and art, served as a quietly conservative balance to Rafi's flighty ways. Somehow Graham kept Rafi from simply floating off on whatever stylish breeze happened to blow down Beverly Hills' wealthy lanes. Rafi stepped over to where he filled her field of vision. "My dear, if confronting your family with the truth frightens you so, why not let us handle this?"

The answer was, Kari wanted nothing more. But her former therapist and closest friend had insisted, in her own gentle and iron-willed manner, that Kari do this herself. And Kari knew the woman was right. Even now, when it meant stripping away the masks that had shielded her all these years.

Graham spoke for the first time since Kari's arrival. "Here they come."

Rafi started in, saying, "Kari, dear, sweetheart—"

"Leave her alone," Graham said.

"Well, really, anyone with eyes can see the poor girl—"

"Rafi, come back here and be quiet."

Graham might as well have shouted a command, given the way Rafi huffed and turned and scuttled back to the gallery's second room. Kari unwrapped her arms and took the three hardest steps in years. And stood by the entrance to greet her first guests.

The instant her father rose from the limo, Kari knew he was in one of his rages. The jerky movements of his body, the clenched jaw, the crouched position there by the limo's rear door, how the driver backed away. Justin rose from the limo's other side and spoke across the roof. Her father chopped the air between them and poured fury into his phone. All the flavors of her early years were on display in the street outside her gallery event. Her father's wrath, her brother's need to play diplomat. She watched Justin round the vehicle and gently but firmly pull the phone from her father's grasp. While Justin poured verbal oil on troubled waters, her father stomped down the sidewalk, stabbing the air with one fist. Kari remained standing there behind the glass wall. Invisible.

Justin, her older brother, was the spitting image of their father, minus the extra eighty pounds from age and living the rich life. They were both dressed in slacks from three-thousand-dollar suits, striped shirts with white collars and cuffs, flash ties. Her father's bark was audible through the closed glass doors, but his words were indecipherable. Both men lived for this. Father and son were now partners in one of LA's most successful agencies. They thrived in the hypercompetitive LA film world, masters of the only universe that mattered.

Kari's attention became held by how her reflection was planted ghostlike between the two men. She studied herself anew, starting with her outfit of midnight-blue silk slacks, matching Ferragamo open-toe sandals, slate-gray jacket over ivory blouse, pearls Kari had inherited from a grandmother she did not remember. And had never worn before this night. Her hair and make-up were courtesy of a shop Graham had selected. As she watched, the scene coalesced. The two men, the limo, Kari's reflection, the door standing between them. A portal to a tomorrow she had strived toward and feared for almost three years.

"Graham?"

"I'm here, darling."

"Would you take a photograph?" She watched him lift his phone. "No, stand farther to your right. Good. Can you shoot me and them without a flash?"

"Hang on and let's see." He clicked his phone's camera several times, then walked over. Showed her the screen. "How's this?"

"Perfect." That would become her next painting. *A good one*, she thought.

Planning her next creative effort granted Kari a remarkable sense of calm. Which in itself was an astonishment, given what she was about to do. Strip away years of ghostlike life. Reveal the woman she was determined to become.

Kari had spent her childhood skirting around the edges of her fractured family. She had had no idea what caused most of the sudden eruptions. Had known only that silence was her safest refuge from becoming a target. Their explosive rages had come with increasing frequency, heightening her desire to maintain a safe distance. When she was eleven, she traded her upstairs bedroom for the pool house. Kari had often suspected it took months before her parents even noticed the change. It was there in her little private space that Kari's dream and direction and life finally took shape.

She was almost ready when Justin handed back the phone and gestured for their father to join him. As they approached the entrance, Kari told the two men hovering behind her, "Thank you both. So much. For everything."

Graham took that as their time to retreat. "We're just a scream away, dear."

Kari took a long breath and opened the glass door. "Hello, Daddy. Justin. Welcome."

Her father entered first, gave her cheek a perfunctory peck, and said, "You look very nice, dear."

"Thank you, Daddy." Kari had mostly dressed for her mother. Wanting to avoid Beatrice's lofty disdain, the sniff, the disappointment, the dismissive shake of her head. All the actions that had scarred Kari's early years. "Would you like a glass of champagne?"

Maxwell Langham shook his head. "Can't. Not tonight." He glanced around, a quick dismissive scouting. No work of any artist on his radar. "I'm trying to understand why you felt it necessary to bring us both here."

Justin stepped up. "Wow. What did you do with my sister, and can I get your number?"

Kari hugged her brother. She had always appreciated Justin in moments like these. His ability to defuse situations with a quick wit and a swifter smile. Words had never come easy to her. "Thank you for making time."

"No problem. But Dad's right." He glanced around the

place. "If you wanted us to buy you one of these, all you had to do was ask."

Kari's father's phone buzzed. Max Langham, senior partner of IAA, International Allied Artists, checked the screen and said, "It's that idiot director again." To Kari, he said, "Sorry, dear. It looks like I'll have to be going."

As usual when her father threatened to bruise her fragile ego, Justin played the diplomat. "One of our clients is about to demolish a sixty-million-dollar tentpole feature with tantrums that defy belief."

Kari knew it was now or never. She took a very hard breath, gestured to the surrounding walls and the artwork, and spoke the words she had avoided saying for years. "This is mine."

Max had already answered the phone. Turned slightly away. Speaking in an angry murmur. But still managing to pay a smidgen of attention as Justin said, "You've bought *all* of them?"

"I *painted* them. These are my pieces. Well, they were. They're sold now."

Those were the words that drew her father's full attention. He pulled the phone slightly farther from his ear but allowed his son to forge ahead. That was their habit. Max let Justin enter the unknown fray first, so Langham senior could hold back, observe, find the weakness. Then together they smashed the opposition to bits. Theirs was an almost perfect partnership.

Justin demanded, "Sis, we don't have time for jokes."

"This is my work," she repeated. Partly for herself. Tasting the words, coming to terms with how it felt. "I paint under the name Kariel."

Her father said to his phone, "I'll get back to you." The phone squawked angrily as he cut the connection, pocketed the device, and frowned as he watched his son step forward.

Not so much to study the art as to scrutinize the *other* things displayed on the walls.

As in, no prices.

Instead, all the unframed items had little red flags attached to the walls beside them. All but one in the front room said simply SOLD.

Justin said, "This is for real?"

Her father's gaze swept around the gallery. Landed on the two men hovering by the second chamber's entryway. Watching nervously. Their gazes fastened on Kari.

There for her.

Justin said, "Pop, check this out."

Kari had expected this would happen. Even so, it hurt. She stood in the room's center and watched the two men step forward. Not toward her paintings. Instead, they were drawn by the items hanging between each artwork.

Rafi and Graham had selected the most explosive articles, then had had them varnished onto stone slabs that matched the gallery's floors. One such news item hung now between each of the front room's paintings.

Max and Justin stood shoulder to shoulder, her father squinting while he fumbled for his reading glasses. The article came from the *Charlotte Observer*. It was Rafi's favorite, which was why it had been blown up to three times its original size and now dominated the wall closest to the entrance. The headline read, INVISIBLE ARTIST DEFIES CRITICS. Underneath was the subheading: THE AUDIENCE HAS SPOKEN. KARIEL IS AMERICA'S PREMIER NEOREALIST.

Justin turned around. Scanned the other articles. Newspapers and magazines from Sacramento, Minneapolis, Vancouver, Houston, Miami. Medium-size cities, second-tier papers. Most acknowledged how the critics despised Kariel's work. They all went on to say basically the same thing.

Despite the critics and their disdain, Kariel's work was a global phenomenon.

Justin pointed to a work on the opposite wall. A young man pushed a laughing child on a swing. The little girl had the faintest hint of wings. The two were joined by a curving rainbow sweep of lavender. "My secretary just hung this poster on her wall."

Rafi couldn't hold back any longer. He stepped forward and said, "We're doing limited signed lithographs of all the works you see here. Most are already sold, but if you're interested, I'm sure—"

Graham said, "Rafi."

"Well, it's true. They need to know."

Kari said, "This is Rafi and his partner, Graham. They own this gallery. And they serve as my managers."

The words emerged just as her mother entered the gallery. Even so, Kari's announcement held both men's full attention. Justin was the one to say, "Your managers?"

"They're responsible for everything that's started to happen," Kari explained.

"What utter rubbish." Rafi waved at the walls, clearly pleased. "All we've done is help find this wonderful artist the audience she so richly deserves."

Kari's mother was followed by her new husband. Pierre Solvang was a highly successful producer, and his Lamplighter Studios was home to Max's highest-profile current project. Which meant Kari's father was forced to behave. Such rare times when LA's social events brought them together normally cost Max dearly. Tonight, however, his attention remained elsewhere.

"How much do these run?" he asked.

Kari had expected the question. Known it was coming. Whenever her father backed projects that were despised by the critics yet were financially successful, his response was always the same. Art was a line at the box office in Kansas City.

Just the same, it hurt. This was the first time Max had ever viewed his daughter's work. And their price was really all that mattered.

Rafi answered for her. After all, he had been shielding Kari her entire career. "Prices vary enormously, of course. But it is a moot issue, I'm afraid. Kariel's work is reserved for the next several years."

"People buy them sight unseen?"

"Oh, no. They can't *buy* a work. The price can't possibly be fixed until the work is completed. They *reserve* the right to acquire."

Father and brother were focused on the gallery owner. Which clearly miffed Kari's mother. Justin said, "And that cost . . ."

"Five thousand dollars," Rafi replied. "Nonnegotiable and nonrefundable."

Her brother pointed to the largest painting in the front room, the only piece without a SOLD sticker. "This one, it says, 'Reserved by the artist . . .' "

"I've begged and begged her to let me have it," Rafi complained. "I've been offered just a *staggering* sum for it. But your sister simply will *not* listen to reason."

It finally dawned on Kari's mother what she was hearing. "Justin, darling, what is this man saying?"

"Kari did these, Mom. She's a painter."

"Well, of course she is. It's all she's ever done with her life—"

Pierre Solvang clapped his hands. "Kariel! Of course! My daughter absolutely adores your work. She has one of your prints in her apartment living room and another in her office!" He walked forward, ignoring his irritated wife. "Kariel. My daughter will go crazy! May I shake your hand?"

"I'm sure I don't understand," Beatrice said. Her response

to any uncertainty was a haughty disdain. "Kari, dear, what on earth . . . ?"

Rafi saw Kari's rising level of anxiety and bounded forward, inserting himself between his client, the producer, and his new wife. "Good evening. I am Raphael, your daughter's manager. I believe Kari has a surprise in store."

"That's all well and good," Beatrice snapped. "But I want—"

"Kari, dear, the gala starts in twenty minutes."

Graham spoke for the first time since the family's arrival. "The waiters need to set up. And our first patrons are standing outside." He pointed to a cluster of elegantly attired people peering through the locked glass doors. "My dear, you need to hurry."

It was the perfect excuse to step away from her family's rising tension. "Please come with me."

The second room's back wall held just three paintings. Kari had long considered Rafi's greatest gift to be how he lit his canvases. The delicacy and precision made the trio appear luminous, as if they themselves possessed a light all their own.

Three and a half years after the first articles had started classifying Kari's work as American neorealism, she remained uncertain how she felt about the label. The concept had originated in South America, where for decades artists had used graphically precise renditions to protest, to rage, to shout defiance at corrupt systems and drug-dominated rebel cultures.

Kari had no desire to rebel against anything. But she kept her comments mostly to herself, since Rafi and Graham both seemed genuinely delighted with her label.

One thing Kari could definitely say for certain was that she had a visceral loathing for art that rejected identifiable forms. Streaks of random colors left her cold. She also disagreed with contemporary artists who rejected any positive emotion and treated their canvases as a means of creating conflict or tension or a looming dark edge.

She despised it all.

So it should have hardly been a surprise that the critics responded in kind.

When the teenage Kari had applied to the top West Coast art schools, she'd had little idea how deeply entrenched the current trends happened to be. She had simply painted what she liked. What she wanted to see.

All the schools had rejected her, of course. Their caustic criticisms, the harsh manner with which they dismissed her work, had very nearly crushed her in the process.

There followed a year of drifting through clouds of ashes only she could see. Until Kari was rescued by her friend.

Everything that came after, all the work and growth and passion, led to this point. Standing in the center of Rafi and Graham's second gallery. Watching as waiters pushed through the doorway leading to the office and the kitchenette, bearing tables wrapped in linen cloths. Glasses clinked as they were lined up along the temporary bar. Spicy fragrances drifted through the open door, and laughter from the chefs preparing hors d'oeuvres.

The three paintings were images taken from Kari's favorite childhood memories. One was on the beach at Malibu; another sailing on Lake Tahoe.

Justin pointed to the third and exclaimed, "That's us."

"It is, yes. All of them are."

"I remember that day! I wanted to talk with . . ."

"Ariel."

"But I was afraid. You said I should give her flowers." He smiled at the recollection, two children surrounded by a springtime garden, the young Kari tying her hair ribbon around a bouquet held by her brother. "Ariel was the most beautiful girl I'd ever seen. I was what? Eight?"

"You were ten. I was five."

"These are great, Kari. Really."

She watched her brother study the painting and remembered. Justin had been her family's lone voice of diplomacy and reason, at least some of the time. He shared their parents' ability to explode in nearly blind wrath. But in his case, Kari could usually identify the reason and knew in advance when to flee. So long as Justin got his way, or no one stood between him and his immediate goal, his attitude toward Kari remained placidly cheerful.

She told her family, "I want you to have them. One each. You decide."

"Really, daughter," her mother protested, "I fail to understand why we're learning about this only now."

Rafi chose the perfect moment to call, "Kari, the press are here. And photographers."

It was a most excellent reason for Kari to rush her words. "I'm leaving LA. I've found what I think will be my new home. I'll contact you once I'm settled."

All three started to protest. But Graham was already ushering her away.

Kari said over her shoulder, "I leave tomorrow."

CHAPTER 3

Kari lingered in the front room, allowing the media to photograph her alongside one painting after another. A television crew positioned her by the front room's unsold picture, Kari's favorite. A reporter whose gaze was as lacquered as her hair asked empty questions. Kari scarcely heard her own answers.

When the pros were done, the fans crowded in. Eager for selfies with the painter who had never before revealed herself. Kari remained mildly astonished at her ability to handle the attention, the conversations, the interviews.

Dr. Indrid Anand, the woman who had done so much to help shape the woman Kari had become, drifted quietly around the two rooms. Kari's parents had never met the woman who had effectively saved her life. To them, Indrid was just another well-dressed visitor. Kari watched Indrid return time after time to the unsold painting. Most times, Indrid found it necessary to wipe her eyes. Which would have probably had Kari reaching for a tissue herself had so many cameras and strangers' gazes not been on her.

Finally, her family prepared to leave the gallery. Quick hugs from her father and her brother. A kiss to her cheek and a final complaint from her mother. Her first ever hug from Beatrice's second husband.

As Kari accompanied them to the door, Justin asked, "Do you know what you're doing, leaving town like this?"

The answer was, she had been planning this step for over a year. Ever since her growing success had offered Kari the financial wings necessary to escape. But she replied as he probably expected she would. "Do I ever?"

Then the door closed, and she responded to her mother's final glare with a smile and a wave. Finally, she could turn away and walk over to where Indrid stood in front of the unsold painting.

Her dearest friend said, "I heard them talking. Your mother tried to be snippy with Raphael."

Which was precisely the sort of reaction Kari had expected from Beatrice. Tonight, though, her mother had probably got exactly what she deserved. No one did snippy better than her manager. "What did Mom say?"

"How nice it was of them to host her daughter's little event."

It should not have hurt as badly as it did. She had endured a lifetime of such comments. But still. "And?"

Indrid did an almost perfect rendition of Rafi at his insulted best. "Oh, madame. It's an *honor*. After all, your *daughter* is a *global star*. You must be *so* proud."

"Rafi just earned the night's biggest hug."

"It left your mother so angry she actually played nice with her ex. They've basically agreed to gang up on you once this is over."

"I'm not giving them the chance," Kari replied.

"Your mother intends to force you to stay in LA." Indrid was watching her now, gauging Kari's response. "She called it just another of your misguided escapades. I fear your father and brother agree."

"I said I was leaving town tomorrow, and I will," Kari said. "But I've already packed everything I'm taking. I won't be going home. Rafi booked me into the Courtyard three blocks from here."

"Booking his star artist into a Courtyard," Indrid said, smiling. "Rafi must have broken out in hives."

"My car is already parked in the hotel garage," Kari went on. "Sienna is sulking in the room."

"Who?"

"My kitten."

"Since when have you owned a pet?"

"Since last month. Rafi and Graham's cat had a litter. Sienna is a Persian-Siamese mix. It was love at first purr."

"A traveling companion. How nice for you." Indrid took hold of Kari's hand. "Now, be a dear and introduce me to your world."

As they slowly toured the two rooms, Kari found herself recalling what she had come to consider the signature event. The moment when her life finally, at long last, began to come together.

Throughout her early years, the fear of unleashing yet another bout of rage pushed Kari ever further into silent isolation. Gradually, this silent drifting around the edges filtered into other aspects of her life. At school she rarely spoke. When she entered her teen years, Kari became ever more focused on the one thing that held her. The one passion that made her feel whole.

But after the shocking and hurtful responses from the art schools, Kari refused even to consider applying elsewhere. At seventeen, Kari had no money, no friends, no apparent interest in leaving home. And in the eleven months after the schools rejected her, she did not paint. Or draw. Not once.

At seventeen, her life was defined by worries. Her mother was defiantly involved in the affair that would soon wreck her marriage. The pool house, Kari's refuge, was lined with half-finished paintings and empty canvases, shards of her former passion. Now that she had stopped painting, what was she to do with all the empty days?

Would she ever paint again?

As she drifted mouselike about their home, Kari began hearing her parents use the I word. *Institutionalize.* At first, she didn't understand what was happening. But days turned to weeks, and the word became an increasingly familiar component of their arguments.

She was almost ready when Justin approached her. Playing the diplomat, seeking an alternative to having their parents lock up his only sister. He gently asked if she might be willing to speak with a therapist.

Knowing the alternative was just beyond the horizon, Kari agreed with a speed that surprised them both.

In truth, what she most wanted at that point was someone who could tell her what to do. Who might show her a way to change all the gray days into something with color. Who could show her a compass heading. Something.

Even so, the closer it came to that first appointment, the stronger grew Kari's dread. When she finally entered the therapist's outer office, she was ready to throw up.

But in that first moment of sitting down across from Indrid Anand, Kari . . .

Settled.

The impossible invitation was there in the room's pastel calm, the woman's penetrating gaze. Indrid Anand's first words were, "Anything you tell me, anything you wish to share, whatever happens within these walls, it remains absolutely between us. Do you understand what that means?" When Kari responded with a nod, Indrid asked, "Can you please interpret that for yourself and tell me in words?"

"Whatever happens in here is confidential."

"Exactly. Very good. Do you believe me?"

Strangely enough, Kari did. "Yes."

"I'm so glad. Just to be clear, anything I discuss with anyone else must first be approved by you. And that agreement will cover only the explicit issues or thoughts you wish to share. Nothing more. Agreed?"

"Yes."

"Very good. So how do we begin? Do you have any questions for me?"

She did, in fact. "Where are you from?"

"My parents are both Punjabi. They fled the disputed territory along the India–Pakistan border. I was born here. Along with my three brothers. I am the youngest." Indrid was in her midsixties and possessed the stately grace of a thousand undistilled generations. "May I ask a question of my own?"

"I guess. All right."

"If you could declare your number one ambition, your true life's theme, what would that be?"

Kari struggled to breathe around the sudden great balloon that had filled her entire being. The therapist probably assumed Kari hesitated because she didn't know how to respond. And before entering this chamber of secrets, that would have been her own true response. Now, though, Kari knew instantly what she wanted to say. What made her hesitate was having this supposed stranger from a far and mysterious land knock on Kari's secret door.

Indrid waited with her. Unblinking. Intense. There with Kari in utter totality.

Finally, Kari said, "I just want to get one thing exactly right."

The words seemed to push Indrid back in her seat. "How absolutely delightful. Tell me, Kari, do you know what that one thing is?"

Whenever Kari looked back on that moment, she recalled actually hearing the secret door open. The portal creaked and shuddered and scattered a year's painful dust.

But it opened.

Kari asked, "Can I use your pad?"

Indrid was seated so close to Kari, their knees almost touched. She reached back and lifted the yellow legal pad from her desk. "Pen or pencil?"

"Either. No, both."

The side wall behind Indrid held shelves, mostly filled with books and a collection of antique bowls in copper and bronze. But there were also two sets of photographs. Both held collages of young boys growing from gap-toothed childhood to marriage. To either side were two additional pictures, both of infants. Kari assumed these were Indrid's grandchildren.

She drew. It flowed so easily, the images and intent so clear in her mind, all those empty months might as well not have existed.

The infants Kari drew in ink. A minimum of lines. Unfinished brilliant blue sketches of new life. Strong and vivid.

Indrid, she drew in pencil. The therapist held both children in her lap, an act not shown in the photographs. In fact, Indrid was not in any of the pictures. Kari drew the woman as Indrid already appeared in her heart—both strong and caring. A woman capable of giving love and showing compassion, no matter what.

Kari drew her leaning forward slightly, studying the two babies. Calm. Knowing. Loving.

Too soon the creative moment ended. Too soon.

"I'm very sorry, my dear. But our time has ended. Perhaps you can . . ." Indrid stopped speaking when Kari handed back the pad.

Kari sat and watched as Indrid's motions slowed. For the first time in what felt like forever, Kari was truly content.

Tight little sparks, aftereffects from releasing the creative energy, jolted her body.

Indrid sniffed. Wiped her face. "I've never cried in a session before. Afterward, yes, not often. But it happens." She looked up and inspected Kari with eyes of rain-washed opal. Even now, so early in their relationship, Kari's new friend knew exactly what to say. "Your family . . ."

Kari nodded. "They can never know."

Kari had long ago realized she was not, and never would be, normal. Whatever that word meant. But in the eight and a half years since first walking into Indrid's office, Kari had found a distinct peace in two hard-learned lessons.

The first was, she was far from unique.

The world was full of fragmented souls. That was especially true for a place like Los Angeles, where the beautifully broken came seeking the film world's special form of redemption.

Drifting around the periphery of her family's universe, Kari had observed any number of so-called stars. Who viewed their newly happy existence through the lens of success. As long as the world remembered their names.

All the others, though, faced the terrible daily challenge of viewing a hard-edged world through crystal shards. Just like she had in those awful months after the art schools rejected her work.

Kari's second realization was she had found a way to knit together all her own broken pieces.

In the hours spent within her creative fire, Kari was as close to whole as she would probably ever come. As a result, her art remained her most precious treasure. And everything came down to protecting the gift. Crafting a time and space and seclusion where the gift could rise up, consume her, and *be*.

Which was why she had not revealed her secret life to her family until the day of her departure. Even now, as the gallery crowd began to thin, the small voice continued the same fretful whisper that had plagued her since she'd agreed to this public display. That she had made a terrible mistake. Revealing herself was an act of self-destruction.

Especially to her family.

Kari let Indrid set the pace as they toured the two rooms. This was her fourth exhibition in Rafi and Graham's gallery. Indrid had attended them all, either alone or accompanied by her husband. This was the first time Kari had ever attended, first time she had allowed herself to be identified as the artist. Before, she had come to the gallery only on the days before the opening and had fretted over the hanging of her work, not complaining, but distraught. Eventually either Rafi or Graham always ordered her out.

Before, she had watched the openings from a coffee shop across the street. From time to time, while her work hung on the walls, she would scurry up and down the sidewalk, passing in front of the gallery. Hiding her face behind a cap and oversized sunglasses. Not going inside. Never, never, never.

The fact that she had cast aside her secret mantle and revealed herself to the world left her breathless.

Indrid asked the occasional question, but mostly, she viewed the works in silence. Kari was beyond grateful for the chance to share this moment with her dearest friend. Indrid had remained her therapist for only nine months. Far too short a time, as far as Kari was concerned. But Indrid had been insistent, repeating the same response to all Kari's pleadings, speaking the words so often they became a mantra. Kari did not need therapy. She needed a friend. Which was what Indrid had remained to this very day.

She had also refused to accept any of Kari's paintings.

Indrid had framed the pen-and-pencil sketch of herself

with the two grandbabies and had hung it in her living room. Anytime Kari had offered something more, Indrid had insisted this memento honoring their first meeting was all she would ever need.

So Kari had painted what she hoped Indrid would be unable to refuse.

The two babies, now nine and ten years old, were again painted in vivid blue. But the brushstrokes were vague; the forms incomplete save their faces. They watched the woman holding them with solemn trust.

Kari had tried a new technique in shaping Indrid's image. First, she had created a hazy collage of grays, an indistinct shadow figure that melded into the background. Kari had then taken an iron-tipped pencil and drawn Indrid's actual form into the wash. A single colorless deep line that depicted the woman holding the infants, meeting their gaze with her own.

By the time they returned to the front room and again stood before the one unsold painting, most of the other patrons had departed. Waiters moved quietly about, cleaning up. Rafi and Graham stood with two old friends in the back room, laughing and gossiping about the latest scandal making headlines in the LA art world.

Kari said simply, "This is yours."

Indrid gazed at the painting and said, "I can't possibly accept it."

"Fine. There's a Russian oligarch who told Graham he'll basically pay any price. Rafi says he's suitably awful. Big and hairy and he smells of vodka. He'll pay cash. Then he'll hang it in some corner of his superyacht. Which he keeps in Dubai."

"All the nice things I've said about you over the years," Indrid said, "I take them back."

Kari struggled to find some way of saying what she felt.

Such words had never come easy, if at all. But this time she needed to knit them into the bond that joined them. "You are why I can do this. Be here. Meet the world. Speak with my family. To say thanks just isn't enough. I did this for you. It would mean the world—"

"Stop. Just stop." Indrid wiped her face. "I could not love you more if you were the daughter I never had."

CHAPTER 4

Morning dawned bright and clear and cool, as if determined to lift Ian's mood. He dressed and entered the breakfast room with a clear head. The night's hard confession had left Ian facing the day with a semblance of calm.

After breakfast he went for a long and meandering stroll through the maze of old San Luis Obispo. The burdens he had carried since his manager's disappearance had not vanished. That would be far too much to ask. But for the first time in what felt like forever, Ian was able to ignore them, at least for a while. The town's heart was charming, a lovely throwback to bygone California. After a time, he had the feeling that Amelia had joined him. Walking the quiet tree-lined lanes. Introducing him to part of her adopted world.

During his early years, Amelia and her partner had lived a fast and expensive life. Soon after her partner's death, Ian's aunt had written to say she was unable to make the promised journey and join Ian for a live concert, because she was short of funds. Ian had sent her a check by return mail, glad his growing success allowed him to be generous. Six months later, his grandfather passed. The old man left the family's Annapolis town house to Ian. His will did not even mention their only daughter.

After weeks of deliberation, Ian decided to keep the home. He brought in an architect and ordered a total redesign, hoping that by gutting the place he could strip away memories of his wretched early years. He sent his aunt a check for half the home's value, never mentioning his grandfather's final vindictive act. Amelia, in her wisdom, did not ask.

When Ian returned to his room at the inn, he found a message from the lawyer, asking him to show up half an hour early. Ian showered, hurriedly dressed in his least wrinkled clothes, and set out.

When Ian entered the law office, Regina greeted him with a smug smile and the words, "There's someone who is desperately interested in making your acquaintance."

A man about Ian's age was already rising from the sofa. "Mr. Hart, I'm Danny Byrd. A real honor."

Ian was swamped by the dread that had been dogging him now for weeks. But Byrd did not look like a reporter. He was tall, well dressed, very fit. And intense. A man on the move.

Danny asked the receptionist, "Would you tell Megan—"

"I'm here." The attorney then stepped into the reception area and offered, "Good morning, Ian. May I call you that?"

"Of course."

She turned to the other man. "Give us a few minutes, Danny."

"Megan, you know how tight our timeline—"

"Danny. Sit. Wait." Gentle but firm. Like she was ordering a well-trained pet. "Ian, come with me, please."

She led him down the side corridor and stopped by the corner office's closed door. "I'm sorry about that. I intended to speak with you before Danny arrived. But he showed up early." She knocked, opened the door, and asked the man inside, "Ready?"

"Yes. Good." An older gentleman rounded his desk and walked over. "Mr. Hart, I'm Sol Feinnes. Can I offer you a coffee?"

"I'm good, thanks."

"Please, have a seat. My wife and I have been fans of your work for years. Megan told me about your current situation—"

"What I know, which isn't much," Megan corrected.

"The sort of tactics you've experienced are a disgrace," Sol settled into a chair opposite them. "I take it you don't have legal representation?"

"I can't afford any," Ian replied. "Not with my assets frozen."

"Like I said, a complete and utter disgrace." Sol was a heavyset gentleman in his fifties, balding and fit. He had the air of an aging boxer readying himself for the next fight. And he seemed genuinely angry over Ian's state. "I'm due in court, but first I wanted to personally address your issues. May I dive straight in?"

Ian glanced at Megan, whose attention was now focused intently on the older gentleman. "Sure thing."

"What you need to understand is this. Opposing counsel has no intention of ever bringing your case to court."

"They've already had the judge set a trial date." Ian pressed a fist to his gut. Fighting back the gorge, an act that had become all too familiar. Sorry that the good feelings had not lasted longer than they did. "Nine weeks from yesterday. My home is scheduled to go on the block five days later. They're already showing—"

"Won't happen," Megan said, interrupting. "Not in a million years will they go before a judge and reveal what they've been up to. Which means their threat of an auction is bogus."

"They seek to pressure you," Sol continued. "They want you to find a way to cover the missing funds. And, if possible, show a direct and ongoing connection between you and your manager."

"I have no idea where he is. Well, I've heard Aruba, but— "

Sol waved that aside. "I've had a word with a friend in Baltimore. She is a well-known trial attorney. She is more than willing to sign on."

"I don't understand."

Megan said, "We want to take your case."

"But I can't pay you."

"We'll handle this on a contingency basis." Sol glanced at his watch. "Sorry. Megan will walk you through the terms. I need to be going."

When Ian remained silent, Megan asked, "Is this agreeable?"

He swallowed hard, forced out the words, "This is amazing."

Sol rose to his feet, offered Ian his hand. "My wife and I saw you last year in Dallas. Your performance, it gave the music wings. Perhaps you'd join us for dinner sometime?"

Ian nodded.

"Good. Now I've got to dash."

After Sol departed, Megan asked, "Are you sure I can't get you something?"

"I don't believe this is happening."

"We're a long way from certainty about how the finish line will look," she warned. "You'll probably be forced into some form of mediation. Which means compromise over reimbursing some part of the missing funds. Right now, it's important you take this in stages. Be prepared for what may be a long haul."

Ian took a long breath. It felt like steel bands had been released from his chest. "Okay."

"First things first. We need to access your accounts, halt their pretense of stealing your home, and show these jokers they can't railroad you into bankruptcy. But that, too, will take time."

"How long?"

"Certainly a few weeks, possibly longer. Which brings up my next question. How will you make ends meet until your funds are freed up?" When Ian did not reply, she went on, "Do you intend to restart your career?"

"No." He felt all the tumult rise until it threatened to cut off his air. "I need a break from the whirlwind my life's become. Desperately."

"Does that mean you wish to step away entirely from music?"

The internal turmoil only grew worse. "It's all I know. All I have." He swallowed, then corrected, "All I had."

Megan spoke with the calm deliberation of a professional long accustomed to handling difficult issues. "Back to the key question. Until we can unfreeze your accounts, how will you live?"

"I haven't thought that far ahead. I know it sounds silly, but all this has hit me so fast . . ."

"I imagine Sol will guarantee a loan, if that's required."

"No. No more debt. What about Amelia's will?"

Megan hesitated, then replied carefully, "You probably don't want to rely on your aunt to see you through this period."

Ian pondered a long moment. "I suppose I could teach. To be honest, though, I'm not happy with the idea. I loathed most of my instructors."

"So you are not intending to back away entirely from your music. Is that what I'm hearing?"

"I can't. Not and eat."

"In that case, I wonder if you'd allow me to suggest an alternative."

"Absolutely."

Megan rose to her feet. "Why don't we shift this over to our conference room?"

They emerged from the office to find the young man pacing the reception area, typing into his phone as he walked. Regina smiled at Ian and said, "Danny, dear, you can stop sweating now."

Danny's head popped up. He stowed the phone and bounded over. "Did he agree?"

"Danny, no, of course not. I haven't even asked . . ." Megan swatted at the young man's shoulder. "Can you dial it down a notch?"

He started to reply, then noticed Regina's grin. "Nice to know I'm entertaining somebody here."

"Isn't that your job? You being the big-time Hollywood producer and all." The receptionist shooed them away. "Go play nice."

Megan ushered them into a smallish chamber holding a pale-wood oval table and six chairs. When they were seated, she started, "Danny is a producer of medium-budget films. He has a problem— "

"Call it what it is." Danny jerked his chair in tight little quarter circles, a drumbeat of nerves. "We're in total crisis mode."

"His current project is for CBS— "

"Correction. The CBS subsidiary Paramount Plus."

"Excuse me. Who's talking here?"

"It doesn't do us any good if you tell it wrong." But they were both smiling now. "Is it my turn yet?"

"Go ahead, then." She pretended irritation. "I'll be ready to interject when and where required."

"Thank you so very not at all." To Ian, he said, "We've been shooting a mystery romance in Vancouver. Which ran over time and over budget. First time that's ever happened to me."

"An old-fashioned flu bug swept through the shoot like Armageddon," Megan said. "Except for the lad here. Who stayed irritatingly healthy throughout."

"Too busy to get sick," Danny replied. "The problem is, we're pushing to meet a fixed airdate. Edits were going solid. Rough cut approved by the studio."

"When disaster chapter two struck," Megan said.

"Three days ago, our music director was felled by a heart attack."

"He's okay," Megan said. "Which is a true relief. He's a wonderful man. And a friend. But he's almost eighty, so it gave us all a terrible scare."

Danny continued, "The problem is, if I tell the studio, they'll send in one of their in-house guys."

"Totally last century," Megan said. "Danny calls their idea of a good score 'creamed strings.'"

"Think Lawrence Welk with attitude," Danny said. "Thanks to our guy, we already have the primary musical elements in place. The opening score is completed, plus five great songs that perfectly suit the key scenes. Mostly old hits redone in a modern style. All unplugged. By that, I mean no electronic—"

"I know what unplugged means," Ian said.

"Right. Sure. What we don't want is the CBS idea of how to score the bridges, the spans joining the major musical moments."

"Danny fears their replacement would serve up a huge helping of musical glop," Megan said. "And because it's okayed by his bosses, he'd have no choice but to use the mess."

"The story's pacing is very sparse, very light," Danny said. "The music needs to match this."

"It's already a beautiful film," Megan added. "When I saw the rough cut, I cried."

"What we need are those musical bridges," Danny said. "We'd like to have five, ideally six, but we can work with three. Link the story's key moments where the anchor melodies play out. Amplify the tempo of these lesser scenes."

"I know this is not what you were expecting," Megan said. "If you need time—"

"I'll do it." Ian had no idea how he felt about the task itself. But against his own financial vacuum was Danny's desperate urgency and Megan's deep concern. This woman who wanted to take on his case. The man she clearly loved. They needed him.

Doing the right thing for his newfound allies was the perfect reason to agree.

Not to mention how he would be spared the need to teach.

The couple took an almost easy breath.

Danny said, "I can pay you six thousand dollars for each segment that we use. I know it's not much, but that's what we've budgeted—"

"Excuse me," Megan snapped. "My client will receive ten thousand. Whether you use the segment or not."

Danny looked horrified. "You know I can't do that."

"You are asking Ian Hart to help you out in a crisis," Megan replied. "You can do it, and you will."

"Megan—"

"Plus residuals."

"What happened to protecting the interests of your client the over-budget producer?"

"You're not my client anymore. I warned you when I accepted this little item." She wiggled the finger holding a diamond ring. "You're Sonya's problem now."

Danny leaned back. "I actually don't know what to say."

"Then we're in agreement?"

"Seven."

"Nine."

"Eight, and that's final."

"Eight per each segment you ask him to work through. What you use in the film's final cut does not enter into this discussion. He gets paid for each segment that you record." She held up her hand. "If Ian's music doesn't suit you, you can stop after the first track. Which we know won't happen. Plus residuals. And *that* is final."

"You are the absolute toughest negotiator I've ever had to deal with." Danny tried for a glare, but his grin broke through. "I agree. But only if we can start this afternoon."

CHAPTER 5

The reading of Amelia's will took no time, really, for the document covered less than three typed pages. Megan then handed over a slender envelope holding a letter. On the envelope was the one word *Ian*. She offered to leave and give him time to read, but Ian refused. Amelia's farewell needed a different setting than a lawyer's conference room. There followed almost an hour of signing documents, for Ian was accepting ownership of Amelia's apartment and taking over her mortgage. Which was ludicrous, given his current financial situation. But Amelia wanted him to have it. Her condo and a small sum in her checking account were all she had to give, and she had left everything to him.

The journey north was pleasant enough, with a crisp, salt-laden wind blowing strong off the unseen Pacific. Ian drove with all the windows down, finding at least temporary comfort in the day. The afternoon sun shone brightly on broad valleys and gently sloping hills. Yet the evidence of drought was everywhere. Verdant lowlands and blooming orchards alternated with parched fields and the white bones of leafless trees. Too many of the slopes held the dark stains of previous fire seasons.

Ian had no idea how he felt about playing music that afternoon. He had not picked up a guitar in almost six weeks, the longest he had gone without playing since forever.

Several of his performances had been adapted into film scores. But he had never helped put one together. He had to assume the work was possible. And that was not the point.

The simple fact was, he needed the money. Megan had assured him anything he made from this point forward could be kept separate from all the pressure the Maryland attorneys were exerting.

And that was not the point, either.

Ian liked how the drive helped him see clearly. Beyond the shame and wounding and loss and stress. By the time he entered the town of Miramar, he felt as if one key element of his day had become clear.

What he had told Megan was the absolute truth. Music was all he knew. But working on the film score represented something far more profound than simply making ends meet. He was entering a new phase. The separation from his former existence was happening. The question he needed to ask now was both direct and perplexing. What form was his life supposed to take?

He followed Megan's instructions, driving along the town's northern boundary, up a gentle slope, and into the parking area fronting three apartment buildings. He left one guitar and carried his other two cases into the central structure. Amelia's one-bedroom apartment was on the top floor, which granted a lovely view over redwoods and magnolias and the rooflines of Miramar's miniature downtown. He stood in the small living room, smelling his aunt's fragrance in the still air. Missing her.

An extra set of keys dangled from a hook by the front door. Ian decided to leave hunting for his aunt's car until later. Danny had stressed the need for punctuality, and he was already late.

Ian took the envelope holding Amelia's farewell letter from his pocket. He was pretty sure how he wanted to read the letter, and it was not here. Nor would it be on some winding hillside road, or while waiting for the next segment of his day and life to take shape. The woman who had seen him through so much deserved a final moment that was in keeping with the life she had cherished. A good bottle of wine, perhaps listening to one of the show tunes she and her partner had so adored. Ian would toast his best friend amid a nice crowd of happy faces and show no shame over the tears he might need to shed.

For the moment, it was enough to prop the unopened letter on the small dining table. He stared at it for a time, then rummaged through the kitchen for a pen and notepad. He wrote the thought that had crystalized during the journey north.

I am done racing toward the challenges of tomorrow, chased by the mistakes of yesterday.

He left his words there beside the letter. Satisfied with how Amelia would like his first act of defining whatever came next.

The hill holding Amelia's apartment backed onto a much higher ridge. They were separated by a broad valley containing orchards, horse farms, and a meandering country road. Following Danny's directions, Ian climbed the steep ridge to the top, then drove north on a narrow lane until it ended at a pair of ornamental gates. Ian rose from the Kia and pressed the buzzer below the camera imbedded in the left post.

"Yes?"

"Mr. Rowe?"

"Who's asking?"

"Ian Hart. Danny Byrd said I should—"

"Yes, yes, I know all about what Daniel said and what Daniel wants." The voice was elderly and British and cantankerous. "I have one question I'm going to put to you, lad. Shift over a smidgen so I can see whether you lie with grace. Now then. Answer wrong, and you can bloody well traipse back down that hill. Listen carefully. Are you going to give me trouble?"

Ian liked the man already. "No. No trouble."

"Because I've heard all I care about you and your antics."

"No antics. Not today."

But the old man wasn't done. "I'm in no mood for some star traipsing in here, putting on fancy airs and acting like king on the hill. You'd be asking for trouble, mark my words."

"I've had all the trouble I can bear," Ian assured him. "All my fancy airs have been stripped away."

"That bloody well better be the truth, or you and Daniel are both going to catch the sharp end of my tongue."

"Are you going to let me in, Mr. Rowe?"

The gates buzzed. "I'm making a terrible mistake. I can feel it in my bones."

The estate was California modern and contained several single-story structures of stone and wood and glass. A bespectacled man in his late sixties or early seventies stood on the flagstone walk, his ratty sweater buttoned up incorrectly, reading glasses dangling from a cord around his neck. He scowled as Ian rose from the car, then said, "I suppose we might as well get this over with."

Ian collected his guitar case from the trunk and followed the man past a narrow lap pool to a cottage by the rear wall.

Its stone façade was almost lost behind a veil of some climbing flower that Ian did not recognize.

According to Danny, Arthur Rowe was a highly successful editor of big-budget films. He had retired to Miramar and now treated Danny Byrd's projects as a well-paid hobby. Danny considered himself the most fortunate of producers and treated the editor with the reverence Arthur expected and probably deserved.

Arthur unlocked the front door and said, "I suppose you'll be wanting tea or coffee or some such. Don't go asking for champagne, because you won't bloody get it."

"Coffee would be great." Ian stepped through the entrance and gaped. "Whoa."

The structure contained a full-scale recording, mixing, and editing studio. Its two rooms were divided by a glass wall, along which ran a digital mixing board, four massive flat-screens, two freestanding keyboards, and an array of electronic editing equipment. This front room also featured a kitchenette, sofa, leather captain's chairs, and a long table. Speakers shaped like narrow pyramids rose on either side of the mixing board, while four JBL professional-grade boxes hung from the room's four corners. Two rear windows overlooked a steep descent, the town of Miramar and, farther out, the glistening Pacific waters.

The second room, the recording studio, held more equipment. Everything had been laid out with a delicate precision. Ian took in the dozens of mikes and stands, the movable walls for either singers or drums, the Steinway grand. "This is an amazing setup."

Arthur busied himself at the coffee maker. "This is hardly the first project that's entered into last-minute meltdown."

"I've recorded albums in worse studios."

The old man was clearly pleased. "I very much doubt that."

"With a full symphonic orchestra."

"Now I know you're pulling my arthritic leg." Arthur kept his back to the room as he continued, "You do understand we won't be using everything you play."

"Of course."

"And there's no score for you to work off."

"Right."

"We're after secondary melodies. Musical bridges that come and go as the story requires. Woven into the film's tapestry. A gentle pastel thread that's always heard but seldom consciously acknowledged."

"That is beautifully put," Ian replied.

"I've wanted to say that for such a long time." Arthur handed Ian a mug. "Sit yourself down and let me play the initial songs we've selected."

The first was Pink's "What About Us," a melody Ian had loved from the very first hearing. The second was Major Lazer's "Lean On," sung by Elise Trouw and backed by the Scary Pockets studio band. Long before the second song ended, Ian understood why Danny's former music director had selected both the tunes and the order. The two songs shared a distinct harmony and the tempo trended upward, hopefully drawing the audience with it.

When the second song finished, Arthur asked, "Again?"

"Not yet. How long is the gap between those key scenes?"

Arthur studied him a long moment, then replied, "Nine minutes, eleven seconds. Too long for the score to go silent."

"How long should my filler run?"

"No idea, lad. Can't answer that until we hear whether you're able to give us something we can use."

Ian nodded. That made sense. "Can I hear the other songs?"

Ian drank his coffee and listened as the soundtrack took shape. Arthur's only comments were to offer the time between melodies. Moxura's "Love of My Life" was followed by Joss Stone's edgy version of "I Put a Spell on You." Then came Paul Carrack's "How Long." Several more melodies followed, ending with Fleetwood Mac's "Go Your Own Way."

When the room went quiet, Arthur asked, "You want the story?"

"Not really. But it would help if you could give me the emotional threads between those first two songs. I'd like to focus on that initial bridge, please."

Arthur tapped a keyboard, drew up a script with his notes in yellow along the side. "The first song begins inside a mounting emotional storm. The two main characters come as close as they possibly can to an almost torrid love scene. They both want to get it on. Desperately. But there are issues. So in the end they don't."

"Got it." Ian rose from his chair. Unlatched his guitar case. "And the setting for the second melody?"

Arthur was watching him now. "Our poor lad grows suspicious that things aren't what they seem."

"Tough."

"He certainly thinks so. As the story develops, things go from bad to worse. Then the lady gets herself into a truly desperate pickle, which is when he finds out he had the whole thing wrong. There's a great deal of drama going on, mind. Action and risk and some very nasty types." Arthur was watching him as Ian tuned the instrument. "Shall I run through the songs a second time?"

"Let's go ahead and get me miked," Ian replied. "Then play me just the first song."

Arthur cocked his head to one side. As if needing to inspect Ian from a different angle. "Sure about that, are you?"

"I am, yes." He opened the door leading to the recording studio. "Soon as you're ready, why don't we take this music for a stroll?"

* * *

Ian settled onto the padded stool at the center of the recording studio and positioned the three mikes according to Arthur's directions: One was directly in front of his instrument and not quite touching the central sound hole. The second was a foot farther back, while the third was positioned ten feet away, high up and pointed straight at the ceiling. The result would be a deeply resonant sound, one Ian had loved from the very first time his music had been taped.

Arthur was seated behind the mixing board on the glass wall's other side. He insisted on minute adjustments to both the mikes and Ian's tuning until his guitar completely matched the song's harmonics. Ian came to admire the editor's professional demeanor. Gone was the caustic grumpiness. They were moving in sync. Like they had worked together for years. Which was both good and bad. Good because Ian assumed whatever he played would be precisely recorded. Bad because the work pushed Ian further and further into unwanted memories. He knew there was nothing to be done about it. He endured as best he could until finally Arthur said, "Ready for take one."

"Play the first song."

"And the second?"

"Not necessary." Ian tapped the side of his headphones. "Play it only through these. Go ahead and start recording now."

Arthur's glare returned. "Ordering me about now, are we?"

Ian was almost grateful for the need to retreat from all the hard memories. "Let's pretend I inserted a 'please' where you think best."

"Right, then." Arthur's hands became busy with his board's many controls. "Take one, beginning in three, two . . ."

* * *

Ian had identified three riffs, or repeated musical patterns, that formed the key emotional threads to that first song. When the melody ended and his headphones went silent, he began repeating them. First one, then the other, then the third. They were simple enough to form a background to his rising memories. He did not welcome the recollections, but here on this hallowed ground, he did not even try to push them away.

Originally, a riff was known as an ostinato. In classical music this formed a subtle repetitive phrase intended to help the listener feel comfortable with the symphony's more complex structure. The ostinato would be played by one instrument after another and would remain in the background until the final climactic movement, when it was taken up by the entire orchestra and shouted in farewell.

The term *riff* was first used by jazz musicians in the twenties. These musical patterns were usually less than four bars long and were intended to stand out from the very beginning. Riffs formed the foundation for most instrumental solos, as well as becoming a key element that was repeated by the singer, often in the refrain.

When he was ready, Ian returned to the first riff and began weaving a tapestry of his own. *What about us*? Pink sang in his head, and he formed contrasting patterns in response. *What about us?* He tried to focus on his music and succeeded at least a little. The memories remained a soft chorus in the background, but for this brief period, they remained free of their heavy emotional burden. Still vivid enough to call across the years. Drawing him back to the early days.

Seven years old, in second grade at the boarding school where his grandparents had deposited him. His class trooped dutifully into the music room. The previous year, they had endured hours of musical appreciation in this classroom, listening to classical music, which most students hated, being interrupted by lectures, which they hated even more. The teacher, Monsieur Lachard, was an acerbic Huguenot who drank. Most of the students loathed Mon-Sewer. The feeling was mutual.

Today the front table was lined with a variety of instruments. Ian endured a dozen or so students who trooped dutifully to the piano in the corner and hammered their way through one awful melody or another. A few others then selected instruments and were defeated by the violin or the flute or the trumpet.

Ian waited.

Finally, the class was dismissed. Ian remained seated as the students gleefully departed. When it was just the two of them, Lachard began wiping down the instruments and packing them away. Then he pretended to notice Ian. "You there in the back. What's your name, boy?"

"Ian Hart, sir."

"I suppose you want to torture me, as well, eh?"

Ian nodded and pointed to the miniature six-string guitar propped on its stand. Waiting patiently in the corner, almost hidden by the portable blackboard on rollers.

Lachard glanced at the instrument, snorted softly, then went back to cleaning the trumpet's mouthpiece. "Go on, then."

The music room was always open, as Lachard's piano students were required to practice at least three hours each week. Ian came before breakfast, when the classrooms were empty and the halls silent. His love for the guitar was already a living, visceral thing. Now he touched the strings one by one, making sure they were still in tune.

That alone was enough to turn Lachard around.

Ian played a rendition of Franz Schubert's "Erlkönig," a song he had loved from the very first hearing. Schubert was best known for combining classical structures with the romantic. He died at age thirty-three, most likely from syphilis, leaving behind more than six hundred compositions. "Erlkönig" was a chamber piece designed around Goethe's poem by the same name, and was one of the instrumental pieces that established Schubert as a genius ahead of his time. Ian had heard some of this in Lachard's lectures. He was most likely the only student that had paid careful attention, hidden there in the rear row. He had loved Schubert's striking use of ostinatos, especially the one depicting the furious gallop of horses that formed the poem's rhythm.

When he finished, Ian discovered Lachard had seated himself behind the front table. There was a moment's silence, and then the teacher demanded, "You accelerated after the coda. That was a mistake."

Now that he had finished playing, Ian could not stop trembling. "I don't understand."

Lachard squinted angrily. "Who teaches you?"

"No one."

"Don't you dare lie to me, boy."

"I come in before breakfast. I sit here. I play."

Lachard studied him a long moment. Somewhere beyond the closed door, a pair of students shouted their laughter. A bell rang, signaling the start of the next class. Neither of them moved.

Finally, Lachard demanded, "When is your free hour?"

"Two o'clock."

"Can you read music?"

"No, sir."

Another long silence, and then Lachard rose and opened the rear cabinet and sorted through stacks of well-worn texts. He drew out one the size and shape of a child's coloring book. "You will memorize every page."

The cover was creased; the pages were sticky from a multitude of hands. "Yes, sir."

"Give me the instrument." He propped himself on the

table, then raised his left leg to support the guitar's body. He played an exercise with drumlike precision. "Did you see what I did?"

"Yes, sir."

"Show me."

Ian took the instrument and copied Lachard. Or tried to.

"No, no, no. That is rubbish." Lachard seemed genuinely angry. "You do not *interpret.*"

"I don't understand."

"You play the exercise exactly as I did. You do not weigh the notes. No emotion, no interpretation, no lazy actions. That way leads to wrong habits. You do it *exactly* as I do. Each note precisely the same as all the others. Give me the instrument." Ian did. "Now listen carefully." Lachard played the exercise through twice more. "Now you."

Ian tried again.

"No, that is awful. It is lazy. It is a child's method. You will come in every morning, and you will play this. For one hour. Nothing more. No exceptions. You will learn discipline and good habits. Your time of lazy playing is over."

And so it began.

Ian remained captivated by Pink's plaintive melody for what felt like hours but probably was only a few minutes. Then Ian gradually shifted to Elise Trouw's softly lyrical version of "Lean On." Ian gently pushed the tempo and elevated the harmonics, and they flowed upward, carried by the melody only he could hear, until it was time for the second song to take center stage.

Finish.

When he went silent, Arthur sat behind the mixing board, watching him through the glass partition. Immobile.

Ian leaned forward and asked through the guitar's upper microphone, "How was that?"

Arthur jerked slightly, then glanced at the digital timer on the wall. He touched a lever on the mixing board, and his voice came through speakers embedded on either side of the connecting window. "You played for nineteen minutes, seven seconds."

"Far too long," Ian said. "Sorry. I was having fun."

"Were you now?"

"It's been a long time . . ." He waved that aside. Not yet. Not here. No need to break the happy spell. "Can you use it?"

Arthur scratched the hair curling beneath his earphones. "You do realize we'll cut that down to two, maybe three minutes."

Ian nodded. "Sorry to give you extra work."

Arthur squinted at him. "I'm thinking we'll add electronic keyboard, maybe a stand-up bass and flute. One segment was crying out for some backup power."

"Sounds like a great idea."

"Does it now?"

"What's the matter, Arthur?"

"'What's wrong?' the man asks. Well, lad, I'll tell you. When Danny called to say he was sending you up, I insisted he was making a terrible mistake. We don't have time to work with some vagrant star like your good self. And I won't put up with tantrums. I told Danny I had left all that sordid mess in LA. Along with stars who think they know enough to tell me my business."

Ian leaned his guitar on the neighboring stool and used a towel draped over the music stand to wipe his face and neck. "I'm glad he insisted."

"Not only that, Danny used the one argument I had no choice but to accept. He said even if you proved to be the complete and utter pain I knew you'd be, all I needed to capture was thirty seconds. Less. Then I could boot your good self out on the street. We'd still have Ian Hart's name to use in the film's publicity. Right in the middle of all the world dining on your misery. Surely I could hold my breath through a thirty-second take, Danny said. Now I ask you. How in blazes was I supposed to argue with that?"

"That's a tough one."

"There you are. So now I'm sitting here behind my little apparatus with *nineteen minutes* of *solid gold*. Shame on you, lad. I hate being made to look like a cantankerous old sod." He began shifting the mixing board's controls. "What say we go for a take with songs three and four?"

Two hours later, Arthur sent him away. There were decisions to be made, he said. Choices that didn't involve a musician who was intent on making Arthur eat his words. Arthur moaned over how Danny would no doubt laugh himself silly and then remind Arthur for *years* how wrong he'd been about Ian. Arthur said all this while resting his hand on Ian's shoulder, accompanying him back around the house.

When they entered the forecourt, Arthur stopped and squinted at Ian's ride. "And what exactly is this?"

"A rental. Old and tired and smelling of too many other hot drivers."

"It's a death trap with four tires. An insult to good cars everywhere."

"With my financial situation, it was all I could afford. I'm pretty sure my aunt has a car I can use."

"A unicycle would be an improvement on that." Arthur watched him settle his guitar in the trunk. "And what were you planning to do tonight? That is, assuming you make it down the hill in one piece."

"Stop by the grocery, go to my aunt's place, open cans, and collapse."

"No, no, we're not having any of that." He pointed at the

unseen town beyond his garden wall. “You hop on down to Castaways. Ask anyone in town, and they’ll tell you where to go.”

“Arthur—”

“Tonight’s a special occasion, one you shouldn’t miss. There’s a local pianist, another star who doesn’t put on airs. I have a place reserved at the bar, but now with what you’ve just handed me, I’ll be too busy to attend. I’ll call and set you up. Go have yourself a good meal on Danny. You deserve it.”

CHAPTER 6

It had all started simply enough.

Several years back, Rafi introduced her to a Santa Monica arts group. There were over a dozen such collectives in her hometown. Hundreds more scattered through greater Los Angeles. But this one was a rarity.

These artists were also successful in some aspect of the film world—graphic arts, storyboarding, CGI formatting, PR design, photography. The reason they gravitated here was the group's rules, which were both strict and rigidly enforced. All conversation was limited to painting. Any mention of the outside world, any pitching of a story, any discussion of a project, any photograph, anything of the sort, and they were barred from the group for life.

The members soon grew accustomed to Kari's reserve. She wasn't the only one who preferred silence to casual conversation. The group contained a number of stars, top directors, senior film executives, and producers. Such people craved time away from the constant chatter and pressure. Successful film people were constantly inundated with tasks and requests—scripts to be read, projects to review, financial packages that needed a name to reach completion, photographs to consider, stories to mull over. The barrage was as constant as rain. Having a place where they could remove themselves from the spotlight, dress down in a floppy hat and oversized glasses, shield themselves behind easels, become part of a group who respected privacy, who shared their passion for interpreting the world with colors and brushes, was priceless.

Monthly dues were steep, and almost everything was spent on travel and teachers. Rafi probably had a word with the art group's director, for any time they brought in a member of the dark-edged artistic elite, Kari was alerted and granted a chance to retreat. Either she did not attend at all or she attached a sheet to the top of her easel, which she would flip over her canvas every time the visiting instructor came within range.

Some in the group knew of her success. They treated her with the same delicate respect they showed the stars. Kari made a few cautious friends, attended a few parties, even went out on dates. She had always enjoyed the company of men, so long as there was no connection to what she called the film world's snatch-and-grab attitude. But her more intimate relationships ended badly. Her first journey to Miramar came after one such breakup. She was astonished at how intense the pain was, how physically ill she felt over a lost love. She signed on to the overnight trip to Miramar in an act of desperation, hoping to flee her misery, at least for a weekend.

Instead, she found a haven. A place she had never dreamed might exist. A world that she desperately wanted to claim for her own.

That first afternoon, Kari declined an invitation to dine with the class and spent hours walking the town's heart. Almost hoping the intense draw she felt would fade. If it didn't right away, this would give her an excuse to stay a few more days on her own. Then she would put it down to a pleasant interlude and travel back by train, her happy memories stowed away, glad to have found a place she might visit from time to time, nothing more.

Ha.

She proceeded down to the shore, strolled along the beach-front path, went back up the main street. It was when she stopped for coffee and a sandwich that she finally admitted defeat.

Every step, every *minute*, the sense of belonging grew stronger still.

The next stage came together with astonishing ease. Rafi and Graham took childlike delight in shopping for houses. This process became a vital means of calming her internal waters, for it was in this same period that Kari accepted Indrid's counsel and agreed to participate in the gallery event. Throw her coveted anonymity aside. Reveal herself to the world.

The idea of a home that might become her secret haven became increasingly important. The online inspection of homes in and around Miramar took on a special flavor. She was doing this. She was doing this *now*.

The home she selected was a case of love at first glance.

The old farmhouse sat at the end of a meandering valley lane. It had been stripped down to a weather-beaten shell and then resurrected as a two-bedroom haven. Old walls had been stripped out, as well as the original ceiling. The result was a series of large, interconnected spaces forming the kitchen, dining room, and living area. A new garage was tucked around to one side. Behind it was a miniature replica of the house itself, intended as a guest cottage. And beside that . . .

Her studio.

The barnlike structure had been plucked from her most secret dreams.

The weathered exterior gave way to a huge internal space, full of light from tall windows on every side, plus a massive skylight, all of which were shielded by electronic blinds. A small bath was tucked in one corner. The video presentation suggested it as either a sound studio, a viewing room, or a gym. Kari knew otherwise.

She bought it the next day.

Kari left her motel room as dawn etched silhouettes from the quiet city. She checked out and poured a coffee from the lobby urn. She had no interest in waiting for breakfast. She was far too nervous to eat. Kari dwelled in some nether region, the borderlands where fear and excitement and dread and joy all met. She settled Sienna's wicker basket in the passenger seat and started off.

As Kari drove along the silent street, she decided the moment and her emotions were all too potent a mix. She was filled with the urge to use these impressions in a new work. A block past Rafi and Graham's gallery, she pulled into a parking space and rose from the car. The electric stabs of fear that had jolted her during the night were gone now. Standing there in the breathless quiet, Kari felt it all gradually come together.

This was why she was leaving her safe little niche in other people's world. So she could have moments like this. Making a slow circuit of Cañon Drive, using her phone to photograph the gray city's silhouette, mentally sketching the artwork to come.

The Beverly Hills street would be a mere shadow image. By contrast, the people would possess a brilliant clarity. A child. No, two children holding hands. A couple walking behind them, also linked. A family so full of happiness and love, they positively shone in primary colors. While the world of shops and cars and wealth, the things other people treated as important, as *real*, was reduced to a vague predawn silhouette. Just like now.

When the new image was firmly fixed in her mind, Kari settled back behind the wheel and started the motor. As she pulled from the curb, Sienna emerged from her basket. The sleepy kitten padded across the central console, settled into Kari's lap, and purred.

Kari joined the freeway and headed north.

Kari had driven the LA freeway system only a few times and never by herself. Her intention was to make it past Ventura before the early rush-hour speeders began their morning commutes. Her only scary moment came after she passed the Getty and started down that steep, steep slope, with two semis and a concrete mixer for company. Her car was nearly new, a Mercedes GLB. She liked the high-up driving position almost as much as the car's color, a metallic periwinkle blue.

Past Thousand Oaks, another climb and descent, then Ventura's multiple exits, and the freeway merged with the coastal road for a long narrow stretch, with cliffs to the east and the Pacific glistening off to her left. She stopped at a Starbucks in Santa Barbara for coffee and a pastry, almost giddy with the sense of adventure just beyond the freeway's next bend.

She had often come up here with her art group and considered Santa Barbara a border territory. Walking the streets, observing the region from behind the safety of her easel, she had recognized any number of people from her father's realm. Santa Barbara was home to many successful denizens of the film world, stars and directors and producers powerful enough to have others come to them. But she was safe here. Such people had not taken much notice of her when she had attended parties and festivals at her father's or brother's insistence. They were blind to her now.

What lay north of Santa Barbara was, quite simply, another world. She had heard locals call it the Middle Kingdom. As far as Kari was concerned, no title had ever fit a region better.

Looking back, Kari was filled with solemn awe at how she had managed the maze of home ownership. The answer was equally astonishing. Gradually, her tight little solitary world had been pried open to include others. People who were there for her. People who went out of their way to make her feel comfortable with the next incredible step.

Graham had dealt on several occasions with an attorney in San Luis Obispo, the closest real city to Miramar. Megan Pierce was fiercely intelligent, with a competent manner that had calmed Kari during their very first Zoom call. Megan had clearly been comfortable representing a young woman who was buying a home sight unseen, for cash, in a town she had visited only once. The attorney had not only handled the required documents but had helped anchor Kari to earth.

As she passed San Luis Obispo and took the county road north, Kari put on a favorite album, *Ian Hart Plays Segovia*. The traffic was very light; the road so empty she could let her mind drift. Kari found herself thinking back over her most recent conversation with Megan. Up to that point, all queries from the building contractor, Noah Hearst, had been passed through the SLO attorney. Kari had refused to involve herself in any details regarding the home's interior. So many areas where Noah had wanted her input—the kitchen cabinetry, bathrooms, floors, windows, lighting fixtures, drawer handles, the walkway, the grout and tile colors. Kari had found the decision-making both frightening and baffling. She had determinedly held her distance. Then the week the home was finished, Megan firmly suggested it was time for Kari to connect with the man responsible for creating her new home.

When the Zoom conference opened, Kari saw the attorney's familiar face alongside a strong-featured man in his forties, tanned and weathered by a life spent outdoors. Megan introduced Noah, then said, "I was in Miramar three days ago and stopped by the house. Noah is both a builder and an artist."

Noah had a surprisingly gentle smile. "Nice to finally meet you, Ms. Langham."

"Noah was a film set designer in a previous life," Megan said.

He nodded. "I know a couple of agents who share your name. Justin and Max. Are they any . . ."

When a flash of very real fear on Kari's face silenced the builder, Megan asked, "Is something wrong?"

Kari began the tragic process of backing away. "Maybe this is all just a terrible mistake."

"Kari, does your family know of this acquisition?" Megan studied her frozen expression, then asked Noah, "How much contact do you have with your Hollywood friends?"

"None at all," Noah replied. "And most of them are no longer friends."

"Noah's company was legally stolen out from under him," Megan explained. "The partner he had trusted with his professional life stabbed him in the back."

"I haven't returned to LA since signing the final documents," Noah said. "I hope I never do."

"My senior partner, Sol Feinnes, is now partners with Noah in a yacht," Megan went on. "Sol is the most honorable man I have ever met. He would never enter into such a venture with anyone he did not trust."

"Say the word," Noah told Kari. "I will never mention who bought the house. Ever. To anyone."

It was the concern they showed her, the respect for her

situation, even when they did not understand, that convinced Kari and allowed her to say, "I am trying to make a refuge. Somewhere totally private."

"I doubt anyone will understand that better than I do," Noah said. "The original farmhouse was where I retreated after leaving the Los Angeles nightmare behind. I'm selling only because my wife is running a surgical ward at the San Lu hospital."

Megan said, "I think you should trust him to honor your wishes, Kari."

A long moment, a pair of uncertain breaths, then, "All right. Thank you."

But Megan wasn't finished. "So your intention is to keep your family at arm's length. Is that correct?"

"My family can't ever know where I am."

"Perhaps you should think about using me as a cutout," Megan suggested. "All contact goes through me."

"This is possible?"

"Oh, absolutely. My firm performs this service for several highly successful individuals."

"I would like that," Kari said. And added, "I need it."

"Consider it done." Megan addressed the builder. "You had something you wanted to ask Kari?"

"Absolutely. Whatever you don't like about the home's interior, anything that doesn't suit, I'm happy to change." When Kari started shaking her head, Noah asked, "Did I say something wrong?"

"If somebody wanted me to repaint a segment of a finished canvas, I'd refund their deposit and ask them to never contact me again."

"Lucky you."

"I want to honor your work the same way I honor other art that is precious to me. I want to study it. Take my time. Absorb everything I possibly can. Let it take its place at the deepest level of who I am."

He wiped one side of his face. Up and down. Very slowly. "Kari . . ."

"Yes?"

"The key will be under a planter by your front door."

Her door. *Her* home. Kari shivered. "Thank you, Noah." As she started to cut the connection, he called her back. "Yes?"

"I was wondering, could I invite you to dinner? A friend of mine is playing at Miramar's premier restaurant this coming Friday."

"It's always a sellout night," Megan said. "The atmosphere is Miramar at its finest. Not to mention the food."

Kari found herself captivated by the sensation of new friends. It required no effort whatsoever to reply, "That sounds nice. Thank you."

Kari had not returned to Miramar since deciding to purchase her home. She wanted to arrive when life's new canvas was hers to paint. She had waited. Worked. Kept herself busy. Endured the nights of fears and thrills and uncertainty. So she could do this now: Turn through the valley gates and drive slowly, slowly down the narrow lane. Savoring every moment of her arrival.

The northern ridge was scarred by fires from some distant season. Down below, everything was silent and still. Watchful. Low-slung houses set on big lots. Several had boats parked in their drives. A dog barked once, then went quiet.

Her new home stood at the end of the lane. The gray-white exterior remained similar to how it had been for three-quarters of a century. The windows were new, as was the railing that framed the wraparound porch. And the rockers. Two of them. Positioned beneath broad-blade fans, which rotated slowly in the hot breeze. Varnished hands waving her forward.

She parked and sat for a long while, not so much studying the house as coming to terms with the fact that it was now hers. She might have remained there all day if Sienna had not planted her front paws on Kari's right arm and mewed.

Kari opened her door, lifted out the kitten, carried Sienna inside. Returned for the padded basket where Sienna liked to sleep, her bowls, food, and covered litter tray. She entered the kitchen without really seeing anything, filled both bowls, then walked back outside. She took a long breath, surveying the silent valley. When she was ready, she entered the house again. And looked.

The home had been kept to its original size, but the interior had been reconfigured into just two large rooms. The kitchen-dining-lounge area and the main bedroom were floored in broad redwood planks. Noah had rescued the wood from an office building undergoing redevelopment. The open ceiling of pale oak was framed by varnished beams. Kitchen and bathroom cabinetry of pale blue with white trim. Gray-blue counters and matching tiles. Kari walked slowly from room to room, the kitten padding at her feet.

The sight left Kari breathless.

Behind the main house rose the three other structures, connected to the rear porch by fired-brick walkways. A new cottage matching the home stood well off, there to house any overnight guests. And a garage built in the same weathered style.

And then there was the third structure.

The old barn had been transformed into a massive single room, lined with narrow cathedral-style windows and floored in polished concrete. The distant ceiling held a trio of skylights and multiple light fixtures that could be dimmed or swiveled by controls set beside the main entry. Another set of switches controlled the pale blinds for both windows and skylights.

As she left the atelier and checked out the guest cottage, children shouted from some yard. A dog barked in response. The sounds made her shiver.

The home, the outbuildings, the space they contained, all this was hers to shape. But first she had to come to terms with Noah's artwork in and of itself.

She imagined most people would think it silly, wanting days and probably weeks to absorb the empty spaces. They would most likely be out already, buying items to fill the rooms, reshaping and decorating and laying claim. Kari saw things differently. Noah's sculpture of wood and stone and space was a delight in and of itself.

The builder had left her an unexpected gift. Four rocking chairs of polished oak, two on the front porch, two out back. Kari stroked the top rim of one and thought it was just like the man she had never met. His silent "Welcome home," an invitation to sit and rest and revel in what was now hers.

The moving van arrived thirty minutes later. As soon as the driver stepped from the cab, however, Sienna fought to be released, squirming and pushing against Kari's hold. She opened the kitchen door and allowed the kitten to scamper inside.

Kari had brought the absolute basics, the very few items required for day-to-day life. A Japanese-style pallet for sleeping, one set of sheets, a few chairs, a kitchen table, the necessary utensils and basic plates and cutlery. Along with that came everything her art required—easels, stretched canvases, drop cloths, paints, brushes. And the paintings she was not yet prepared to part with, fourteen in all.

When the movers left and Kari returned to the home's rear porch, Sienna stood inside the rear screen door, mewing. Kari picked up the kitten and seated herself in one of the polished rockers, overwhelmed by the enormity of it all.

Her home.

CHAPTER 7

Ian returned his rental car to the local office and took an Uber back to Amelia's. The keys hanging in her foyer fit a Honda CR-V he found in the main parking area. It had more miles on it than the Kia, but Amelia had always treated her car as a pet. He showered and dressed in his last remaining clean clothes, retrieved her letter from the kitchen table, and took a long look at his own scribbled declaration. *I am done racing toward the challenges of tomorrow, chased by the mistakes of yesterday.*

Then he set out for town.

Miramar's main street was a gentle slope easing its way toward the Pacific. Castaways Restaurant occupied a lovely position near the town's center. The old-timey California structure's smiling hostess apologized that she could not offer him a table, as they were fully booked, and declared that for Arthur to have given up his customary spot at the bar meant Ian must really be in good with the old grouch.

Ian assured her a seat at the bar would suit him fine. He accepted her recommendation of sea bass in a white wine reduction, with saffron rice and fire-roasted asparagus, then ordered a glass of wine, waited until her attention turned elsewhere, and brought out Amelia's letter.

Even before he unfolded the two pages, he knew he had been right to wait for this time and place. She was there with him, savoring the noise and the people and the fragrances and the laughter. Amelia had always loved a good party.

Dearest Ian,

It's just as well we have this final chat by letter. You and I were never much for harping over the sad times. Of which we've both had too many. I hope you're reading this somewhere fun and happy. All in all, I've had a good life. And though I'll miss you so very much, these days everything hurts, and it's time. Writing does not come easy, for these very same reasons, which means I must be both quick and to the point. If I hurt your feelings as a result, I apologize, dear boy. Know I do so out of love. I hope with all my heart that you will find your own way to joy. Something I fear you have not experienced nearly enough.

This past year, I've watched you change. Your music remains good enough to fool most people. But sooner or later, they'll recognize what I'm already seeing. They always do. And unless you see this first, they'll come down hard.

I'm leaving you my little place in Miramar, hoping you'll stay here long enough to find yourself. And do so before it's too late. If the wolves of your world have already attacked, come here and heal.

I have always thought of Miramar as my midnight harbor. It's the place I feel you need now, the haven where you can retreat when the winds are harshest, life's storm is at its most violent, and no other place offers the refuge you so desperately need.

You possess a very special creative fire, dear boy. It is so very rare, so uniquely yours. You lost it somewhere in the rush and stress of your life, and you must find a way to rekindle this. You must. It is your most precious trait.

I asked Megan Pierce to try to make you come out for the reading of my will. I did so because I feel you need to step away from your world. May you find a healing peace, as I have, here in Miramar. If so, stay until you are certain the fire has been restored. In the meantime, enjoy life, the wonderful Pacific, the people. Raise a glass of something special. Play a favorite tune in my memory. Know I will love you always.

Amelia

Ian slowly folded the letter and slipped it back into his pocket. His aunt might as well have swept him up in one of her embraces, she felt so intensely close. Ian felt as though he breathed for both of them. The woman who had done so much to shape and shield him, even now, after she was no more.

Ian asked the bartender for a second glass of wine, one to rest where his aunt should be seated. As he settled it in place, an attractive woman with reddish-gold hair emerged from the ladies'. She took up position by the side wall, drew out her phone, and began taking Ian's picture.

Ian did his best to ignore her entirely. He knew from bitter experience that confrontation only made things worse. He reached into his pocket and touched Amelia's letter as he would a talisman.

Wishing the good feelings had lasted just a little bit longer.

Chapter 8

Castaways was a work of art, aged and weathered, filled with good cheer and a rainbow of fragrances. Long before their first course arrived, Kari grew certain she was in the company of genuine people. There were five of them crammed around a table meant for four. But the entire restaurant was overfull, and the confines somehow added to the atmosphere.

Noah was accompanied by his wife, Jenna Greaves. The two had been married only a few months, and their love surrounded the table in a soft luminescence. Noah, the artist with wood and stone, and Jenna, the . . . what? She had described herself as a nurse, but the way the others watched her as she spoke, the depths to Jenna's gaze, Kari was fairly certain Jenna carried secrets. She and her husband both. Just the same, they showed her a genuineness that no amount of hidden elements could taint.

The other couple was equally fascinating. Noah's half brother, an African American county sheriff named Amos, and his Latina wife, Aldana. Silent and strong and entirely comfortable in their own skin. The harmony that bound these four people was a quiet force that welcomed Kari yet held the rest of the world at bay. What was more, the sheriff lived just down the valley lane from Kari. Soon as Noah revealed this, the couple went out of their way to assure Kari that they would not bother her or probe or come by when they weren't invited.

Aldana told her, "Privacy is one big reason why people move to our valley."

"We go out of our way to be good neighbors," Amos assured her. "And invisible most of the time."

Midway through the second course, Kari found herself struck by how she was the one who was not being honest. As in, refusing to reveal who she truly was. Forming her own version of the falsehood she had grown up with. Fashioning a lie through her silence. Keeping the truth of who she was hidden. She sighed, confronted by how Miramar was already making changes in her life.

She heard herself say, "There's more to this than just my need for privacy. Which is really important. I'm an artist. A painter. I go by the name Kariel."

"Kari Langham," Noah said. "Wow."

Aldana said, "You're famous."

"I've never been comfortable with that," Kari said. "Fame."

The four exchanged a long look, and then Amos said, "Somebody needs to tell the lady."

"You *ask* her," Aldana corrected. "There is no telling. This is a request."

"You know that's exactly what I meant."

"Then you should have said it."

"I'll do it." Jenna turned to Kari and said, "We have very dear friends. Ethan is a banker here in Miramar."

"And an artist," Aldana said. "He builds miniature houses. A few go to children, but they're mostly for film sets and such."

Amos was already busy with his phone. He held out the device so Kari could see a brightly painted palace in the softest pastels. "This is three feet high."

Jenna said, "His wife, Ryan, is a detective on the Miramar force."

"We're all very close," Aldana said. "The four of them, Ryan and Ethan and Noah and Jenna, they got married in a joint ceremony."

"We all own an ocean cruiser together," Amos said. "Love to take you out someday, if you're interested."

Noah said, "Ryan has a son from her first marriage. Liam. He's twelve and a truly gifted kid."

Amos scrolled swiftly through his phone and showed Kari a sketch of his wife, one that was precise and clear and vivid. A minimum of lines. Remarkable maturity, incredible depth.

Kari asked, "The person who drew this is twelve? Truly?"

"Liam thinks the world of your work," Jenna said.

"He has two of your posters on his walls," Aldana said. "Children on the swings. A baby at the surf's edge, bound by the mama's legs. The first time my Amos saw that picture, he wept."

"I did no such thing," Amos protested.

"Inside, where only I saw." Aldana nudged her husband. "Where it means the most."

Jenna said, "Some of Liam's work was used in Noah's last television project."

"Back before my LA world got shredded," Noah agreed.

Kari studied the four faces. Saw the intensity of the concern for a child not their own, a shared bond, which somehow left her wanting to cry out loud. Shout to her own past, demand to know why she could not have been gifted with such an upbringing.

She knew what Indrid would say. That her past and her longings had all combined to make her and her own art what they were today. Just the same, she had to swallow hard before she could say, "I would be delighted to meet him."

They breathed in unison.

Jenna said, "It will mean the world to that child."

"You need to understand," Noah said, "Liam is the quietest kid I've ever known."

"He can go for hours without saying a word," Amos added. "Days, even."

"The best word to describe Liam is *solitary*," Aldana said. "I don't think he has any idea just how lonely he is."

"The child needs contact with another artist," Noah agreed.

"I have no problem with silence," Kari said. "May I make a request of my own?"

Amos and his brother shared a look, then chorused, "Sister, just say the word."

"I would like to use you and this moment in a new work."

"You mean paint us?" Amos grinned. "Like we're somebody?"

"Exactly like that." Kari took the phone from her purse and rose. "Could you just take a few moments and talk among yourselves?"

She went into the ladies' and splashed water on her face. She'd hoped to clarify her thoughts, but it proved futile. Her first evening out in this new hometown, and already she felt the ground shifting.

Kari thought most of the successful people in her family's film world were manically self-absorbed. Miramar and these new acquaintances were so different, she felt threatened. As if all the assumptions she'd made, the walls she'd built to shield her creative fire, simply did not fit in this place. She stared in the mirror and wondered if here in Miramar, she was the imposter.

She reentered the dining room and stopped. The bar formed a brass-rimmed island to her right. Their table was directly ahead, against the far wall. As hoped, the four of them deep in conversation, her presence momentarily forgotten.

Kari raised her phone, brought the table into focus, and shot each individual several times. She had no idea how she would use these images. Only that they represented a seismic shift, a direct honesty, even when they clearly held secrets. They were *honest* secrets. She couldn't say it any better than that.

She then widened her focus and photographed the table. She then pivoted in order to shoot the surrounding tables, the entrance, the grand bay window, the bar. . . .

Then she saw him.

Ian Hart. The guitarist whose music had framed a backdrop to so many of her most precious creative hours. Here.

Kari had a sudden certainty that he knew she was there and that he assumed, mistakenly, that she was shooting his photograph. He looked so sad, so resigned. . . .

She walked over and said, "I wasn't taking your picture."

He looked over.

"I'm an artist. I wanted . . ." She gestured in the vague direction of her table. "There's something very special about this place, these people. I wanted to capture it. Not you."

He nodded slowly. "I know what you mean. About Miramar. I've been here only a few hours, and already I feel . . ."

"Disconnected," she offered. "From out there."

His gaze cleared. He did not actually offer her a smile. But Kari had the distinct impression he came as close as he could just then. He asked, "You're an artist?"

She nodded. "Kariel."

"Are you really?" Ian Hart swung fully around. "Sorry. Of course you are. It's just . . . I love your work."

"That makes two of us." She swatted at the words. "That sounds vaguely nuts. I mean, I love your music. I've heard you twice. I mean, in person." She stopped. "Maybe I should just shut up and run away."

"No. Don't go. Where did you see me?"

"Hollywood Bowl. And Toronto." The only reason she had agreed to accompany her father and brother to the film festival. To hear Ian Hart in person. Who was now so into their conversation, she felt the restaurant slip into vague shadows. "You were wonderful. Your music totally captivated me. Sometimes when I listen to your albums, it's like I'm hearing the pieces for the very first time." Kari stopped because her words had somehow brought his sorrow back to the surface. Suddenly, all she had said seemed so feeble and out of place, including, "I'm sorry."

He made a genuine effort to clear his gaze and offered another almost smile. "I have one of your oils. At least, I did. Now . . . you've heard about my current situation?"

Of course she had. But Kari had no interest in talking about things that belonged to the outside world. "Which one?"

"The ballerina dancing on the ocean wave. The first time I saw it . . ." Ian drew a tight breath. "It's a long story."

"I understand. A little. Really. And I'm so sorry. It's just . . . I've never spoken with a buyer before."

"What? Never?"

She shook her head, mostly in wonder. Ian Hart.

"I bought it sixteen months ago. Just as I was beginning to see . . ." Another hard breath. "I needed a break. Your painting reminded me of what I'd lost. What I needed to get back."

Kari breathed a soft, "Wow."

"What are you doing here?"

"I've just moved here."

"No kidding. When?"

"Yesterday."

Ian came closer still to a real smile. "Okay, that's spooky."

"You've moved here?"

"This morning."

"Wow again."

"You said it. Why Miramar?"

"I've always wanted a refuge. A place where I could be safe." She could scarcely believe the words she heard herself release. Her secrets shared with a man she knew only through his own art. A total stranger. Now in possession of intimate details. She wanted to take a step back, maybe just offer a soft farewell, until . . .

Ian said softly, "Sheltered from the harshest storms."

She shivered. *Wow* did not go far enough.

"My aunt called Miramar her midnight harbor," Ian said.

What Kari thought was, *I'm going to paint that.* "Your aunt lives here?"

"She did. I've inherited her apartment. As of today."

"I'm so sorry for your loss." Kari watched the waiter approach with Ian's meal and said, "I should get back to my friends."

"Wait. Kariel . . ."

"Just Kari. Kari Langham."

"Thank you for speaking with me. Really."

"I'm so glad I did. Really."

"Can I see you again?"

Apparently, this was a night made for the shivers. "I'd like that."

"Coffee tomorrow? No, wait, I'm booked . . . A glass of wine tomorrow evening? Here?"

"Seven o'clock." Kari brought her smile back to the table, slipped into her chair, and announced, "I have a date with Ian Hart."

CHAPTER 9

Ian ate his solitary meal, lifted by the sudden appearance of his all-time favorite painter. He would like to think Amelia had had a hand in the introduction, though that was probably going too far. Just the same, he drank in the restaurant's shared atmosphere with his wine as a heady cheer enveloped even him.

As he set down his fork with a satisfied sigh, a man's voice said, "Excuse me, Mr. Hart?"

"Yes?"

"Connor Larkin. This is my wife, Sylvie. Arthur is a neighbor. And a friend. He called us and said you'd be coming."

"Sorry we couldn't offer you a table." The bright-eyed woman shared her husband's smile. "We're booked solid whenever my husband tries to upstage the food."

"A place at the bar suits me just fine." Ian accepted the man's hand. "You're the actor."

"Guilty as charged."

Sylvie said, "Arthur mentioned you're helping out with a certain crisis we're not supposed to know about."

"Trying to."

"We're both big fans," Sylvie said. "Of you. Not Arthur. He's a sweetie pie when he's not being Miramar's number one grump burger."

Connor said, "Sylvie's been playing our twins your music since before they were born."

"I'm partial to swing," Sylvie said. "Compliments of dear old dad. I'm hoping early doses of classical music can prod these two in a loftier direction."

They were both seasoned pros at introductions. No gushing, no awkward pauses or comments about events that had no place in the evening.

"Arthur insisted on treating you tonight," Connor told Ian. "But you've got to come back again as our guest."

"Next time we might even find you a table." Sylvie pointed her husband toward the stage set by the front window. "Now you need to excuse my guy. He needs to go earn his keep."

Ian could actually feel Amelia's finger prodding his ribs. Doing her best to touch him at the heart level. "Would it be okay if I joined you for a song?"

Both faces lit up, two people illuminated with the sort of delight that Amelia would have loved.

Connor said, "Are you kidding? It would be an absolute honor."

Sylvie warned, "My husband doesn't have a clue when it comes to classical music."

"That's both true and not true. I know how to listen," Connor said. "I know how to love it. But from the audience's standpoint only."

"I've always enjoyed swing." Ian glanced at Amelia's wineglass sitting there on the bar. He missed her terribly. "My aunt, the reason I'm here in Miramar, she was hooked on big band."

"This has the makings of a great night," Sylvie said. Then

a head popped out the kitchen door, and a hand waved in her direction. "Ian, promise me you'll come back when we can chat."

"I'd like nothing better," he replied and meant it. Friends already.

"Let me play a couple of intro numbers. And then come up with the band." Connor clapped him on the shoulder. "This is going to be a session to remember."

Ian slipped from the restaurant and retrieved his guitar from the Kia's trunk. The bartender was now playing hostess. She introduced herself as Marcela and offered to carry his instrument up front. Ian returned to his place by the bar and watched as Connor spoke to a trio occupying a table by the stage, then slipped behind the piano and adjusted his mike.

As soon as Connor launched into his first song, Ian knew he had been right to ask. Any doubts he might have harbored, all arguments regarding his present state or the fact that he had spent the afternoon in Arthur's studio, simply vanished.

The song was Nat King Cole's "Stardust," which Amelia had played every time the blues descended. *Love is now the stardust of yesterday, the music of the years gone by.* He could actually hear his aunt humming along with Connor.

Connor was an excellent pianist, but his voice was the standout. Ian had met any number of such talented people who had the potential to achieve stardom. But for one reason or another, they had remained on the periphery of commercial success. Ian looked around the restaurant, took in the rapt expressions on so many faces, then caught Kari's eye. A look from across the room, her face glowing in the candlelight. He lifted his glass in salute and was warmed by her smile.

Connor segued directly into a second melody, this one by Norah Jones, entitled "Come Away with Me." He finished the song, waited through the cheering applause, then motioned for his band to join him. They settled into place, only now there was an empty seat, with two mikes on booms placed between the drummer and Connor's baby grand. Ian's guitar rested in an oversized frame that was meant to hold a bass.

"We have a special guest joining us tonight," Connor said. "I can't hardly believe I'm saying these words. But here goes. Ladies and gentlemen, it's my genuine pleasure to introduce Ian Hart."

Their first song was one written by Carole King and her husband for the Drifters: "Up on the Roof." As soon as Connor Larkin counted them down, Ian sensed his aunt slipping through the audience and settling at the table the trio had vacated. He cast his invisible friend a silent greeting. Memories flooded in, only this time they carried the bittersweet flavor of his aunt's smile.

His parents had departed from Ian's life when he was just four. A mother's suicide, a father's swift descent into the dark pit of drug-addled sorrow. His father's parents had been the only so-called stable family available, so they had reluctantly made room for their grandson. Sort of.

Three weeks after his sixth birthday, they shipped him off to the Annapolis boarding school. They never visited. Amelia became his only connection to family. His aunt traveled down from her Philly home at least twice each month, always bringing with her those singular rays of love and sunshine. She treated him to a day of whatever suited their fancy. Christmas and twice each summer, he secretly made the trek north. Amelia faked the school's letterhead and wrote her parents that Ian was on a school holiday, spending time with another student's family, whatever. She always added that additional funds were required to cover the period. They both took secret delight in stowing the money away, adding to what Amelia gleefully called his runaway fund.

Once that first spring, Ian asked her why her parents were that way. Colorless. Silent. Settled into tight little grooves that shaped their every waking hour. A couple who could go days without speaking. Who considered Ian's presence a noisy and distasteful invasion of their tightly perfect world.

For once, Amelia lost her brilliant smile. "It's not you, if that's what you're asking. They were the same way with me. And your poor dear father. We both ran away, in our own secret hearts. They loathed your mother. Thought her the worst possible choice of a mate. Which made her perfect in your father's eyes." It was doubtful Amelia could see him any longer. "You know your grandparents both worked in the Department of Agriculture."

Ian nodded. "When I was little, I thought it was called the Department of Oatmeal."

Amelia had a bell-like laugh, a musical shout. "I love that! It's perfect!" She wiped her eyes. "Is it okay if we don't talk about your grandparents? Not ever again?"

Ian only ever mentioned them once more. He was ten and was entering his second year of study under Lachard, whom Amelia referred to as "the discipline freak." Far too much like Ian's grandparents for her taste. Lachard was tolerated only because of the fire he strengthened in Ian.

Amelia was a fanatic when it came to Broadway musicals. But show tunes of any kind left Ian cold. They attended a couple of live performances and saw a few musical films. Ian barely tolerated the experiences. Finally, Amelia admitted defeat. "I hate throwing away a hundred bucks. The problem is, I can't take you to a classical concert."

"Why not?"

"Because if you like the performance, you go into a trance. If you hate it, you are a total pain to be around." She shifted her large frame around in the ice cream parlor's chair, like she had an itch she couldn't reach. "This is you when you don't like the music."

"I like the music. I just don't like what they've done with it."

"Same difference."

"I didn't think anyone noticed."

She smiled with genuine pleasure. "Your sphinx act might fool most people. But not your aunt Amelia. What other kind of music do you like?"

"I don't know any. Granddad and Grandmother hate all kinds . . ." He stopped when a shadow flitted across her broad features.

Amelia said, "Let's not taint a perfectly good afternoon with their poison."

"All right." And that was it. The last time those two people ever came up in polite conversation. "Lachard says I can listen only to my assignment. Plus, he hates modern music. He calls it amplified trash."

"I'm liking this tyrant of yours less and less."

"He's teaching me a lot."

"Maybe so. But a little bit of tyrant goes a long way in my book." She reached for his half-finished sundae and thought her way through two spoonfuls. Then, "What about jazz?"

"I don't know it." It was only then, as Ian watched her consume her second sundae of the day, that he realized feeding her bulk was Amelia's way of cushioning the hurt she carried from her own early years. The new awareness brought such a surge of emotions, he almost wept. "Lachard says jazz is a corruption of the classical discipline."

"Well, he's at least partly right." She waved her spoon in a broad arc, dripping chocolate across the tabletop. "Do you see Lachard around here somewhere? No? So I want you to forget everything the little Frenchified tyrant is force-feeding you."

"Okay."

"I bet the man likes yogurt." More sundae. "I've never met a yogurt lover who wasn't hiding something twisted in their personal closet."

"I have no idea what that even means."

She pushed his sundae aside with a satisfied sigh. "Let's go see if we can find some undisciplined degenerates playing jazz."

Over the years that followed, Ian grew to love jazz and a great many directions and artists of contemporary music. This was partly due to how they released him from the rigorous discipline and artistic snobbery present in so much of the classical music world. Now, though, as he softly accompanied Connor Larkin and his band, Ian found it easy indeed to remember only the good. Only the laughter. Only the rich joys that remarkable woman had brought into his life.

Next they performed a lighthearted rendition of Paul Anka's "Tonight My Love, Tonight," followed by the Righteous Brothers' "Unchained Melody." For each selection, they made room for one member of the group to perform a solo. Piano, sax, Ian, bass, then a rousing version of Ray Charles's "Hit The Road, Jack," where the drummer brought almost everyone to their feet. The longer they played, the more clearly Ian could see Amelia's smile.

Afterward, Connor spoke into the mike. "We're going to take a short break. Before we go, who here thinks it's time we give our guest a chance to stretch his wings?"

During the applause that followed, Connor covered his mike and leaned toward Ian. They had a swift discussion about song and tempo and key. He played a soft chord. Another. A third. Then he nodded to Ian and mouthed the word, *Fly*.

The song was another by Carole King, "Will You Love Me Tomorrow." A folksy blues number with enough jazz undertones to remain one of Amelia's absolute favorites.

Ian created a continual riff from that awful question, one he had seen in the gazes of far too many lovely ladies. But tonight was not made for sorrow, especially after Amelia left her comfortable perch, climbed onto the stage, and settled in there beside him. Which brought to mind her reaction whenever sadness had threatened to overwhelm him; Amelia had cradled his head in both strong arms and drawn him close.

Close to the heart that beat no longer.

He was scarcely aware when the trio joined in, soft murmurs of accompanying music and beat. Then Connor began to sing, and finally the song ended, and Ian forced himself to look out over the restaurant and smile at the applause. Though he could scarcely see anything beyond prisms of memory and love.

CHAPTER 10

When Connor began his second solo melody, the two other women at Kari's table shared a smile over the first line, *Come away with me*.

Aldana, the sheriff's wife, said softly, "Sign me up."

Several women at neighboring tables laughed in response. One murmured, "Get in line."

Amos pretended shock. "In case you hadn't noticed, this is your husband sitting here."

"Oh. Right." Aldana patted his hand. "What was your name again?"

The song ended to long and rapturous applause. Connor invited his band onto the stage, waited while they settled, then invited Ian to join them.

Kari studied the faces around her, warmed and lit both by candlelight and sharing this special hour. Some people showed confusion over Ian's appearance; others utter astonishment. She wondered if she was the only one who felt chills.

The Drifters' "Up on the Roof" was played with an upbeat jazzy rendering that had many dancing in place. Kari wrapped her arms around her middle, thrilled by the shape this moment was taking. Her first evening in her new hometown.

Ian held back through the first few songs, playing so lightly he merely punctuated Connor's lead. Even so, he created a special magic all his own. Kari was certain this was not merely her own sentiment, seeing her favorite musician in such intimate surroundings.

Then Connor invited their guest to play lead on the set's final song, a second Carole King melody. Ian generated a melodic force that elevated the music to an entirely different level. This was Ian Hart's gift, offering the audience wings of their own, inviting them to soar with him. Kari had tasted this same energy in his albums and while seated in a captivated live audience. But the restaurant's intimacy created something else entirely.

Kari felt herself pierced by his music. She looked out over the audience, saw the rapture. She had spent her entire life in artistic solitude. Only now, in this moment, she yearned for what would never be hers.

When she woke the next morning, Kari was ready to paint.

She rushed through the morning routine, throwing on whatever clothes were at the top of her unpacked case. Brewing coffee took forever. Her fingers made an impatient mess of feeding the kitten and then pouring yogurt and granola into her own solitary bowl. She forced herself to eat, knowing otherwise she might faint before realizing her body's needs. The kitten became infected by her frenetic energy, mewing and threading its way around her feet, twice almost bringing her down. Kari plucked up the feline and her coffee and rushed down the brick walkway, fumbled with the atelier key, stepped inside, and breathed.

Sunlight spilled through the skylights and the eastern slit windows. The pattern cast upon the empty room's vast space was an artwork all its own, so beautiful she might have wept if she had not felt such an urgent need to begin.

Every now and then, she worked on two or more canvases simultaneously. The ideas and emotions all crowded in, forming a huge jumble that could be clarified only by sifting through them together, isolating one fragment after another. Kari set up a pair of easels and got to work.

She loved sketching directly onto the canvas but seldom did so, because too often her initial ideas were miles removed from the final concept. Too much work on the canvas, and she became defensive. As if she needed to protect what she had done thus far. Working first on her pad was liberating in that sense. She had once heard a teacher declare, "An artist needs room to doubt." That was how she viewed her sketch pad. As a book of doubts.

Today was different.

The first canvas was based upon her view of Justin and her father through the gallery door. Graham had forwarded his photographs, but her memories were so vivid, Kari found no need to bring them up. Her recollection of that night was merely a jumping-off point; she knew that now. Studying the images would only muddy her vision.

She sketched out the two men raging into their phones, then began swiftly adding color and form. First, to the background, then to the ephemeral image reflected in the glass. She had not yet decided whether to actually paint the two men so they resembled her father and brother. That needed to wait. Nothing could be allowed to hold back this creative torrent. So the two men were almost faceless, at least for the moment. The clearest element was their matching dark sunglasses, square and large and impenetrable. Almost as an afterthought, she then swept the brush along the left side of their profiles. As if an unseen wind, a tempest of rage and pressure matching their internal state, threatened to pull them away.

She was far from finished when she shifted her attention. The second canvas called to her with silent intensity. On it she sketched a memory, one that had woken her at daybreak.

Kari had not thought of the incident in years. Which was hardly a surprise. It had occurred the weekend before her sixteenth birthday. The week after, she had received the art schools' responses. Her hand froze momentarily, her heart again captured by the words that had branded her spirit. She had always suspected the handwritten notes attached to one of the rejection letters had been forwarded by mistake. The professor's comments had quenched her creative fire for almost a year.

Pollyannaish, the instructor had written. *Not without some small talent, but absurdly immature, nowhere near ready for higher learning.* Nine comments in all. Each stabbing her with those blades of contempt and rejection.

Then the kitten mewed, drawing her back to the here and now. Surrounded by a vast clean space, a confirmation in itself that the instructor's opinion was not shared by many others. Kari shuddered, breathed, refocused, and sketched.

After the first few lines, the happy memory became so vivid she might as well be viewing it through clear glass, instead of rendering it onto an empty canvas.

Justin was six years her senior, but when they were growing up, he'd seemed much older. As if his single-minded ambition, his aim to join their father's agency had aged him a full generation. He had never understood her desire to paint. Which was why she had never shared the art schools' rejections and the devastation they had caused.

Every now and then, Justin had done his best to bridge the divide between them. On this day, all he had told her was he had a surprise in store. He'd dragged her out of bed at four in the morning. Kari kept whining as she dressed because it made him laugh. She had always cherished her brother's rare good moods. This morning was one of the best.

Three of them traveled south at dawn that day. Brother and sister were accompanied by Justin's most recent flame. As Kari sketched, she tried to remember the young lady's name. Tessa sounded right. Her handsome brother maintained a revolving-door attitude about his female companionship. Tessa was beautiful, of course. They always were. But there was something to this one, a unique flavor or depth, something about the quiet way she observed everything. As if she was not as easily taken as the others Kari had met.

They stopped for breakfast at a Long Beach diner, a throwback to a different era. The place was filled with a remarkable blend of people. All ages, many races, all quietly sharing a fizzy, ethereal joy.

Afterward, they joined others from the diner, walking a narrow path between houses and businesses, skirting under two freeways, a long line of happy people trekking westward. They arrived at the entrance to El Dorado Nature Center just as the sun peeked over the eastern ridge.

The world exploded in a rainbow of colors.

Migrating monarch butterflies occasionally used the preserve as a waystation on their annual migration from the Mexican highlands to California's Central Coast. Recently they had skipped an entire decade, and people had assumed it was over, just another nearly forgotten California legend.

But this year they had returned. When daylight warmed their wings, they rose in a silent thunderclap of color. Thousands upon thousands of them. Billowing rainbows that serrated the rising sun.

Tessa, her brother's momentary flame, shed her years and reserve. She shrieked with unbridled delight. She danced with abandon. She sang a lilting melody, so captivated by the moment that Kari doubted the young woman was even aware of the music she added to the moment. Or how people turned and smiled and clapped in time to her antics.

The butterflies seemed to be attracted to her joy. They settled on her hair, her face, her arms.

Tessa froze, captured by the feather brushes. Tears streamed down her face. Kari watched as the brilliant creatures extended their proboscises and drank her tears like nectar.

When it was over and they were driving home, Kari watched from her position in the back seat as Tessa said, "I will remember this forever." When Justin glanced over and smiled, the young woman remained solemn, almost sad. She went on, "I can never see you again."

Kari sketched the woman's outstretched arms, the momentary ecstasy, the joy that had infected everyone around them. Even her avaricious brother. As she rendered the memory on the canvas, she felt the art schools' painful rejection crowding in. But she was well armed now. Both by her creative fire and the almost forgotten young woman's joy.

What was wrong with wanting to fill cracks in the world with hope? Or love? Or joy? Why shouldn't she use these as the themes for her life's work? Why couldn't an artist reveal her innermost self and become lost to the glory of momentary abandon? This was what Kari loved most about her work. A dropping of defenses, a release of all barriers. Finding a temporary center point of joy. Sharing it with the world.

CHAPTER 11

Ian slept well and rose with the dawn. He took his coffee out on the apartment's stubby balcony, which overlooked the town and the mist-wrapped horizon. Amelia had written him several times about this wonder. How the shoreline and much of the town was blanketed by a marine layer, sometimes for hours, and occasionally all day. Yet from his perch, Ian could see how the main street emerged from the haze as it rose gently from the Pacific. The first structure to be seen clearly was Castaways. Ian wondered if this was why the sea captain had built it where it stood, just beyond the drifting tendrils. Up where he sat, the sky was a pristine, cloudless blue, the daylight and colors both gradually taking on strength.

He stared at the old building and recalled his stint on the Castaways stage. He had wound up playing both sets, melding easily with the others. Connor's band members were all experienced studio musicians, well accustomed to accepting changes on the fly. Ian finished his mug, reentered the kitchen, and filled it a second time, then returned to the dawn. The fire he had always taken for granted was still gone. And yet, for the first time in months, the taste of ashes was absent as well. Strange as it was to admit, Ian looked forward to another series of studio takes.

What was more, he had an idea how the session might take shape.

Ian decided to call Arthur and treat it as a sort of test. Involve himself in the work to come. See if this mildly pleasant sensation remained intact.

Arthur greeted him with a typically bitter "I suppose you're ringing to ruin my day. Something to the effect you're going to be late. Or not show up at all."

"I hope I'm not calling too early."

"What, you think perhaps if I'd finished my morning constitutional, I'd be more open to your version of bad news?"

"You mentioned bringing in studio musicians, adding some depth to portions of my first session."

Arthur snorted. "Having second thoughts, are we? Looking to make fresh misery for me and Danny both? Seeing as how we're already working the segments into the film's final cut."

"Is there any chance you could bring the musicians in today?"

"What exactly are you saying?"

"I have an idea about the next scenes."

"And?"

"Could we hold off discussing this further until I'm in the studio?"

"Am I going to bitterly regret saying yes?"

"Hard to say." Ian was grinning as he added, "One more thing."

"Yes? What further misery have you concocted to ruin this perfectly good morning?"

"Your neighbor, Connor Larkin."

"I've already heard about your invading his rare appearance onstage." Arthur grumbled, then allowed, "Wasn't altogether a bad night, by all accounts."

"Could you phone him, ask if maybe he'd be willing to join us?"

There was a moment's silence, followed by a faint gurgling sound.

Ian asked, "Are you laughing?"

"Certainly not. You've got some bloody nerve, I'll give you that much."

"Is that a yes? Hello?"

But the old man had already hung up.

Connor Larkin was already there when Ian arrived. The actor was sprawled on the front room's leather sofa, cradling a mug of coffee. "Vanessa, Larry, and Leo are on their way," he said in greeting. "They all live in San Lu. Be another half hour or so."

Arthur demanded, "You asked your band to trek north on the basis of a few words from this one?"

"Nobody required convincing," Connor replied. "I mentioned Ian's name, and they were already moving."

"Terrible idiots, the lot," Arthur said.

"I'll tell them you said so," Connor replied. To Ian, "What's up?"

"The song Danny has slated next, 'Every Breath You Take.'"

"Sting and his former band. I forget their name . . ."

"The Police," Arthur said.

"Great song," Connor said. "What about it?"

Ian addressed Arthur and his deepening frown. "The next major scene is after the breakup, correct?"

"Where'd you hear that?"

"You told me."

"Did I, now?" Arthur picked up his flow-chart, flipped pages, fiddled with his spectacles. "So?"

To Connor, Ian said, "What if we did a slow bluesy-jazz rendition? Say, four takes with different levels of backup. One with just you singing and piano. Another just your voice and my guitar."

Arthur was aghast. "Tell me you're not suggesting we dump the selections made by an Academy Award-winning music director."

"Not dumping," Ian said. "Reworking. A new version."

"After the original was approved by the producer. Already edited into the film."

Connor ignored the editor. "Third take, full team, add a sax solo."

"Slow and plaintive," Ian said, liking how they were already in sync. "Maybe bring in some backup singers if it works."

"Danny will scream bloody murder," Arthur said. "Rightly so. Especially when he's faced with extra costs on a project that's already gone over budget."

Ian offered, "I'll give up my share."

Connor started to object, but Arthur was faster. "No, you bloody won't. What's more, you won't mention any such blasphemy in Danny's presence. Are we clear on that, mate?" When Ian did not respond, the old man rose to his feet and pointed to the sound room. "Now shift yourselves over and let's see if we can give him a useful addition to this project."

Connor remained where he was. "You think the film has potential?"

"I think it's going to blow the roof off the summer releases. But what do I know? I'm just an old field hand with almost fifty years in the trade." Arthur made a vague sweeping gesture. "In you go, now. More work, less chatter. That's my motto."

But their first take did not go as planned.

Arthur was busy setting up mikes and sliding in transparent sound baffles for the drum set so they could all play together. Ian and Connor were playing quick segments, talking more than making music, when the song came together. It happened so fast they ran through the first attempt while Arthur shifted back to the controls and set the gains. Then they all had to stop, because Connor's drummer and bass and sax players had arrived and had to be miked and brought up to speed. They all lent a hand prepping the studio, impatient to begin work on a song that already seemed half done, at least to Ian.

With the drums positioned behind Arthur's movable glass partitions, the sound was both clear and baffled. This allowed the drummer to play in the same room with them, rather than them having to add his work later. Arthur fiddled with the mikes' gains and issued a steady stream of complaints over the studio speakers. Connor finally lost patience and ordered the producer to start taping. Arthur responded with more of the same, but Connor walked to the connecting door, leaned in close to the old man, and spoke one word. *Enough.*

With that first stanza, the drummer set a low heartbeat of a rhythm, using just the tom-tom and bass drum. The stand-up bass player amped the beat, hammering the string with the knuckle of her right thumb, then softly plucking the next three notes. Then hammering again.

In the second stanza, Ian entered in, a soft refrain of minor notes. Three and sometimes four strings together. Timed to match the drummer.

Oh, can't you see, you belong to me? When Connor began the second refrain, the sax entered. The sax player blew just a few quiet reedy notes, little more than a rasping confirmation of Connor's sorrow. Ian thought the sax sounded like a strong man trying hard not to weep.

Three takes and the song was done.

When they filed back into the control room, Arthur asked

Connor, "Could you hang about a bit longer? Danny wants to have a word."

Connor busied himself making a fresh pot of coffee. "He's heard our rendition?"

"I fed the second take through the film set's sound system. Danny's dropped everything and is on his way up."

Ian asked, "It's good?"

"Good?" Arthur swung around to his board. "Have a listen to this."

"No," Ian said. "Please. Not until we're completely finished."

Connor asked, "A superstition?"

"Something like that." In the silence that followed, Ian found himself wanting to offer the truth. "It's been a long time since I've felt this good about my work. Felt anything at all, really. I'd like to hold on to that for a little while longer."

Arthur's response surprised him. The old man stared through the glass wall at the empty recording studio and mused, "The bloke who taught me the ropes was Andy Johns."

"I know that name," Connor said.

"And well you should, lad. He recorded the likes of the Stones, Free, Eric Clapton, Jethro Tull. When he was in his cups, Andy liked to talk about the band that gave him his big break. Led Zeppelin."

Ian found himself able to step away from the strain of partly confessing his secret. He was mesmerized by the sight of this irascible old man putting aside his grumpy mask. Revealing his own quiet passion for the craft.

Connor asked, "What did your friend say it was like?"

"Pretty much what we've had here," Arthur replied, still searching the empty recording studio and the skeleton shadows of mikes and drum set and piano. "Most groups, they show up with a fistful of ideas and half-finished songs. They spend days messing about, trying to find what they're after."

Ian had heard of such nightmare scenarios. Big-name groups booking entire orchestras for backup, then forcing them to wait for hours, sometimes days, sometimes even weeks.

Connor asked, "Zeppelin was different?"

"They came in, set up, completed one take, sometimes two, and the song was done and dusted. Mind you, Jimmy Page brought together four blokes who'd spent years working as backup studio musicians. They all knew to watch the ticking clock."

Leo, the drummer, spoke for the first time. "Go in, set up, shut up, get it done, and leave. That's how a studio musician survives."

"There you go," Arthur said, still watching the empty room. "I suppose I only half believed studio takes could ever run the way Andy always claimed they did with Zeppelin. Until now."

Ian was so moved by the moment's quiet intensity, he confessed, "I lost it. The passion. The fire. It's gone out."

Connor asked quietly, "When did it happen?"

"Started about fourteen months ago," Ian replied. "Last month, I finally admitted defeat. I told my manager I was totally burned out and needed to take a year off. But the truth was, I wanted to try and rekindle the passion that had taken me this far."

Connor guessed, "Your manager didn't take it well."

"He screamed at me. For days. When that didn't work, he stole all he could, including advances on three projects I didn't even know he'd committed me to handling. Then he fled the country."

The actor's response surprised him. Connor leaned back so far, his head collided with the wall. He directed his words to the ceiling. "You mind some advice?"

"I guess. Sure."

"This comes from the eye of the hurricane. You understand what I'm saying?" When Ian remained silent, Connor asked, "Those three surprise commitments . . . Who is heading the project left in the absolute worst position?"

That required no thought whatsoever. "Kiki Kerkorian, head of the Miami Music Festival."

"What's their start-date?"

"Little less than a week."

"You one of the event's headliners?"

"I was. Again, without my knowledge or okay."

Arthur huffed softly.

Connor asked, "When did you find out?"

"Six days ago. After their lawyers froze my accounts."

"So you haven't actually spoken with the lady?" When Ian shook his head, Connor went on, "Call her directly. Pretend the lawyers and their actions don't exist. Lay the whole thing out."

"She's heard it all by now," Ian pointed out. "Seeing as how I'm the latest bad boy on all the entertainment channels."

"The lady hasn't heard it from you, which is the only thing that matters. Tell her you'll do the gig."

Ian opened his mouth to protest. But the words didn't come.

"Do the gig," Connor repeated. "Tell her you'll do it for free. No charge."

"Connor, I'm broke."

"Hear me out. Make sure she understands what this is costing you, both financially and personally. In exchange, all you're asking is that she spread the word about what happened. Have her tell the music world your side of the story." He rose and crossed to the coffee maker. "I'm pretty sure she'll pay you what you're owed. But her coming out publicly on your side will mean more in the long run. To have a senior figure serving as your new ally, this could save your career. Keep the doors open for when you're ready to return."

Ian wanted to protest, say he didn't know if he'd ever resume his career. But as he was still mentally shaping the words, a chime sounded from the wall console.

Arthur walked over and pressed the button to open his front gates. "Danny's made it here in record time."

But it was not the film producer who approached the studio. Instead, three very large and cheerful women stopped outside the door. When Arthur merely sat there and stared at them through the window, the closest woman tapped on the glass with a purple fingernail as long as a talon.

Arthur opened the door, asked, "May I help you?"

"Danny Byrd said you needed some backup singers."

"Did he? How astonishing." Arthur stepped away. "Then I suppose you'd best come in."

Each member of the trio easily outweighed Ian by a good fifty pounds. Everything about them was huge—face, hair, limbs, smile. One Latina, one Black, the eldest an Asian beauty, with the broadest grin of all. She pointed to Connor on the sofa and said, "Look what we have here, ladies."

"Lunch," the Black woman said.

The Latina was the largest of all. "Honey, you know who that is?"

"Of course I know." She addressed both Connor and Ian. "If you two sing as good as you look, we're in trouble."

Ian pointed to Connor. "He sings. I watch."

"Great heavens above," the Asian woman said. "You're Ian Hart."

"Who's that, now?"

"Don't you ever watch anything but those silly game shows? This here is the baddest of the bad boys." To Ian, she added, "Sugar, you're way better looking than those awful pictures they're showing."

Connor asked Arthur, "Danny didn't say anything about this?"

"He mentioned wanting to add some personal input to today's session. I said since he was the boss with the checkbook, he could do pretty much whatever he liked," Arthur replied, studying the women now compressing the air in his control room. "I've been known to make the occasional mistake."

The Latina demanded, "Who're you calling a mistake?"

The Asian lady said, "You don't watch, old man, I'm gonna tie a knot in that ratty sweater, with you still inside."

Connor pointed to the cottage door. "Here comes Danny. Right on time."

And it wasn't just Danny.

The producer arrived with three others in tow, a videographer and two lighting gaffers. The four of them were all loaded down with cameras, tripods, lights, cables.

As Danny followed his crew into the recording studio, Arthur told Connor, "I suppose it would be too much trouble to inform the guy whose house he just invaded."

The Latina asked Connor, "Does the old man always register so high on the crankometer?"

Danny set down the camera, slipped the cables off his shoulder, and returned to the front room. "My aching back."

"You didn't mention bringing the circus act," Arthur said.

"Apparently so," the Latina said.

Danny greeted the ladies, said, "Why don't you go get miked up while I have a word." When the women went next door, Danny addressed the three men and Connor's band, "You don't need me to tell you the song is first rate."

Connor told Ian, "Something tells me there's a big ask hidden in that compliment."

"You're not as dumb as you look," Arthur grumbled.

Danny went on. "We can run through a couple more takes of what you've already done. Work up a nice little video we can use as a feeder for the film's release. Everybody goes home happy."

Connor asked, "And the alternative is . . . ?"

"The story ends with them coming back together," Danny said. "Sort of. The final scenes are a romantic cliff-hanger. A lot of heat and possibilities and uncertainty. Myron and I went back and forth over the last melody."

Connor asked, "And Myron is . . . ?"

"Myron Riles," Danny replied. "Multiple Oscars, Emmys, the works. We never found exactly what we were after. So we went with what sounded, well, okay."

Arthur demanded, "Why am I only hearing this now?"

"Do you want polite or the truth?"

"Polite will do just fine, thank you very much."

"We didn't want to trouble you with issues unrelated to the final cut."

Arthur gave that a moment. "That will do, I suppose."

Danny asked, "Would you be open to recording a second song?"

Connor asked, "And that is . . . ?"

"It hit me listening to your take," Danny replied. "I think a new rendition of 'Fever' might just knock our film's ending into next week."

Arthur said, "Oh, well, now."

All eyes turned to him.

Danny asked, "You like?"

"I actually have chills." Arthur seemed to gather himself. "Of course, I might just be coming down with a fever of my own."

Danny Byrd played director. It was a relatively new role for him, and his nerves were evident. Ian did not mind. Nor, apparently, did any of the others. Even Arthur set aside his irascible nature and calmly followed Danny's cues.

Written by Eddie Cooley and Otis Blackwell, "Fever"

was originally recorded by R & B artist Little Willie John in 1956. Since then, the song had been covered, or restructured and sung, by over a hundred recording artists, including such standouts as Peggy Lee, Ray Charles, Natalie Cole, Michael Bublé, and Beyoncé.

For the intro, Danny positioned the videographer behind Arthur's shoulder. They shot the film's editor making his final adjustments to the mixing board, then using the arthritic fingers of his right hand to count in the band.

When you put your arms around me, I get a fever that's so hard to bear. The lighting was as sultry as the song. Two brilliant spots were positioned on Connor's face and the keyboard. Another spot on the heart of Ian's guitar. One on the snare drum, touched by the feather strokes of the wire brushes. One on the bass player's right hand. One on the sax—the instrument, not the man.

The three ladies Danny had lined up behind the piano, almost beyond the spots' reach. They swayed in unison, one large amorphous mass, joined together by the song's gentle heat.

Connor almost moaned the words *You give me fever.*

In response, the ladies shouted a one-word chorus.

Fever.

The second time, their cry was matched by the sax and Ian and the bassist and the drummer. All of them adding their own thumping emphasis to the word.

Fever.

Second stanza, the trio clicked fingers and came as close as they could without moving to a full-body strut.

Fever.

The beat rose to a grinding force. Connor's voice was now a controlled shout of pure, unadulterated lust. *You bring me . . .*

Fever.

Ian then played the solo that had originally been played by a trumpet. As he started, the spot on his instrument broadened to where his entire body became illuminated. Midway through, the sax entered, and they began alternating the lead, racing each other through faster and faster riffs, until the ladies halted them with the passion and the harmony of that one incredible word.

Fever.

The next stanza had Pocahontas saving her lover from her father's wrath. But now the trio sang it, each one taking a line, almost bellowing it with the sheer joy of saving the man. Connor added his soft backup, then joined with them to plead in intense harmony for her lover's life.

Fever.

The room stopped. Took a silent breath lasting three impossibly long beats. Then Connor came back in alone for the final verse.

The final chorus was their first time singing in tandem. A magnificent harmony.

Ian was genuinely sorry when it ended.

Two more takes and Danny declared, "I have all I need. Arthur?"

"I suppose it wasn't overly off-key."

Danny grinned at Connor. "You heard the old man. That's a wrap."

CHAPTER 12

Kari finally stopped work at five that afternoon, exhausted and famished and eager for the evening ahead. As she showered and dried her hair, the kitten remained sprawled on her pillow, as close to pouting as a cat could possibly come. Kari carried the beast into the kitchen, fixed another half bowl of granola, then sat, settled the kitten in her lap, and ate with one hand. The night held an electric promise, at least for her. It was not merely that she was meeting her favorite musician for a drink. Kari had grown up surrounded by stars and their oversized egos. There was something distinctly different about Ian Hart, a vulnerability that suggested he might actually be one of those rare gems. The sort of people she hoped might populate her new world. Individuals who were the same inside as out. Impossible as that might seem.

She dressed and left for town, impatient and hopeful. The drive was made more special still by the echoes of her creative flow. As the hills gave way to Miramar's outskirts, yet another idea struck, one with such potency that she halted on the roadside and opened her sketchbook and worked.

The waning light finally warned her she was beyond late. Reluctantly, she closed the sketchbook, restarted the car, and continued on. Quietly ecstatic.

As she started along the downward-sloping central avenue, the phone in her purse rang. She received so few calls, she had forgotten it was even there. She pulled into a space opposite the restaurant and answered. "Hello?"

Graham demanded, "Are you so important now that you don't bother to check your messages?"

"I've been painting."

Graham said in an aside, "She's painting." To Kari, he replied, "In that case, all is forgiven."

Kari spotted Ian as he stepped out of the restaurant's entrance and searched the street. She said, "Just a minute, Graham." She rolled down her passenger window and called, "Ian, hi. I'm sorry." She held out her phone, then added, "Three minutes." To Graham, she said, "I'm back."

"And who, may I ask, is Ian?"

But she wasn't ready to talk about that. "I'm working on two new canvases. I think they're good."

Graham said to Rafi, "She changed the subject. Something about new work."

"They're really, really good, Graham."

"She says they're special works, both of them." To Kari, he said, "When can we see?"

"I should finish them in another day or so."

"What, both?"

"I've worked all day. Things are going well." She studied the restaurant's empty doorway. "I like it here."

Graham's silence was punctuated by Rafi's whine. "I'm happy for you, Kari. Truly. We both are," Graham told her.

"Thank you, Graham."

"You'll send us pictures?"

"Soon as they're finished." She used her free hand to caress the sketchbook's cover. "And I've started a third."

"Wonderful." To Rafi, Graham said, "Hush now, else I'll banish you to Starbucks. Yes, of course I'll ask her."

"Ask me what?"

"Oh, it's a silly nothing sort of thing. Rafi, just stop. It's only that we've been contacted by Miami's premier art fair. They've heard about your coming-out here at the gallery. Don't ask me how, but I suspect it was that television journalist who would not let you go. They want to showcase your work." He paused while Rafi hit a high note, then went on, "Apparently, several of their biggest clients collect your work. They're offering to put on a retrospective. I told them no, of course."

She knew Graham expected her to refuse out of hand. Which was no doubt why he was making the call and not Rafi. But the day's exhilarating rush, the sense of entering a new life chapter, made her pause. She shut her eyes, trying to bring back the fearful reserve. Instead, she saw herself standing there at the gallery's front door. Only now it was a portal, open to the night, leading her to . . .

What, exactly?

"Kari?"

She opened her eyes. "From Rafi's song and dance, I assume he wants me to do this."

Graham huffed a laugh. "Add a double measure of sheer desperation and you might have an idea of what I'm going through here."

"Why Miami?"

The fact she had not responded with an immediate rejection caused Graham to accelerate. Zero to ninety in one sentence flat. "Rafi has been six times. Six. Trying to insinuate himself into the event. Everything but walking the carpet on his knees, doing penance for being a successful Beverly Hills gallery. They have never given space to one of our kind before. But here they are, contacting *us*. Being the ones to beg.

Literally." He waited through a pair of audible breaths, then said, "Kari?"

She was already in the process of opening her car door. "I have to call you back."

Ian returned to the restaurant bar and ordered a glass of wine. He sat staring at the orchestral beauty of a Miramar sunset, set within the bay window's varnished frame. He could have been seated in the aft cabin of some great sailing vessel, bidding farewell to another mysterious dusk. He was meeting a lovely and talented artist. He was tired from the unexpected pile of events. Exhausted, really. A red-eye flight, a drive north, a first recording session, followed by an evening on the restaurant's cramped stage. No single night's sleep could erase all that. Not to mention today's long session.

But none of that was what had left him so hollow.

Kari rushed through the entrance and hurried over. "I'm so sorry to be late . . ." She inspected his face. "What's wrong?"

"Nothing at all." He slipped from his seat and fashioned a salesman's smile. "It's so nice to see you. What would you like to drink?"

"I don't care." She pointed at his glass. "What is that?"

"A local pinot."

"Fine."

Ian signaled to a waitress, and when she made her way over, he ordered another glass.

Kari waited until they were alone again, then demanded, "Ian, tell me."

Hours later, lying in a bed too large for the narrow room, Ian wished he had deflected. Told her something else. Taken a different path. One that carried them away from the intimate moment that honesty revealed.

But what he said was, "I've been lost for almost a year now. Since I've gotten to Miramar, things have been better. Nice, even. Today was great. But the moment ends, and I'm left . . ."

She took his hand. Held it while the waitress deposited her wine. Then said again, soft as the gathering dusk, "Tell me."

Ian looked at her. This woman with the power to isolate them in the heart of a restaurant. Make an island of light and warmth. All with the touch of her hand, the look in those impossibly clear eyes. Kari Langham was not a beauty in any standard sense of the word. She was tall and strong, with a face drawn too sharply for today's taste. But to him, she was as lovely as the night. Her pale blue eyes struck him as too frank and open and intense for this world. Hers was the clearest gaze he had ever seen.

"There was a time . . . ," he said. Hearing himself shape the words, he took hold of his glass, set it back down. Watching it all from the distance of fatigue and something else. A lonely man calling out from the depths of his sad cave. "I never took it for granted. Not really. But it was just a part of me. The only time I was alone, the most important moment before a concert or session, I shut myself away and ran through a practice routine. I've done it ten thousand times. More."

He knew he wasn't telling it well. Part of him, whispers from his own dark corner, cried for him to stop. Be silent. Keep it hidden away. Nothing good would come from this barstool confession. He heard himself continue, "Before every session, I'd keep at it until I just . . . disappeared. Me, the guitar, the place, the audience, the recording studio, all the outside things that didn't matter. When it was just the music flowing through me, I was ready."

He stared at the fingers resting on his. "Now it's gone. My playing is a lie. Even on a day like this, as special as I've had in months. I'm performing. I'm doing what I need to do. Getting it out there. But inside . . ."

Kari's hand retreated. She whispered, "That's terrible."

Ian looked up and realized that her expression had gone from concerned to horrified. "You understand."

"Ian, I'm so sorry."

"I don't know what to do." Even the plea was not enough. "I said I wanted to take a year off. Now I'm dragged back in. Only I didn't fight it. A couple of studio sessions, playing here, and now Miami."

She jerked upright. "What?"

"Connor thinks I should agree to play in Miami's annual music festival. My former manager committed me to it. They're probably desperate to find . . . Kari, what's the matter?"

"When is the festival?"

"Five days."

She opened her mouth, but no sound came.

"My manager signed me up, then forgot to tell me. Or maybe he did, but I wasn't listening. The events definitely weren't in my calendar. Two performances. Now he's gone, and—" Ian stopped his rambling discourse because Kari was off her stool and backing away.

"There's something . . . I need to be going," she said.

"Kari, I'm so sorry. I should never—"

"I asked. You said." She was already heading for the door. "Sorry, sorry, it's just . . ."

She was gone.

CHAPTER 13

Kari returned to her car and took a meandering drive down Miramar's main street, almost allowing the car to guide itself. She pulled into the seaside lot and parked facing the Pacific. Rollers crashed so far out, the sound was softly muted through her open windows. A sliver of moon cast its feeble light, turning the long streamers of foam into silver-white blankets. She welcomed the chilly, salt-laden breeze. It helped anchor her to this new place, helped her make sense of these incredibly confusing new events.

Despite her racing mind, Kari remained filled with an eerie calmness. She felt as though she was being realigned at the atomic level. Her life had entered into a series of subtle changes. But all she could see were the external elements. A new home. A new town. An invitation to Miami. And now . . .

Her purse was an old-fashioned Fendi she had found at the back of her mother's closet, forgotten and forlorn. Her own years of hard use had rendered the shoulder bag shapeless and baggy. She rummaged through an assortment of pads, pens, colored pencils, cleaning cloths, and PowerBars, which she bought and seldom ate, and retrieved her phone.

Kari sat there a long moment, cradling the device in both hands. The moon rose another notch; the waves beckoned and whispered. Finally, she made the impossible call.

Graham answered with, "Kari, is everything all right?"

She opened her mouth, breathed again, then asked, "When do you need to tell them?"

It was Graham's turn to go quiet. Then, "Just a moment, dear." Rafi spoke in the background, and Graham replied, "It's nothing, really." A door closed, and he said, "There's no need to shorten Rafi's life span. Which we very well might, if we're talking about what I think we are."

"I'm just asking."

"The fair starts in five days."

"The same as the music festival?"

"How did you know that?"

"It's hard to explain."

"Well, to answer your question, the two cities' annual calendars are still jumbled by COVID. Before, the music thing was strictly Miami, and the art fair was Miami Beach. Those places were often at each other's throats."

"How do you know all this?"

"I was born in the next city north. A dreary place called Fort Lauderdale. Where the very old and feeble go to visit their parents."

"I feel terrible not knowing that."

"It's not something I advertise. You're not the only one who was eager to leave the past behind. It's why Rafi travels there on his own."

"So things are different between the two cities now?"

"At least for this year. Next year they might be taking aim across the Intracoastal Waterway. For now it's all huggykissy. The art exhibition has locations in downtown Miami, and the music festival is at both their main venues."

"But you're willing to go back?"

"With you? Showcased by the biggest art fair on the East Coast?" Graham gave that a beat, then said, "Is that your idea of a joke?"

This same bone-deep calm continued to override her frantic nerves during the drive home. She remained oddly fixed in the storm's silent eye as she fed the kitten and made herself a salad. Kari felt able to observe herself from a distance, while remaining intensely involved in the moment. When her meal was over, she settled Sienna in her lap and placed the night's second call.

Indrid answered with, "Kari, is everything all right?"

"I'm sorry to call so late."

"Nonsense. I'm delighted to hear from you. How are things?"

"Things," Kari replied, "are very confusing."

"Tell me everything."

As she began, Kari could see the older woman now, settled on the ivory love seat, placing her reading glasses on the coffee table, tucking her feet up under her, draping a cashmere throw over her legs. Ready to listen forever. Her dearest friend.

Kari started with dinner at Castaways, the remarkable foursome, wanting to photograph them for future work. Meeting Ian, their conversation. Painting all today. She acknowledged to herself as well as to Indrid that the creative surge was at least partly due to agreeing to a drink with one of her favorite music stars. Which led naturally to Graham's phone call. Entering the restaurant, finding Ian wrapped in his sad solitude. As she recounted Ian's explanation, she was silenced by the resurging terror. Losing her creative way, watching helplessly as her life's passion went away. Forever.

Indrid brought her back with "What happened next?"

Kari recounted Ian's agreement to play in Miami. At the festival. Timed to the event where they wanted to showcase Kari's work.

When she was done, Indrid did not respond. Kari stroked the purring kitten and welcomed the silence. The sensation of balanced calm versus electric rush was stronger now. As if she had taken a further step toward the nexus of this strange force.

Finally, Indrid said, "I think it's time I came up for a visit."

"Really?"

"Tomorrow," Indrid said. "I want to meet this gentleman for myself. Can you arrange that?"

Kari started to say it was impossible, since she had no idea what his number was or even where he lived. In the end, though, all she said was, "I'll try."

CHAPTER 14

The next morning found Ian back in Arthur's studio, drinking overly strong coffee and reviewing the final segments they needed for the film's completion. It was just the two of them discussing the day's work in musical shorthand, interrupting the songs with quick punctuations of what might work and how. Two professionals comfortable with each other and the work ahead.

The next four scenes that Arthur and Danny wanted Ian to bridge formed the lead-up to the film's climax. This was where far too many stories crashed and burned. Too slow, and the audience lost interest in following the drama. Too fast, and the emotions required for an explosive third act never developed. In the first bridge, both characters felt the other had let them down. In the second, they broke up. Again. Which was a terrible move as far as the story went, because the only way they might survive was by forging ahead together.

As Arthur fiddled with the microphones and their relative gain, Ian stared out the rear windows and thought about the previous night. The morning was still, not a breath of wind. Another Pacific mist blanketed the world below the ridge, sparkling gray and silver in the rising sun. Ian had traveled and played in over two dozen countries. And here he was, spellbound by a central California sunrise.

Playing with Connor in Castaways had seemed so natural. Amelia's presence had been so intensely close. She would have liked seeing him here, doing this work, extending himself in a new direction. Amelia had always felt the classical realm was overly constrictive, far too disciplined and stilted.

And then there was the night's other little surprise.

Kari Langham. Of all people. He had never even seen a photograph of the artist. And up she had sprung, feeling a need to apologize for not taking his photograph. Talking with him as if they had known each other for years. There was an ethereal quality to the lady, as if she was not truly comfortable with the world.

He liked her already.

Which made the previous evening's lightning-fast conversation all the more regrettable. He should never have burdened Kari with all his sorrowful confusion. Never, never, never.

Arthur broke into his reflection with, "All right, lad. Let's see if we can avoid making a complete and utter hash of this."

The rainbow heritage of Spanish classical music for guitar was rich in connections to the nation's varied past. The centuries when the Islamic Empire ruled the region, the Castile monarchs who conquered them, the years of conflict and strife all played a role in creating one of the most varied and challenging arenas for classical guitar.

Early in his training, Ian had found opportunities to escape through Spanish music. Teacher after teacher had demanded an attitude that gripped Ian as firmly as an iron straitjacket. "Don't stop," they said, and they repeated this with the firm confidence of one quoting holy verses. "Don't stop, don't think and, most important of all, don't feel. Just play the notes." When Ian complained that the fun was stripped away, along with his reason for wanting to play the music at all, he was punished, sometimes severely. "Fun is the enemy." They said that, as well. "Fun will not take you where you need to go."

He endured, and he learned. He made slaves of his hands, playing with a precision that eventually silenced his most ardent critics. And he found escapes when he could. Jazz and contemporary concerts with Amelia.

And the treasures he discovered in Spanish compositions.

Of those composers who became his secret allies, the most important was Isaac Albéniz, who had actually composed for the piano. Later interpretations, including Segovia's work, which Ian played on numerous occasions, focused upon Albéniz's use of *cante jondo*, the Romany method of singing. Albéniz incorporated themes from Andalusian folk music into his compositions. And most delightful of all, he used the exotic scales associated with flamenco music.

A flamenco guitar had a thinner top and less internal bracing than a classical guitar. It also featured what was known as a tap plate, which permitted the combining of drumbeats to the music. Ian had worn holes through the varnish of several classical guitars by copying the staccato beats required for such melodies. He had secretly considered these scars badges of honor.

The scenes Arthur and Danny wanted him to bridge were both heavy and hot-tempered. Ian took pleasure in bringing forth those hard-earned lessons, taking the melodies he was meant to bridge and tearing them apart.

He played the rage.

Raw, unadulterated, a crescendo of riffs filled the studio and resonated deeply. The music echoed his internal tumult. The conflicts he felt over his current state, the shame he had carried since learning of his manager's defection, the fury. His guitar wept for all he had lost. He shrieked his fear of all the empty tomorrows. For a very brief moment, the internal flames ignited once again. For all the wrong reasons. But still.

Too soon, it was over. He drove all the unwanted emotions back into their internal cage. He rejoined the second melody, forming a bridge for the song that would help carry the audience into the film's climax.

He stopped.

The silence resonated so deeply, he remained as he was, head bent over the silent strings. Seeing the sweat drip from his face and puddle on the guitar's upper rim. Feeling the fire gradually fade to ashes. And for once, he did not mind.

When he looked up, Arthur was seated behind the controls, solemn and watchful. Connor stood behind him, arms crossed, mouth slightly open.

Arthur cleared his throat, then said, "I believe we have what we need."

Ian stood by the chest-high rear wall, staring out over the vista. Rooftops and trees gave way in the distance to a trio of lines: first, the coastal road, then the seaside walkway, with its intricate connection of paths and bridges, and finally, the sandy shoreline, sparkling in the afternoon light. A slight trace of Pacific breeze cooled him as the sweat dried and the salt crinkled his skin. It was a beautiful moment, a good end to a fine session. One where his fear had no place. Even so, Ian stood cradling his phone in both hands, wishing he could find the strength to do what he knew had to be done.

Footsteps scrunched on the path, and Connor stepped up beside him. He sipped from his steaming mug, then said, "You did good in there. Arthur is as close to doing backflips as I've ever seen him."

"That was fun."

"Does that surprise you?"

"Totally. I can't remember the last time I enjoyed music this much."

Connor used his mug to point toward Ian's phone. "Scared of calling Miami?"

"Terrified."

"I take it you know the individual on the other end of that conversation you're not having?"

"Kiki Kerkorian's staff calls her the genteel assassin. She runs the festival and is also head of MISO, the Miami Symphony Orchestra," Ian replied. "When all this broke, she didn't call. She didn't try to find out what had happened. She ordered her lawyers into attack mode. That is basically all the introduction you need to Kiki Kerkorian."

Connor gave that a moment, then said, "But that's not really what's kept you frozen to the spot, now, is it?"

Ian swung around.

Now it was Connor's turn to stare at the sunlit vista. He sipped from his mug. Waiting.

"Excuse me?" Ian said finally.

Connor pointed behind them. "Why don't we move this inside, find you a nice quiet spot where you can enter meltdown in private?"

Ian hesitated, then followed him down the path. "That's not funny."

"Weird. I thought it was."

Arthur glanced up from his mixing board when they entered. At a motion from Connor, the old man slipped his headphones down around his neck.

Connor asked, "Can we use the studio?"

"For what, exactly?"

"You don't want to know."

"In that case, be my guest."

"Arthur, be a gent and turn off all the feeds."

The old man slapped a pair of switches. "As if I have any

interest whatsoever in your private affairs. Inside what was formerly my private space."

Connor motioned Ian inside the recording studio and closed the door. "Make yourself comfortable."

Ian selected a chair by the side wall. "Why are you doing this?"

Connor settled onto the piano stool. "I'll tell you. But mind if I ask a question first?"

"I suppose."

"Yesterday you said you'd lost the passion that fueled your music and your rise. When did that happen?"

"I can't say for certain. I claim it was fourteen months back. But really that's just when I couldn't ignore the change any longer. It was so gradual, I didn't actually notice at first. Then one night, after a concert in Montreal, I got back to my dressing room, looked in the mirror, and there was this cadaver staring back. Lifeless."

"Scary."

"Awful."

Connor studied his empty mug. "So maybe what you're really frightened of now is going back into that same desperate moment. Isolated and empty. Nothing but dust and ashes. A blanket so thick, it cuts off your air."

Ian pressed a fist to his gut. Swallowed against the rising gorge. Wanted to ask again how the man knew. But the words did not come.

Connor went on. "As far back as I can remember, all I ever wanted was to be a singer. Play the soft jazz, the swing, bring all those old hits to life in a new age. So I moved to LA, made the circuits, played the gigs. Then one night I performed at a wedding reception for a big Hollywood producer. You know the line. I hoped this might be my big break. Only the hope wasn't really there. I was telling myself the same old lie I'd repeated a hundred nights before."

Connor swung the stool around so that he stared at the

piano keys. "Midway through the second set, a lady started this drunken jag, screaming so loud she shut us down. Then she flipped over her table, sent glass and plates and cutlery flying everywhere. Everybody started scrambling and shouting. I looked at my band, ready to suggest we take another break. And I really saw them. Maybe for the first time. All three were so stoned, they barely noticed. Helpless and lost. Just like me."

Ian uttered, "Wow."

Connor nodded to the keys. "That same night the agent who still represents me came up and said I might have what it takes to make it in film. As an actor. Not a musician. And I did. Make it. And I'm happy. I love my family and my life. Mostly." He pointed at the silent instrument. "When I'm not off on another shoot, every month or so, I sit in Sylvie's restaurant and live a tiny shred of my dream. Until one day my neighbor phones and says there's this star doing some work for our pal Danny. Would I like to sit in? And between takes I look at his face, and I see exactly what I went through."

Connor looked at him for the first time since entering the studio. "You haven't lost your gift. If you have any doubt about that, go have a word with Arthur. Sooner or later, you'll find what's necessary to rekindle that precious flame. It may not be in the way you expect. But it will come. Right now, in this moment, all you're doing is repairing a hole in your commercial world. That's all. Nothing more." He gave Ian a moment to respond, and when he didn't, Connor asked, "Ready?"

Ian nodded.

"Good." Connor walked over, opened the door, said, "Make the call."

There was no logical reason why Connor's confession would render Ian so calmly resolute. But logic held little sway in that remarkable moment. Taking a willful step back into the world from which he had fled. All arguments to the contrary, Connor was right. He needed to do this.

A young man's voice answered, "MISO. How do I direct your call?"

"The director's office, please."

"Who do I say is calling?"

"Ian Hart."

A pause, then, "Really?"

"Yes."

"Hold please."

Eons passed. Ice ages began and retreated. Then, "Ian?"

"Hello, Kiki."

"You have thirty seconds."

"I didn't know I was booked to play your festival until the MISO lawyers went on the attack."

"So the rumors are true."

"There are so many, at least some of them have to be."

"I'm not calling them off. Our attorneys can tear you apart, for all I care. So don't bother begging."

"That's not . . . Okay, it would be nice to have my life back. And my home. But I'm calling to say I'll play." When Kiki did not respond, he went on, "A friend suggested I ask that in return, you help rebuild my good name. But I'm not asking. If you want to do it, fine. But my offer is without strings."

Ian heard the woman breathe through pursed lips. "Our advance . . ."

"Is in some Aruba bank, as far as I know. And no, I'm not asking for that, either. I'm coming, and I'll play. If you still want me." He stared through the studio's glass wall, over to where Connor and Arthur were both doing their best to look anywhere but at him. "This is about honoring commitments."

"Well." Another breath. "Few things astonish me in this

business. And most that do are dreadful." Then, "Rehearsals start in three days."

"I'll be there. What am I playing?"

"You truly don't know?"

"I have no contract, no alert, no note on my calendar. Truly."

"If your louse of a manager ever returns, promise you'll let me skin him."

"No."

She might have laughed. "You're starring in our opening concert. This year's festival coincides with the delayed art fair. You've been sold out for months."

He asked again, "Kiki, what am I playing?"

"This is the oddest conversation I've had in thirty years."

"Kiki."

"Rodrigo's Concierto de Aranjuez. And Vivaldi's Concerto in D Major."

He knew them both. Intimately. Had performed them countless times. "Who is conducting?"

"You really don't know, do you?" When Ian did not respond, she said, "Israel Saban."

"Good. Wonderful, in fact."

"Not really. Israel is furious. He's demanding that I ditch you. Bring in someone who doesn't threaten us with a last-minute tantrum." A pause, then, "Should I?"

"No tantrums," he replied. "I'll give you the best that I have."

"You better."

"I'm sorry, Kiki. Really, really sorry."

"Enough to do the second gig?"

"I heard about that. I don't remember where. Maybe I saw it online."

This time her laugh was clearly audible. "Your ex-louse booked you for 'An Intimate Conversation with Ian Hart.' Just you and several hundred of your closest admirers."

"What am I playing?"

"In this case, whatever you like."

Ian studied the two men beyond the wall and sensed an idea taking form. He opened his mouth, tasted the air, decided the idea was a good one. Better than that. He asked, "Do I have to play classical?"

Another longish pause, then, "It's not polite to render me speechless."

"I've been working on a film score with Connor Larkin."

"The film star?"

"And pianist. And singer. He's good, Kiki. Outstanding, in fact. His specialty is soft jazz and renditions of late-era big band."

"You. And Connor Larkin. An intimate evening on Miami Beach's New World Center stage."

"I haven't asked him. I just came up with the idea while we've been talking. But I'm pretty sure he'll say yes."

"Go ask. I'll wait. And, Ian . . ."

"Yes?"

"Oh, nothing. Hurry. I'm quite sure I'm late for something vital. I just can't remember what."

Ian decided he wasn't up for a solitary meal in his apartment. He headed for the diner, then decided a bar was more in keeping with his mood. So he returned to the same stool at Castaways and sat nursing another glass of excellent local grape, reviewing the day.

Everything about it rang true. It was an almost silly way to describe the work and the repetitive takes and the people who crowded in. But Ian felt those words best fit the long and tiring day. Especially given how he was left with a distinct sense of making new friends. Finding his own place in a town where he already felt at home.

His thoughts then veered back to the previous evening.

Sitting here in this spot. Sending his favorite artist fleeing into the night.

He reviewed their too-brief conversation and decided he had done nothing wrong. She had asked; he had answered honestly. If honesty was a reason to run off, well, so be it.

Just the same, Ian wished things had turned out differently.

He asked to see the menu and ordered the lamb. The restaurant was lively but far from full. When his meal was ready, the bartender, a lady with dark, dancing eyes, offered him a table. Ian replied that he was happy where he was. She offered a flirtatious smile and said, "That makes two of us."

As he was finishing, Arthur walked in. "Mind some company?"

"Not at all. Is this a coincidence?"

"Hardly." Arthur grimaced as Sylvie emerged from the kitchen and kissed his cheek. He asked, "Where's our lad?"

"Driving the nanny back. She wasn't feeling well." To Ian, she said, "Our boys spend the morning at home. Most evenings they're shifted into the apartment upstairs. I like to be the one who tucks them in at night. When we close, Connor and I swoop them up, and they wake up in their own beds."

The bartender offered, "They'll either be great travelers or seriously schizoid."

Arthur said, "That's actually not a proper term, Marcela."

"Of course it is. You'll find it in the dictionary, right after *seriously grouchy*." Marcela smiled at the old man. "Hi, Arthur."

He grimaced. "I suppose you'll be wanting to kiss the old wattled cheek."

"Been waiting for this moment all day."

Sylvie asked Ian, "How was the meal?"

"Great. Better than that."

"What we like to hear."

Danny Byrd entered the restaurant, accompanied by his fiancée, the attorney Megan Pierce. Connor arrived back two minutes later. As the greetings and laughter grew, Ian had the sense of being drawn into a clannish community. Old friends who gladly made room for him. He found himself wishing Kari were still there, that it was the two of them together being welcomed into this group.

Which was when Arthur said, "I suppose we'd best tell the man of the hour what's going on here."

"Not just yet." Sylvie said to Marcela, "Open a bottle of that stuff we couldn't unload last New Year's Eve."

"On it." Marcela went through a professional's process of icing seven glasses, setting them out on little starched napkins, then uncorked the champagne with a flourish. They watched in happy silence as she filled the glasses, picked up the last one for herself, and asked, "What do we toast?"

"I've always been partial to Winston Churchill's comment," Arthur replied. "'Champagne should always be cold, dry, and free.'"

"I'm not toasting another old grouch," Marcela said. "Especially one who's dead."

"Here's to friends, old and new," Sylvie said.

Connor lost his smile. "And dreams long dead."

Sylvie used her free arm to embrace her husband. "Not dead. Never dead. Just dormant."

"No longer," Danny said. "Right, Ian?"

"Absolutely," Ian said, feeling vaguely ashamed over how he missed a woman he did not actually know.

They drank; then Megan nudged her fiancé. "Go on, then. Say your say."

Danny said to Ian, "I've had a word with the powers that be."

"He means the folks running Amazon Prime," Arthur said. "And it was more than one word. Several hours' worth.

First, they talked. Then Danny showed them a revised rough cut of the film, now including some of your musical bridges. Then they talked again."

"They're impressed with what we're doing here," Danny continued.

"Blown away, more like," Arthur offered.

"Who's the guy telling this?"

"You are, mate. Megan and I are just filling in the blanks."

"They're going to give my new film a limited theatrical release," Danny went on.

Megan said, "Enough to make the project open to possible film awards."

"So I went ahead and played them another rough cut, this of the video we shot of your and Connor's music," Danny revealed.

Arthur said, "Against my strident objections. I hate music rough cuts worse than a rash on my unmentionables."

"They want me to ask if we can film you and Connor playing in Miami," Danny said. "Put together a documentary. Amazon wants to release it along with the film."

Ian shrugged. "That's not for me to say."

"Ahem," Megan said. "May the lawyer have a word?"

"Whenever does a barrister ask permission?" Arthur tapped the side of his empty glass. "Oi, barkeep."

Marcela plied the bottle. "Somebody ought to teach you manners, old man."

"Not worth the trouble," Sylvie said.

Megan said, "Danny asked if I'd help with that. So I phoned Kiki Kerkorian. Just in case you might be willing to let this happen."

"Megan put her on speaker," Danny said, smiling. "Kiki didn't actually do handsprings. But she came close."

"The Miami Music Festival, an Amazon Prime special," Arthur said. "Starring Ian Hart and Connor Larkin. What's not to love?"

Danny added, "Recorded and mixed and edited by none other than the winner of three Oscars, Arthur Rowe."

Arthur accepted his refilled glass, toasted Marcela. "Oh. Him."

Danny said, "So now's the moment when we ask if you might be willing to let this happen."

All eyes were on Ian now. All save Connor's. The actor stared at his wife's hand, the one anchoring him to earth. Not sad, not really. Just the same, the man's expression brought a lump to Ian's throat.

He managed, "I would be honored."

As they broke up, Danny drew Ian to one side. "Megan tells me you're short of money."

He hated having to admit, "Very."

Danny handed him a check. "Full payment for your initial segments."

The simple act should not have moved him as it did. "Thank you so much."

"Your attorney has the new contract ready for signatures. This one covers the documentary, a possible album, and residuals. There's a signing bonus, which should ease your way through the next few months." Danny's smile was more a grimace. "Just ignore the tearstains I left in the margins."

CHAPTER 15

That night Kari dreamed she was painting. And yet she was also inside the work itself. She painted a mist-clad road through an indistinct scene of low, half-formed structures. Inside the painting, Kari was scarcely able to see her next step. She wished she could tell herself to make things out more clearly. But, of course, no figure in a painting could be given a voice.

Up ahead, an individual walked, holding a lantern. The light was diffused by the drifting fog coming from this location, then from somewhere else, shifting points and directions. Just the same, Kari was not worried. She was almost happy to follow in the path laid out by this half-formed figure. The curious meandering journey captivated her.

Then she woke and discovered the kitten had crawled onto her pallet and was breathing softly on her neck. Kari dressed and picked up the kitten and padded through the house. She left by way of the rear door and crossed the starlit path. There was no mist here, just dry sorrel flavors of a clear California night.

Inside the atelier, she set up another canvas and sketched swiftly. By dawn the dreamscape was taking shape. The canvas showed a woman rushing forward, hand outstretched, desperate to take hold of a man she could not quite see.

Kari slept until half past ten and probably would have gone much longer had her phone not started ringing. She rose from her pallet, took the phone from her purse, and saw on the readout that it was Indrid who had rung her. Kari decided to wait until she had fed the mewing kitten and prepared coffee before calling back. She knew why Indrid had phoned. That conversation definitely required coffee.

Fifteen minutes later, Indrid answered with, "Did you find him?"

"I just woke up. I spent most of last night painting."

"As far as excuses go," Indrid said, "that one is close to top of my list."

"I don't know if I can find him." Kari knew she sounded petulant. There was nothing she could do about it. In the clear morning light, the entire idea sounded ludicrous.

"If you can't, you can't." Indrid refused to budge. "Do what you can."

"I can't see why it's so important."

"Can't you?"

"We only talked twice. Thirty seconds each time. Less."

"And the amount of time is so very important, is it?"

"Well, of course it is." The previous day's calm was gone now. Kari opened the kitchen door, nudged the kitten back inside, then walked into the atelier and stood staring at the new canvas. The first traces of colors were almost dry. She had started by painting the mist-shrouded man and his brilliant lantern. The glow reached out of the canvas, warming her.

"Kari?"

"The painting I started last night. I think it's very good.

Actually, I've been working on three more or less together. They feel—I don't know—different."

Indrid surprised her then. Almost always the older woman used such moments to draw Kari back to the topic at hand. Not allowing her to evade the uncomfortable by changing subjects. Only today she asked, "Is this normal, your working on so many projects all at once?"

"No." She stood directly beneath the central skylight, which meant the easels were spaced around her. Kari inspected each in turn, then shivered. "Almost never."

"Is it possible this gentleman has something to do with your creative surge?"

She felt herself being ejected from the atelier. She stepped back into the sunlight, closed the door on all the unfinished works. "Certainly not."

"Just asking."

"It has nothing to do with Ian. And everything to do with Miramar."

"I see."

Kari stared at the small structure set farther from the house. "Speaking of which, I want you to stay in the guest cottage. But there isn't any furniture."

"You have a guest cottage? That's perfect. I worried about disturbing your routine."

"Indrid, I mean what I say. I have one pallet, two sheets, a blanket, two towels, two plates, one pot. A table and two chairs. And the things I brought for Sienna." She felt both defiant and ashamed. "I want to take my time with everything else."

"I understand."

Kari pressed on. "Find things that suit me and this home. Besides, I like the empty space. It breathes with me. I know that probably sounds a little nuts."

"Don't say that. Don't even think such a thing. It sounds divine. May I bring something?"

"If you're staying here, you have to."

"Not for me, silly. For you. Can I bring a gift? So you have something of me in your new home."

"I would like that more than anything."

"Then it's settled," Indrid said. "Now go see if you can locate your young man."

"He's not my anything."

"Kari."

"All right. All right. I'm going."

Kari parked just up the main street's gentle slope from Castaways. The instant the car stopped rolling, she cut the motor and opened her door and started walking. She was giving herself no time to argue her way out of this next step. She had no idea what to say. Asking some stranger for a way to contact a man she didn't know, after having run away from their first real conversation? Absurd.

Yet as soon as she entered, Kari was glad she had come.

Connor Larkin was seated at the piano, with Ian on a barstool facing him. Ian had his guitar propped on one thigh and a notepad stationed on the baby grand's closed top. He and Connor were both making notes and talking softly. Three heavyset women occupied more stools between the piano and the big bay window. The woman closest to Connor nodded in time to something Ian said and made her own notes.

Two more men occupied a pair of front tables, pages and phones and computers spread out before them. The woman Kari had last seen managing the restaurant sat at the table closest to the piano. She bottle-fed one infant, while another was held by the bartender. Four other people moved slowly about the restaurant, setting up for the night ahead.

A young Latino spotted Kari and said, "Sorry. We don't open until six."

Which was when Ian looked over.

He settled the guitar in its stand, jumped off the stage, and rushed across the restaurant. He moved so fast, he collided with the bar. Just bounced off it, ricocheted with a chair, and forged on. "You came."

All the words she struggled to half form, all the excuses and reasons for being here, just dissolved. "I'm so sorry."

"You're apologizing?"

"Well, of course."

The man looked impossibly handsome when he laughed. "I've spent hours racking my brain, trying to figure out what I did wrong."

"Nothing." The words gushed out, almost without thought. "You didn't do anything wrong. It's just . . . When you started talking about next week, it scared me."

He showed confusion. "Next week?"

"Yes."

"You mean the festival?"

She nodded. "They want me to go."

The older man at the front table called back, "Ian, we're waiting here."

Ian showed no sign he had even heard. "They want you to go to Miami?"

"For the art fair." She breathed around the enormity of it all. "I just found out. When you saw me in the car . . . It was my agent. That's why I was late. Well, that and I was sketching a new concept. I needed to get the idea down on paper while the emotions were still fresh. And then my agent called. And said the art fair wants to do a retrospective."

Ian shocked her then. A simple moment in time, but somehow her view of this man changed entirely when he asked, "Did you bring it with you?"

Kari needed a moment to realize he meant her sketchbook. "I carry it with me everywhere."

"Can I see?"

She drew the sketchbook from her purse, astonished at

how easy it felt. And *right*. Showing this almost stranger what she kept hidden from everyone. Kari turned to the sketches she'd done before Graham's call. "Here. These."

He turned the pages. So very slowly.

The old man called Ian's name a second time. Connor spoke too softly for Kari to understand the words. The three women laughed.

Ian turned the next page, revealing a blank sheet, and sighed. Closed the cover. Didn't hand the sketchbook back. Did not look up. Just stood there.

She had to tug the sketchbook to get him to release it.

"Kari, these are amazing."

It was beyond easy to confess, "I'm terrified of going."

He breathed once. Like he was awakening. Only then did he look up. "You don't want to go to Miami?"

"I've never been anywhere. I don't . . . I revealed myself as Kariel only last week. It was part of my leaving LA and starting here. Being honest."

She felt like the words had jagged edges. Just the same, she was glad she had spoken.

Especially when he nodded once and softly declared, "You need to protect your gift."

She opened her mouth, but no words emerged.

"If you decide to go, I'll do all I can to help." This time, his smile was weighted down by the sorrow in his gaze. "It's a lesson I need to learn myself. If there's still time."

"Have dinner with me tonight."

"Of course."

"I have a friend coming up. Her name is Indrid Anand. She wants to meet you." Kari realized how that probably sounded. "Not because of who you are. She's my oldest and dearest friend."

"She wants to help protect your gift. Which means meeting me."

Having Ian understand her and connect with her secret

needs at such a level that it made him sad left Kari so intensely conflicted that she didn't know whether to embrace him or flee. "Yes. Only we can't meet at my new home. I don't have any furniture. Yet. It's just . . . I want to take my time."

Ian seemed to find nothing amiss with her living in an empty home. His only response was, "We can eat at my place."

"All right."

"Or we can go out." He smiled. "I know a great restaurant."

"No. Your place is better."

"It's very small, Kari. Kind of cramped, even when it's just me."

"Better than sitting on my kitchen floor."

"A little. Maybe." He walked back to the stage, retrieved his pad and pen. Spoke a few words, then returned.

"This is my address and number." He wrote, tore out the page, handed it over. "Thank you for coming today. So much."

"I'm glad I did. Really."

He started toward the stage. Then turned back long enough to say, "Kari, I wish I had met you years ago."

Kari stood there a long moment, captured by the torrent of emotions. Finally, she stepped to the bar and pulled out her sketchbook. Swiftly she drew a new image. One of a man seated on a stool, playing a classical guitar. A storm of smoke and burning cinders surrounded him, whirling with hurricane force.

A heart's flame flickered in feeble defiance to the tempest.

CHAPTER 16

Ian drove straight from the session with Connor to the town's main supermarket. He could have ordered another meal from Castaways, but he wanted to show a bit more imagination. The way Kari had spoken this newcomer's name, Indrid Anand, suggested a special bond. He bought the deli's own kiln-smoked salmon and fresh-baked bread. At the bottle shop next door, he selected a pair of California whites and added a bottle of French champagne. He then walked down to a Lebanese restaurant that anchored the outdoor mall's far corner, and ordered traditional meze, a myriad of small dishes. He hoped Kari and her guest would approve.

Back home he put the wines in the fridge and the bread and the meze in the oven to warm. He mixed together a cabbage salad with mayonnaise, lemon, and a hint of horseradish, then hurried into the bedroom to shower and change. He returned and spent a few minutes cleaning the front room before the doorbell rang.

Kari arrived bearing flowers and a very nervous air. Her

guest, however, was something else entirely. Indrid Anand was a rather small woman and held herself impossibly erect. Ian guessed her age at midsixties, but he could have been off by a decade either way. Her dark hair was laced with silver; her eyes were piercingly alert. She accepted Ian's welcome with solemn grace, inspected him a long moment, then stood in the stubby foyer and swept her gaze over the living-dining area.

She declared, "This is a woman's home."

"My late aunt's," Ian replied.

"A woman of taste and heart," she said, nodding approval. "She was close to you?"

"The only real family I ever had."

Indrid's gaze rested on the framed poster of Ian, a promo shot for his second album. "And you cared for her as she did you?"

"So much."

"I am sure you were both enriched as a result."

"We were, yes." Ian assumed the formal air he adopted before his European events. "Please. You are both most welcome."

The meal flowed from there. Any awkward moments that might have arisen between Ian and Kari were avoided by them making Indrid the focus of their attention. Just the same, they shared a few intense glances, along with small smiles and occasional comments. As Ian removed the first course, he caught a glimpse of Indrid nodding approval to her friend.

Toward the end of their second course, Indrid asked about his aunt. It seemed the most natural thing in the world to Ian to describe the role she had played in his life. Which led naturally to why he was here at all. In Miramar. Trying to find his way back.

Indrid proved an excellent listener. Neither by word nor gesture, but rather with a stillness and intensity. He genuinely liked speaking openly with this woman. Even when it hurt to confess, even when he wondered if he was dominating the conversation, and perhaps pushing Kari away again. Even then.

When he finally went silent, Indrid responded by murmuring, "Good. Very good indeed."

The words propelled him from the table. "I would call my situation anything but."

"You misunderstand me." Indrid rose with him, and Kari followed. Together they began the process of clearing the table. "Of course, I am sorry for the distress you've faced over these many months. But to have arrived at this point, and to *know* you are there, this is a singular achievement."

Ian would have said the kitchen was too small for the three of them. Yet here they were, moving in sync, the ladies loading the dishwasher while he made coffee. "Achievement."

"Indeed so. Very few artists ever realize this wall you're confronting even exists."

It seemed his role now was to repeat each key term. "The wall."

Indrid closed the dishwasher and leaned against the counter. "This awareness is quite rare, especially with someone at your level of fame. You understand?"

"I'm trying."

"The temptation is to remain willfully blind. Most artists glimpse the internal storm, and they flee. They rush into whatever comes next, the concert, the photo op, the drugs, the . . . whatever. You must have recognized this, no?"

He was glad for the need to pull out cups and saucers, retrieve milk from the fridge, anything to avoid meeting the woman's dark gaze. "Why does it make me feel so ashamed to admit that?"

"Because you are being honest and open both. And doing so with a stranger. For which I am indeed grateful."

He stared at the coffee maker, intensely aware of the women now standing to either side. "Sometimes I wish I had done just that. Run into the next big thing."

"But you didn't. And your task now is to accept that you are strong enough to be aware. To face this struggle. Accept it as both real and vital." Indrid tapped one long fingernail on the back of his wrist in time to her words. "This is an *opportunity*. Your spirit is telling you, you have taken this previous course as far as you possibly can. Now it is time for the *next* challenge."

"That absolutely terrifies me," he confessed.

"I am sure it does. But you are taking the right steps. Forging ahead. Making your way through the wall."

Ian poured them coffees and indicated the sugar and milk. He did not bother making one for himself. Just then, his stomach would not have taken it well. "How can you be so sure?"

"Because, young man, I have witnessed this struggle before. Not often. But enough to see the signs of success in you and your words." She accepted her cup and moved back to the table. When Kari joined her, Indrid went on, "I often wonder if this is perhaps why so many artists die young. They'd do anything rather than take this dread step, examine themselves honestly. They seek a way to flee altogether."

Ian remained standing. "What do I do now?"

"Precisely what you are currently doing. Accept the quest." She patted the table by his empty chair. Only when he was seated did she continue. "Simply because you can't see the road ahead, this does not grant you a reason to stop walking. You understand what I am saying?"

A big breath, then, "Can we talk again?"

"My dear young man." Her smile took in the two other people at the table. "It would be a distinct honor to share this journey with you."

CHAPTER 17

That night Kari gave in to temptation and googled Ian Hart.

Sixty million options for her to choose from.

Kari scrolled through all the recent junk, the scandal and the delighted way in which the fanzines trumpeted how the star was brought to earth. Further back she went, until she was looking at Ian the star.

And his ladies.

So many of them. All so lovely, glittering, smiling, showing the world how thrilled they were to be with this man. Stars and fashion models. Women who looked perfect in whatever.

She could not get a clear impression of how Ian felt about it all, however. Not even about the one rumored to be his fiancée. A model. From Bulgaria . . .

Kari cut off her phone and pressed it to her middle. Willing herself to calm down. Swallowing against her queasiness.

When she could, she returned to her little pallet. Wishing she could take it back. Not know what she did now.

Ian Hart belonged to the world she had fled.

* * *

She was woken by sounds in the kitchen. The kitten was still asleep, nuzzled up to the nape of her neck. Kari slipped from the bed and found full, late-morning sunlight streaming over the eastern hills. She washed her face and slipped into her clothes. But when she opened the bedroom door, Sienna remained sprawled on Kari's pillow, staring up at her.

"Aren't you hungry?"

Sienna's only response was a minute twitch of her tail.

Kari waved toward the open door. "Indrid is my oldest and dearest friend."

Another twitch.

Kari left the door open and followed the smell of fresh-brewed coffee to the kitchen. "Sienna is being shy. Again. Maybe I should carry her in."

"Perhaps she's a one-woman cat," Indrid said. "Then again, many young animals are shy."

Kari made herself a cup, sipped, and followed Indrid to the rear porch. "I checked out Ian online."

Indrid settled into one of the two rockers Noah had left. "When?"

"Middle of the night." Another sip. "I didn't get back to sleep until dawn."

Indrid gave the sunlit hills a long look. "And now he wants to be with you."

"For the moment."

The older woman shook her head. "I don't think that's the case." A sip, then, "And neither do you."

"He thinks I'm special."

"Because you are."

"You've always said that."

"Because it's true."

"Have you seen the women he's been with?" Kari almost wailed the words.

"No. But I can imagine. And here's the plain and simple truth, dear one. Now he wants to be with you."

"But for how long?"

"None of us can ever know the answer to that. Which only makes our time together more special." A final sip, and then she rose to her feet and started for the door. "More coffee?"

Kari passed over her cup without looking up.

When Indrid returned, Kari said, "You sound so . . ."

"Calm? Pleased?" Indrid settled back in the rocker. "Happy for you?"

"Glib."

Indrid rocked a long moment, then asked, "Have you called your managers?" When Kari remained silent, Indrid added, "Your friends?"

"I just woke up."

"My dear, those two are no doubt wearing grooves in the gallery floor."

"How can I call anyone? I haven't decided whether I'm going or not."

"Now you're being silly. Of course you are. It was clear enough in your gaze last night. You want to go. You want to be with him. There. At this event." Indrid's gaze was warm. Beckoning. Filled with good humor. "You want to know if he prefers you over all these fashionable ladies who litter his past, no? Fine. Call Graham and Rafi. Let those two wonderful men celebrate with you."

"Indrid—"

"Dear one, go inside and make the call." She turned back to the day. "I need to be heading home. But first, I want to see what you've been working on since your arrival."

That next morning, Danny shifted their session to Arthur's studio. Connor was reluctant, but Ian wholeheartedly agreed with the move. He knew it was a far better spot for the whirlwind to come, and so did Arthur. It was crucial that they pull Connor away from the stage, where he was most comfortable. Where playing with his little group was fun. As Ian's former instructors used to say, fun would not take them where they needed to go.

It was one thing to perform for a group of longtime enthusiasts in Sylvie's restaurant, where any small error would be happily overlooked. The same easy state also existed during recording sessions, where multiple takes were common. But they would face an entirely different situation in Miami. They would be playing in front of a highly critical audience who had paid a hundred dollars or more for a seat. Not to mention the professional critics and journalists eager to headline the next chapter of Ian Hart's fall from the lofty heights.

Danny had gently insisted their backup group be expanded to include the three women. Arthur complained mightily, but Ian suspected he was equally pleased. The women's voices and professional manners would go a long way toward smoothing out any rough edges. Which there were bound to be.

With Arthur's silent agreement, Danny asked for the musical lineup to expand beyond the film's soundtrack. Woven into this were numbers from Connor's existing repertoire, with a focus on songs that fashioned a seamless musical tapestry.

Over an early lunch of sandwiches and coffee, Connor asked how large Ian thought their audience would be. "That is, assuming anybody shows up."

"No question there," Ian replied. "Kiki says the gig's been sold out for weeks."

Connor dropped his sandwich back on the wrapper. "How many?"

"I've never played the small salon. Three-fifty to four hundred is my guess."

Trish, the eldest of the ladies, asked, "And the big place where you have your first concert?"

"Just over two thousand," Ian responded.

Lucinda asked, "Can we come?"

"If you want, sure."

"Is that a joke?" This from Maxine, the de facto team leader. "Do we want. Huh."

"It's classical music," Ian pointed out, only half joking. "No jive. Very little beat. Hip-hop is barred at the door."

Lucinda raised a hand the size of a skillet. "You're looking for a taste of Dominican heat, you don't watch out."

Trish asked, "Didn't you say that first gig is sold out, too? How can you find us seats?"

"They almost always assign me a box," Ian told her.

"A box?" Lucinda.

"He means one of those little rooms with the balcony." Maxine.

"It will be a tight fit, but I think we can probably get everyone inside." Ian addressed Connor. "Sylvie is welcome, if she's coming."

Connor continued to inspect the sandwich he wasn't eating. "The wife says it all depends on the babies."

Maxine leaned in close. "You all right there? You've gone all green."

"Connor will be fine," Arthur said.

"If there's room, Megan would love to join everyone in the box," Danny said. "But I'll probably be stationed by Arthur's control board. You know. In case the man here needs reminding which knobs to twist."

"There's probably some polite way to describe just how unwelcome a producer is in my box," Arthur replied. "It just doesn't come to mind."

"I'll have a word with Kiki soon as we're done here." Ian's phone rang. He checked the readout and instantly rose to his feet. "I need to take this."

Ian left the studio and took the path around to the rear wall. "Kari?"

"Hello, Ian."

"Is something wrong?"

"I have no idea."

"You sound worried."

"I'm so scared."

He took a long moment, savoring the view and the words. There was no longer a wise older woman playing go-between. This was him and her. "How can I help?"

"I don't know if anyone can. I don't even know why I called."

"I'm glad you did." He paused, then added more softly, "Let me try to help. Please. I really want to."

Her next words came in a breathless rush. "Indrid is out on the porch. She thinks I should call Graham and accept. You know, Miami. I think . . . she might be right. She probably is. But everything is moving so *fast*."

"I understand."

"Do you? Really?"

"Totally. I came here thinking I'd step back from the mad rush. Do a big nothing for as long as I needed. Instead, it's been full speed ahead since the moment I walked into Megan's office. Doing what I ran from and more besides. A lot more."

She was silent. Her breaths puffed against his ear. As intimate a moment as any he'd known in a long while.

"Kari, I understand," he repeated. "You're facing your own hurricane. You're worried about what happens to your gift."

She did not respond.

"So here's what I think. Take as long as you need. You're the only person who can decide whether it's right to go."

"Indrid thinks I should. That I need to."

He softly pounded a fist on the wall. Marking time for his words. "Maybe she's right. But this is your decision. Not hers. And the key here, the absolute most important thing, is what impact this will have on your *next* work."

Kari did not respond.

"Not what you've already painted. Your people see the outside. The commercial. They're focused on what is already done. Already out there. You're worried about your next work of art."

Kari remained silent.

"And you're right to be worried, Kari. Because that's the most important issue of all. What happens when you come back from the hurricane, and you're working on your new painting?"

A long silence, then, "I'm going to Miami."

"How can I help?"

"Be my friend."

"Kari." It was his turn to pause for a soft breath. "I want that more than almost anything."

"I don't even know what that word means. *Friend.*"

"You know," Ian replied. "You just don't know what it means with me." When Kari remained silent, he went on, "Thank you for trusting me, Kari. So much."

CHAPTER 18

Kari stood staring at Indrid's gift. Her oldest friend had brought an antique French cabinet called a commode. The slender legs were curved, like the delicate steps a ballerina might make. The side panels and the two front doors were inlaid with polished burl. The top was sheathed in ormolu, the gold alloy carved with designs from the reign of Louis XIV. Kari's living room was now redefined by this work of art, in the way that a beautiful painting might give meaning to a wall.

She felt herself filled with an eerie calm. She had expected to be shaking in her bones, knowing that she was about to put her newfound liberty and creative fire on the line. Instead, she merely flowed into the next moment. Speed-dialing Graham's private line. Listening to his phone ring.

"Kari?"

"I think I should do this."

"I need to sit down." Silence, then, "Are you sure?"

"No. I'm a billion miles from certain about anything." She breathed around the immensity of her words. "But it feels right."

"Is it all right if I share this with Rafi?" Graham's voice was unsteady.

"Yes."

"Just a minute, dear." He did not cover the phone, which meant she could hear Graham say the words, "We're going to Miami."

Rafi snapped, "Give me the phone."

"Rafi . . ."

"Don't you 'Rafi' me. I need to hear this for myself." A long moment, and then Rafi asked her, "This is for real? Really real?"

"Yes, Rafi. Really, really real."

His silence carried an emotion, an energy, something strong enough to cause her to shiver. Then a trembly, "Here's Graham. And, Kari . . ."

"Yes?"

"Oh, nothing."

Graham said, "We've been fielding calls every hour or so. The fact that you haven't said no has had them dumping ever more chips on the table."

"I have no idea what you're talking about," Kari responded.

"Incentives, dear." Graham sounded eerily calm now. As if her own weird state had passed through the phone and infected him. "We are now up to your having the premier suite at the Ritz Carlton South Beach, and quite a nice one for us, as well. Private jet to sweep us all up as soon as you give the word. Hot and cold running limos."

She heard Rafi cry from the background, "Ask her about the paintings!"

Graham said, "They'd like to include samples of your recent work. Your friend Dr. Anand was scheduled to have her painting delivered tomorrow. Your brother is moving and wanted us to hold his until he's settled. We were wondering . . ."

"I'm sure Indrid will agree." It was her turn to hesitate. "Would you mind asking Justin for me?"

"Not at all, dear. Anything else?"

"No. Well . . ." She stared at the hand stroking the purring kitten. Tiny flecks of paint rimmed one fingernail. "I have some works you haven't seen."

"You mean your current paintings?"

"No. Well, yes, those too. But I kept others back from the past two shows. I brought them to Miramar with me."

A longish silence, then a very weak "How many?"

"Fourteen, plus those I've been working on here."

"Oh. My."

Rafi shrilled in the background, "*Tell me*!"

"Kari has been hiding work from us. Fourteen paintings, plus her new ones." A pause. Then he told Kari, "Rafi is now prostrate on the floor."

"I have no idea if any of these fourteen are up to exhibition standards," she cautioned. "I just felt a special bond . . . something. I wasn't ready to give them up, so I kept them hidden. You'll need to come up and decide for me."

"We would like nothing more. You'll be able to complete the others in time?"

"I can't say for certain. But things are going so well, I might have them finished. When do we leave for Miami?"

"Three days. When can we come up?"

She breathed around the enormity of it all, then said, "Does tomorrow work?"

Kari carried her phone into the bedroom and settled on her pallet, her back against the side wall. Sienna padded over and climbed into Kari's lap as she placed the next call.

Ian answered, "Hello?"

"It's me."

"And?"

"I'm going."

"Wow. Kari." A silence, then, "Are you okay?"

"I have no idea." Kari stroked the purring kitten, the world a distant silence beyond her closed door. "I'll probably come down with the screaming meemies in a little bit. Right now . . ."

"Yes?"

"I want to go finish a painting. Maybe two."

He laughed. "I'd take that as a good sign."

"This rushing forward, it ought to terrify me. I've spent so long holding tight to one little space." In the quiet moment, voices sounded in Ian's background. "I took you away from something."

"Kari, nothing is as important as . . ."

"What?"

"Being there for you."

She formed a silent *wow*.

"Did that sound totally lame?"

"No, Ian. It sounded nice."

"Did they say where you'll be staying?"

"The Ritz Carlton, on some beach."

He laughed a second time. "You're staying at the Ritz Carlton South Beach?"

"Is it nice?"

"At two thousand a night for the standard room, it better be."

"They say I'll have a suite on the top floor."

He laughed again. "No kidding?"

"And another for my managers." She loved having the ability to draw laughter from this man.

"I guess you must be somebody important. Thank you so much for speaking with little old me."

"Stop."

"I'll call Kiki and ask if they can put me in the same hotel. That is, if you want."

"Very much. I need—" Her voice caught then. Trapped by all the wrong moves she'd made with other men.

Ian said softly, "You need a friend nearby. Just in case."

"You understand."

"Yes, Kari. I really do." A man's voice called Ian's name. Sharp and loud. "I have to go."

Kari cut the connection and sat there. Stroking the kitten. Coming to terms with this shift in the world's axis. Trying, anyway.

When she was ready, she rose and carried the kitten through the house, out the rear door, and said to Indrid, "I need to paint."

"Is it done?"

"Yes." Kari started down the walk, then turned back and said, "If you're coming, come."

There was no question about which painting to work on. It was a decision of the heart, taken without conscious thought.

She painted the man.

A vague portion of her mind sensed Indrid moving about the atelier, inspecting each canvas in turn. Then the woman left and returned, Kari assumed with a chair from the kitchen. But she couldn't be bothered to check.

The structure came to her so clearly, the work might as well have already been completed.

The borders became a swirling mass of gray flecked with black sparks. Pale and incomplete, like smoke in the wind, cold cinders thrown aloft and spinning with the intensity of dervishes.

At the painting's heart was the man.

He sat upon a musician's stool and held a guitar. His face was turned slightly toward the instrument's neck. But he could not see where his fingers were placed. Because he had no eyes.

A tight golden flame was set deep inside the man's heart.

Despite the tightening intensity of smoke and cinders, his illumination defied the gloomy storm. The light seared outward, so that the man's right hand, the one playing the strings, was on fire.

Kari then took a metal stylus and began drawing half-formed people in the stormy background. They writhed; they danced; they did all they could to pluck away the man's flame. Turn him from the music toward the storm. Wreak havoc in his creative life.

As she painted, Kari listened to a softly lyrical internal dialogue. She had witnessed the marvel of true love, but only from a distance. It was there in the shimmering exuberance of a happy child, the gentle affection of a good parent. She had glimpsed it in how longtime lovers cared for one another. She had watched an old man pushing an ailing woman's wheelchair, his gaze mirroring the sorrow that creased his lover's features. For Kari, the difference between young romance and true love was night and day. The love she found in such moments pointed toward an elevated state of existence. Far more refined than a simple end to loneliness or the momentary spark of sex between lovers. In her finest pieces, as she painted the last few strokes, she felt she approached a true understanding of love. A softly yearning call to what she feared would never be hers.

Kari had no idea how long she worked. Time's passage was meaningless. When she stepped back from the canvas, her neck and shoulders and right arm formed one continuous ache.

Kari realized she was alone.

Then footsteps scratched along the path, the atelier door opened, and Indrid entered bearing a tray. "Your cat is very unhappy."

Kari walked to the house, opened the rear door. The kitchen was filled with the aroma of fresh-baked bread.

"Sienna!"

The kitten scampered toward her, mewing plaintively. Kari picked her up and started back. As soon as she entered the atelier, however, Sienna began squirming. Kari let her down, and the kitten ran to the chamber's far corner and slipped beneath a canvas drop cloth.

Indrid said, "Many young animals grow out of shyness as they become aware of their own strength." Indrid had brought in a second chair, which, like hers, faced the new work. "Come sit down."

Kari sat and accepted a plate holding buttered bread topped with chunks of crumbly cheese and sliced tomato. "I'm starving."

"I'm not surprised." Indrid filled a mug and set it on the floor between them. She sipped from her own mug and studied the painting. The colors gleamed wet and alive in the afternoon light. "This is extraordinary."

Kari ate and drank and watched her oldest friend approach the canvas. The man's boundaries swam in and out of focus as clouds passed over the sun. One moment he was almost lost to the gloom; the next, his defiance seemed ready to push him from the canvas.

When her plate was empty, Kari set it on the floor and said, "I make such a total mess of my relationships. It's only in those first moments of coming together that I realize . . ."

Indrid stepped back two paces, still facing the canvas. "What?"

"How lonely I am."

Indrid nodded slowly. Her gaze still elsewhere.

"So I grow frantic. Desperate. Clingy. I want so much. And then . . ."

Indrid spoke to the gray-shrouded man. "You run."

"It doesn't matter what they do. How nice they are. How right it feels. I don't . . . I can't . . ."

Indrid walked back. Seated herself. Assumed a position so as to face Kari directly. "The relationship's intensity threatens your world. It isn't the man at all. Your enclosed space, your creative drive, becomes endangered by what they represent."

Kari wiped her face. "How do you do that?"

"My dear young friend, has it occurred to you that you are facing your own wall?"

When Kari did not respond, Indrid went on, "You came here to Miramar expecting one thing. But your current state, your immediate needs, won't be satisfied by more of the same. The solitude you needed to protect yourself in Los Angeles, it has no place here."

Indrid's words pressed against Kari from every side. Just the same, she could not deny the truth. Or deflect.

Indrid reached over, gripped Kari's hand, and said, "Just know you don't walk this road alone."

Kari waved Indrid off, then stood and watched the silent valley road, so tired her thoughts felt congealed. When her phone rang, it required genuine effort to pull it from her pocket, find the proper function, make the connection, lift the device, speak the word hello.

"Hi, Kari. It's Aldana, your neighbor."

Only then did Kari notice the woman standing a half dozen homes away, waving in her direction. Kari waved back. "Yes?"

"You remember at dinner, we mentioned the young artist who's the son of our friend?"

Kari searched her memory. "Liam, is that right?"

"He's coming over this evening. We're grilling burgers in the backyard. I was wondering . . ."

"Just a moment." First things first. A nap before anything. Kari checked the time, decided. "Would six be okay?"

"Perfect!" Aldana waved once again. "See you then."

CHAPTER 19

Ian waited until they had finished the afternoon session before he went back out to the rear wall again, a sweat-stained towel wrapped around his neck. He dialed Kari's number and waited. When the phone rang and rang, without an invitation to leave a message, he grew worried.

Then a sleepy voice said, "Hello."

"Kari?"

"Ian?"

"Did I call at a bad time?"

"What time is it?"

"Almost five. Kari, what's wrong?"

"Indrid was here. I started painting. I fell asleep, and now I'm due at the neighbors for dinner in an hour. Why are you calling?"

"Oh, nothing. I was just wondering if you'd like some company." He smiled at the gathering dusk. "But that was before."

"Before what?"

"Before I heard you've been working. Can I see?"

"I never let anyone see my work like this. Never, never, never." He was fairly certain he heard a smile in her voice. Then she said softly, "I suppose . . . if you really want."

"I do. So much."

"It's just . . ."

"What?"

"The painting is about you."

He steadied himself on the stone wall. "I actually don't know what to say to that."

"My neighbors have a friend. Her son is an artist. They want me to meet them. Why don't you join us for dinner?"

"I'd love to. But are you sure I'd be welcome?"

"They were at Castaways when you played with the actor."

"Connor Larkin."

"They'd be thrilled to bits." The smile in her voice was clear as the sunset. "But they'll probably ask you to play for your meal."

When Ian started back toward the studio, Danny's crew were packing away their gear. Connor waved a farewell from his car and pulled through the open gates. Ian hurried home to shower and change. He waited until he was through town and heading south to make the call.

"Ms. Kerkorian's office," the receptionist said.

"It's Ian Hart. I'm sorry to be calling so late. Could I set up a time to speak with Kiki tomorrow?"

"Hold please."

Which was why Ian had phoned. This close to the festival's opening, it was unlikely Kiki would stop working before midnight. The phone clicked twice. Then, "You just saved me a dime."

"What's up?"

"Your new attorney, Megan. She's impressed me. Which doesn't happen often. Especially with lawyers."

"I'm glad to hear it. I like her," Ian said.

"Is she your new manager?"

"I haven't thought beyond the festival, Kiki."

"Well, maybe you should. You could do worse."

"I'll definitely take that into consideration. What were you discussing?"

"No time. Ask her. What do you need?"

"Two quickies. First, I'm concerned about people coming to the second event, expecting to hear classical music, and being disappointed."

"Already covered with your lady lawyer. We're billing this as a night of soft jazz. Show tunes, hits from the fifties and sixties, like that. Anyone who wants a refund is welcome. Which isn't happening."

"How can you be certain of that?"

"Ian, darling, there is nothing that attracts a Miami crowd like fresh scandal." A pause. Then, "We're thinking of shifting you to the main hall."

He could come up with only "Oh."

"Naturally, your attorney is demanding a second pound of flesh." Kiki was clearly enjoying herself. "What else, dear? I'm due on a conference call with Israel Saban. Please tell me you've been in contact with the conductor."

"One of the most difficult conversations I've had in years."

"You deserve nothing less. Go on. Point two."

"I would like to coordinate things so I can stay at the same hotel as a friend."

"Oh. Is that what they're called these days? Does this friend have a name?"

"Kari Langham."

"Should I know her?"

"She's an artist. Kariel."

A silence. "It's not nice to plant your boss on the floor."

"She's staying at the Ritz Carlton. Can you book me a room there?"

"You do realize this is Miami in the high season, dear."

That was good for a pause. "You've never called me that before. Dear."

"A slip of the tongue. Forget it happened. I'll do what I can. Must run. Bye." A pause, then, "Dear."

CHAPTER 20

Ian liked Kari's home long before he arrived. Her residence anchored the end of a long valley road. The builders had either modeled a new house after a local farm or had actually held on to the old place and built around it. When he rose from Amelia's car, Kari was there, standing in the doorway. Despite the screen door separating them, he could see something was wrong. As he climbed the four steps, her tension became clearer, the tight way she wrapped her arms around her waist, the rigid stance.

He halted on the top step. "I can wait out here if you'd like . . ."

"No." She shoved the screen door open with a jerky motion. As if she fought against her own will. "You can come in if you want."

"Kari, no, really, I'll just stay and enjoy the evening until you're . . ."

His words were cut off by a plaintive yowl from inside the house. Before Kari could swing the door shut, a cream-and-cinnamon kitten shot between her legs and scrambled across the porch. She halted by Ian's feet, looked up, and mewed a constant sorrowful note. Crying with almost humanlike clarity. Demanding to know why ever it had taken him such a long while to arrive. Finally. At long last.

There was nothing to it. One moment he was standing there, wishing he had not climbed that first step. The next, Ian was down on his knees.

The kitten responded by flopping on her side and just lying there. Two paws in the air. Belly exposed. Crying.

Ian lowered himself farther still, until his face was just inches from the mewing kitten. Stroking the soft coat. Marveling at the artistry of her fur. A creamy near-white everywhere except for her cinnamon socks, the tips of her ears, and the little nose. Like she had played in a bowl of the spice. And those eyes. Crystal blue, watching him as she purred.

He felt as much as saw Kari step closer and lower herself. But the kitten held him. That and the memories. "I always wanted a cat," he said, talking mostly to the little beast. "My grandparents hated the idea of a pet. For them, it was just another awful part of being forced to take me in."

Early memories rushed to the fore. The utter loneliness. The nausea of having no place and no people who wanted him. His grandparents' silent rages over any wrong step. The shadows in that miserable home, ready to reach out and capture him. Being shipped off to the boarding school. Becoming marooned with other too-young, too-lonely boys. The school's principal had had a cat, a mangy tabby who growled at Ian's approach and seemed to resent his petting.

Ian watched the kitten roll back over and rise to her feet, but only so she could climb into his lap. The purr was intoxicating. Then he realized he was crying.

"I don't understand." Kari reached over and stroked between the kitten's ears. "Sienna runs from everyone."

"Sienna." Ian wiped his face with the hand not stroking the kitten. "It's the perfect name."

Kari rose to her feet. Stood there beside him. Then said, "Come inside."

Ian lifted the kitten, intending to set her back on the porch. But she responded to his hands by going utterly limp. Like she'd been waiting all her brief life for this very moment. Ian rose to his feet and carried the purring, limp bundle into Kari's home. At least, he made it six steps. "Oh. Kari. Wow."

"I wanted to take my time . . . I've already told you that."

Reluctantly, Ian set down the kitten. Sienna mewed a soft protest, then began undulating around his feet. "Kari . . ."

"What?"

The westering light bathed the living room's polished floor in soft honeyed strokes. "It's like the room is breathing."

Suddenly, she was excited. Kari gripped his hand and pulled him toward the living room's only article. "My first real furniture. It's from Indrid."

"Beautiful. Kari . . ."

"Yes?"

"Can I do that, too? Give you a new-home gift?"

She was silent a moment, still holding his hand. Then she tugged on, pointing down a stubby hallway as she aimed for the back rooms. "Through there is my bedroom. Here's the kitchen."

She gave him a moment to appreciate the Shaker-style cabinetry, then guided him through the rear door. Kari used her foot to firmly nudge the kitten back. Sienna planted her forepaws on the screen and cried in protest.

"I spend a lot of time out here on the porch."

"I would, too." Ian pointed to the mewing kitten. "Can I bring Sienna?"

Her smile held a piercing brilliance. "I'll get her." She opened the door, scooped up the kitten, then retook her hold on Ian's hand. "This is crazy. She's hidden herself away from everyone."

"I'm honored." He pointed. "That must be your garage."

"And that's the guest cottage."

He pointed to the third structure, the largest of all. "And your studio?"

"I call it my atelier."

"Atelier," he repeated. "The word suits the building, and it suits you." But as he started forward, he realized Kari remained planted on the top step. "What is it?"

"My new painting."

"You said it's about me."

She nodded. "Ian . . ."

"Kari, if you don't want to show me, I understand. Really."

"No. It's not . . ."

"Tell me."

She replied with little-girl softness, "I want you to like it."

This time, he was the one to reach out and take her hand. "Show me."

As he entered the barnlike structure, a final golden thread shimmered through one of the skylights.

Then he saw it.

"Let me turn on some lights."

"No. Not yet. Please." He scarcely heard what he was saying. The painting drew him forward until his nose almost touched the canvas.

The oil colors were still damp in places. They glistened, adding a surreal effect to her work. Ian stepped back far enough to study the swirling gray cloud. The flecks of black stood out so sharply, he could almost feel them pelting his neck and shoulders. And those spectral images caught within the gray mist. He felt as if Kari had reached inside him and drawn out the childhood terrors. In the room's murky depths, the wraiths danced, mocking him, pouring scorn on the heart's flame, the music, the sheer intensity captured by the central image. They were just waiting, Ian knew, ready to attack and pluck away what remained of his flickering passion.

Kari stepped up close to him. “Ian, do you . . .”

He swung about and gripped her with a fierceness that shocked them both. As did his kiss.

He knew it was probably wrong. But words simply did not fit into this space. Then she sighed, or softly moaned, and relaxed in his embrace.

She reached around and held him with just one arm, since the kitten was still cradled in the other. So they stood like that, the three of them entwined, two kissing, the kitten purring happily there between them.

CHAPTER 21

The kitten started crying soon as Kari opened the rear door and deposited her on the kitchen floor. Mewing like she was forever lost.

"I don't understand this." Kari seemed genuinely mystified, watching Sienna claw at the screen. "Before tonight she fled from everyone. She wouldn't let Indrid get within ten feet."

Ian still felt slightly intoxicated from their kiss. Added to this now was Kari's relaxed closeness. "Maybe it was just a phase. You know, new home and all."

"I suppose." She reentered the house, rummaged through a drawer, then told Sienna, "If you're coming, you have to wear the leash."

He watched Kari settle on the floor, heard the kitten begin to purr. "I've never seen a cat on a leash before."

"It happens. Not often. I was told to start her young." She rose to her feet, opened the door, and asked the kitten, "Are you walking?"

As if in response, the kitten trotted over and planted her forepaws on Ian's leg. And mewed.

Kari said, "This is just unbelievable."

Ian lifted the kitten, allowed her to nuzzle his cheek. The leash was attached to a harness that fit in front of and behind the forelegs. "I feel like I've just made a new BFF."

Kari studied him, her eyes glowing in the porch light. "We should be going."

As they came around front, Ian recalled, "You said they might want me to play for my meal."

"I was kidding. Sort of. But I'm sure they would be delighted."

Ian handed the kitten over, unlocked the Honda, and drew out his guitar case. "I was wondering if you'd like to come hear us tomorrow night. We're doing a complete run-through of the Miami gig. Danny is bringing in videographers to shoot the performance."

"And Danny is . . . ?"

"Danny Byrd is producing the film that started this whole thing. You saw him at Castaways. Amazon has contracted him to make a documentary of our Miami concert. They want to release it as a sort of promo for the film itself. An evening with Hart and Larkin. Something like that."

She nudged him with her free arm. "Try to be a little more casual, the way you say all that."

"It's all a mask. Inside I'm quivering."

"I don't believe that. Not for an instant."

"Between us, I suggested this full dress rehearsal in front of an audience. I'm a little concerned about Connor." They walked the valley road, so close together, they made contact with every other step. Two friends sharing an evening stroll. With her kitten purring a softly emphatic note. "Today was our last session. Toward the end, Connor started sweating like he'd run a four-minute mile. His voice broke twice on the last song."

"Why can't you practice more?"

"I leave day after tomorrow for Miami. I'm scheduled for full rehearsals with Saban and the orchestra . . ." He realized she was watching him. "What?"

"I was hoping . . . I don't know. That we'd travel together."

"Kari, that's so sweet. I'd like nothing more. But I have to go."

"I understand."

"I could come meet you at the airport."

"That's being silly."

"No it's not."

"Ian Hart. The star. Hanging around Miami International. Waiting. For me."

"With balloons. And flowers."

"You're very sweet to offer, Ian."

"Is that a yes?"

"It's a 'Don't talk silliness.'" The kitten started squirming, so Kari set her on the pavement. When Sienna fell into step between them, she said, "I'm not letting her outdoors off the leash. Maybe in time, but I don't think so. I've heard animal sounds at night. I'm afraid something might get her."

"That's probably wise."

The evening held them in a balmy embrace. The homes they passed were illuminated and welcoming. Conversation and laughter and the sound of chattering televisions drifted in the otherwise still air. Then through one screened door came the sounds of a full orchestra.

"Debussy," Ian said. "That piece is called Arabesque. He never wrote for guitar. But I did a rendition of one of his pieces."

"'Claire de Lune,'" Kari said. "I have the album."

"Okay, now I'm really impressed." When she merely smiled in response, he added, "If you're coming to our concert in Miami—"

"Don't be silly. Of course I am."

"Tomorrow night will be an exact duplicate. Assuming we don't mess anything up."

"Why should that bother me?" Two steps, then, "Ian, I listen to your albums all the time."

He had no idea how to respond, except to reach over with the hand not carrying his case and rest it on her shoulder. Drawing them closer still.

As they approached the last house before the valley gates, he could see families filling the backyard. "Who are these people?"

Before she could respond, however, Kari's phone chimed. She checked the readout and said, "It's my manager. Which reminds me. Can they come tomorrow?"

"Of course."

"Great." She handed him the kitten. "Go on inside and introduce yourself. Tell them I'll be in soon as I'm done."

Which was how Ian wound up entering the house full of strangers. Carrying his guitar in one hand. And a cinnamon-dappled kitten in the other. He might have made more of a stir if he had been accompanied by a full marching band.

Then again, maybe not.

CHAPTER 22

When Kari entered the backyard, Ian was surrounded by ladies of all ages. Sienna had made herself small and had squirmed into the crook of his elbow. The kitten silently tolerated the attention. There was certainly no purring. But at least she didn't hiss as one hand after another stroked her head. Ian stayed where he was, midway between the long trestle tables and the backyard grill, and watched as Kari was welcomed into the gathering. She then knelt beside a boy seated at the porch table, a sketch pad open in his lap. Kari spoke softly, then accepted the pad and leafed through the pages. The boy made himself as small as the kitten, watching Kari without turning her way. Ian found himself deeply moved by the care she showed, slowly examining his work, offering soft comments, which caused the silent boy to respond with a nod and a small smile.

As soon as she rose to her feet and looked his way, Ian realized something was genuinely wrong. While she spoke to the boy's parents, Ian excused himself and walked over. The closer he came, the clearer he saw she exuded the same tension as she had upon his arrival at her house. He greeted the adults and the boy named Liam, gave them a few polite moments, then excused himself and drew Kari away. Not insisting. But close.

Kari followed him to the rear hedge. He asked, "What's the matter?"

She gripped her arms across her middle. Just like before. Kari stared, unseeing, at the families. Silent.

"Kari, I don't know how to say it better. I'm here for you."

She breathed around the enormity of one word. "Justin."

"Who?"

"My brother. He's been talking to Rafi. And Graham. Both of them."

"And they are . . . ?"

"My managers. They want to show a painting I gave Justin in Miami. But . . ."

"It's complicated," he offered gently. "Anything to do with family is a bundle of knots."

She blinked. Drew the evening into focus. Looked at him. "How do you do that?"

He said, "Tell me how I can help."

"Justin is coming to Miami. He wants an invitation to a gala." Her voice grew tighter still. "That's the first time I have heard of it. This gala . . . Rafi says the art fair is doing this gala for *me*. And now Justin *insists* on being there. It's all so *complicated*."

The people standing by the grill glanced over, then away.

Ian said, "You thought they would show your work. You'd shake some hands, do some interviews, have your picture taken, come home."

"I don't even know what that means. *Gala*."

"Yes you do. You just don't know what it means for you."

"I think I'm going to be sick."

The kitten started squirming, as if sensing Kari's need for

comfort. Ian handed her over, watched the two of them bond. "Better?"

"No. A little." She stroked the kitten. "They're displaying a collection of my paintings at the gala. Which is inside some ballroom. Not the exhibition hall."

"That makes sense," Ian said. "The hall is rented by vendors actually trying to sell new works."

"That's what Rafi said. After I freaked out."

"I'm sure you looked lovely doing so." He waited for a smile. When none came, he went on, "When is the gala?"

A few strokes of the kitten, then, "The exhibition's opening night. Three days."

"Which is the same night as my main concert. I assume you might still want to hear me do my classical gig?"

"Ha. A joke." She nudged the purring head. "Double ha."

"Listen to what I'm saying. So you and one of your managers come to the concert. The other one goes to the gala and explains why you're showing up fashionably late. Because you're the honored guest of the night's star performer. Who will then accompany you to the gala." He paused. "I assume that will be okay, me coming?"

"Look at the funny man."

"So here's how it will play out. There's a reception after the concert. I have to go, at least for a few minutes. Then we'll hop over to the gala. We show up together, you smile, you chat to a few people, you let them gush, take a few pictures, you wave, and you leave."

A few more strokes, the kitten's eyes now almost entirely shut. "You'll really come with me?"

"To your gala? I wouldn't miss it for the world. It's the main reason I'm going to Miami."

"That's the worst joke of all."

"Not that bad."

He could feel her tension easing away. "You'll be there? With me? Really?"

"Kari, I've asked them to book me into your hotel. We'll show up together. Do the gala thing. Then scoot."

"The gala thing."

"I'll be firmly attached to your side throughout, if you like." He nudged her. "Was that a smile?"

"No. Definitely not."

"I also think it was." He pointed toward the people pretending to ignore them. "I also think it's time we go play like we want to be here. Have some dinner."

"I left my appetite out on the street."

"So long as you hold the kitten, nobody is going to notice."

CHAPTER 23

Over dinner, Ian learned they all were coming to the next evening's concert.

"Don't think that lets you off the hook, playing tonight," Aldana warned. "Not for a single teeny-tiny instant."

Amos, her husband, said, "Not the most polite request I've ever heard."

"He brought his guitar. It's there in our front room." Aldana smiled across the table. "If you want some begging, honey, just say the word."

"It's fine," Ian said.

And it was. The evening was warm, and the insects were being kept at bay by torches rimming the dining area. Their welcoming acceptance was as clear as the rising moon. Ian played two pieces; then the younger children started to squirm. He accepted their applause, played an encore, then bid them all a good night.

During the walk back to Kari's new home, Ian told her about his conversation with Israel Saban, the conductor. On the surface, it had gone much as expected. Saban had broken down the two pieces into their component parts. He had focused almost exclusively on the orchestral score, identifying themes and highlighting elements that flowed into Ian's primary guitar work. The only time Saban had delved into Ian's actual playing was at those points where he wanted something different from how Ian had played them on his CDs.

Under other circumstances, Ian would have thanked the conductor for taking such care, as Saban had obviously listened to Ian's earlier performances with the scores in his hands.

Instead, he had remained almost completely silent.

Saban had addressed Ian with frigid scorn. The conductor started their conversation by recounting the upheaval Ian's actions had caused him, the orchestra, the festival, even city officials. Everyone involved had been pushed to the limit by this detestable guitarist. Well, his spoiled-star attitude had crossed the line. Saban would not put up with any more such antics. He wanted to make sure that was perfectly clear.

Which was the one time Ian spoke during their conversation. "Perfectly."

When Ian finished relating the worst part of an otherwise good day, they walked the night-clad lane linked by far more than their hands. The only sounds were the kitten's constant purring and their footsteps along the pavement. The quiet was as comfortable as the starlight.

Ian marveled at the ease he felt over confessing his shame to this remarkable lady.

Finally, Kari asked, "What will you do? I mean, during the performance." When Ian did not respond, she added, "Playing for a conductor who hates you, that must be terrible."

"Knowing the pieces helps. Which I do. Backward and forward." Another few steps, then, "I'll do my best to focus on the music. My role especially. Once we get going, it will be okay. I hope."

She tightened her hold on his hand. It was her turn to ask, "How can I help?"

They stopped there in the middle of the starlit lane. "Do you really want to?"

"Yes, Ian. Very much."

"Be there. On the stage. Where I can see you if things go bad."

Her eyes glowed in the dim illumination. "You can make that happen?"

"I'm the soloist. It's a rare request in a classical concert, but I've seen it happen. I'll ask them to give you a stool, so you're high enough for me to see you. You'll be positioned back behind the curtain, stage left."

"I actually don't know what to say."

"Yes would be nice."

"Of course, yes. I'm honored, Ian. And so deeply touched."

It was the most natural thing in the world to kiss her. He kept his arm around her as they continued on.

"Can I make a suggestion?" he asked after a while.

"Of course."

"Kari, I hope you won't take this the wrong way."

"I won't know about that unless you tell me."

"You might want to go shopping. For an outfit. You know . . ."

She took another few paces before finishing for him. "For the gala."

"Well, yes."

"This just gets worse and worse."

"Forget I said anything."

"No. You're right. And it's not the clothes."

"It's everything. I know."

Another few paces, then, "Rafi will go nuts when I ask him to help me shop."

"And Rafi is . . . ?"

"My manager. He and his partner Graham own a gallery.

They're two of my closest friends. Graham will enjoy shopping, too. But with less volume."

"Rafi is excited about Miami?"

"Oh no. *Excited* doesn't even come close." She stopped where her drive met the road. "They'll be thrilled to learn about tomorrow's concert."

"It's not a concert. Not even close."

"I know. A dress rehearsal."

"With cameras swooping around the place. And no food. One round of drinks only." He explained their aim to run through the program, start to finish. No stopping or reworking if something went wrong. Danny and his team were going to shoot it, so they would hopefully have footage they could splice into the concert itself. Add atmosphere and a sense of momentum both to the documentary and the film. Ian finished, "They'll be hearing exactly the same lineup in Miami. That is, assuming they'll want to attend both concerts."

"It's too late for jokes."

"Okay, so I'll speak with Kiki. Make sure there's room for two more in the box."

Kari's smile held a lantern glow. "A private box. So they can watch Ian Hart in concert. They'll die. They'll just die."

Another kiss, far too brief in his mind. A quiet word of thanks for including him at the dinner. How nice it was to meet her new friends. And her wonderful, beautiful kitten. A final soft kiss. Then he set his guitar in the back and slipped behind the wheel. A wave, a flash of lights, and he was gone. Leaving Kari standing there, clad in the starlight's silver gleam, stroking a feline that would not stop purring.

CHAPTER 24

Kari rose early and painted all morning. For the first time ever, she actually applied oils to two canvases during the same session. The butterfly girl was on the easel to her left; on her right stood the woman chasing the man and his lantern. Somehow the two paintings felt interconnected. Or they balanced each other in some illogical manner. Whatever it was, the longer she worked, the more she became convinced that in reality she was working on just one large project.

She became utterly caught up in her work, something that had been happening with increasing regularity. Such that her ringing phone was a jarring irritant, until she remembered why she had brought it with her.

"Rafi?"

"No, dear. Graham. Rafi has been breaking out in hives ever since we passed Santa Barbara. It's his customary reaction to entering a frontier zone."

"Where are you?"

"We just left San Luis Obispo. Wherever do they come up with these names?"

"Can you stop somewhere and buy us lunch?"

"Kari, it's four o'clock in the afternoon."

"No wonder I'm starving. I've been painting since daybreak."

A pause, then, "Well, as long as we're not required to watch them shoot and skin some poor animal. What will you have? Bison tongue on sourdough?"

"You're loving this. I can tell."

"I do confess the scenery is rather fetching. Mind you, in an utterly primitive fashion." A second voice muttered something. "Rafi wants to know when you'll be moving back closer to civilization."

"Never, never, never, never."

"She says it will be a few weeks yet." To Kari, he said, "We'll be with you soon. Unless the road gives out and we're forced to hire a pony."

Kari rushed into the house, where she was greeted by a loudly complaining kitten. She opened a tin of food, then carried it and Sienna to the rear porch. Kari seated herself so that she was facing the atelier and fed the kitten off the tip of one finger. It was how Graham had directed her to make Sienna's acquaintance the first time they met. Ever since, it remained Kari's way of apologizing.

"What am I going to do with you? Do you want to come with me to Miami?"

Sienna replied with her remarkable ability to eat and purr simultaneously.

"I don't like carting you off so soon after you've arrived here. And you hate being around almost everyone." She scooped out another finger's worth. "Ian will be there. Which I think we both agree is a plus."

Sienna licked the finger clean. Purring. When Kari did not offer more food, the kitten head bumped her and purred.

"Liam—he's a young artist—he and his mother have offered to come feed you. And it's only for a week at most. Should I leave you here? Alone?" She lifted the kitten so they were eye to eye. "Pay attention. This is important."

Kari returned to her atelier, settled the kitten in her basket, and resumed painting. She stayed there, immersed in her work, until Sienna bolted for the corner drop cloths. Then Kari heard a car-door slam, and a man called her name. She set down the brush and palette, wiped her hands with a paint-stained cloth, and told the kitten, "Don't you start. You were born in their home."

The kitten remained invisible. Silent.

Kari walked out front, kissed the two cheeks, and demanded, "Where's lunch? I'm so hungry."

Rafi said, "You've waited this long, you can just starve a while longer."

Graham said, "We're going to pretend we've viewed your lovely new home."

"And we're enjoying your company," Rafi said.

"Now that the trivialities are out of the way," Graham said, "why, yes, Kari dear. We'd love to see your secret stash."

"And you can explain why we had to come all this way to see work you should have shown us years ago," Rafi said.

She studied the two implacable faces and knew they were only half joking. "They're not secret. I just wasn't ready to give them up."

Rafi looked at his partner. "I don't find that explanation the least bit satisfactory. You?"

"Kari. Really. Please."

"Well, if you're going to be that way about it," she said.

"We absolutely are," Rafi said.

"All right, then." She led them back to the atelier and pointed to the four packing crates stacked beside the drop cloths. "Careful not to step on Sienna. She's hiding back there."

Kari watched them unlatch a crate's top and begin setting out her work. They gradually rimmed the walls with paintings, some of which she had not seen in over a year. Longer.

"Do you want tea?" she asked a little while later.

"Kari, be a dear and go for a walk. Pet the cat. Something. Just . . ." Graham watched Rafi set the next painting down in the line. "This one?"

"Definitely," Rafi replied.

Kari decided her only real option was to ignore them and paint.

To her surprise, the day's intensity resumed almost instantly. She was mildly aware of the two men as they moved about and talked in near whispers. She knew they occasionally shifted paintings about. She noticed when Sienna emerged and drifted about the room's periphery, finally settling by the north wall, as far from the men as she could get and still remain within the late afternoon sunlight.

The sun moved. The kitten moved with it. Not purring. But there where Kari could see her. She painted.

Then she realized her two friends stood to either side. Watching her. Studying the two canvases.

She set down her brush and palette, cleaned her hands, waited. "Well?"

"You are growing up," Graham said.

"And there's one more." She walked to the corner opposite where the crates had been stacked, and carried back the easel holding the storm-clad guitarist. With Graham's help, she settled it to the left of the pair.

"Our precious darling girl," Rafi said. "Coming into her own."

"I could weep," Graham said.

"Go right ahead," Rafi said. "Why should I be the only one getting all teary-eyed?"

Kari settled her arms around their two shoulders. "They're not finished."

"They will be," Graham said. "Not long now."

They made a picnic on the atelier floor, facing the three easels. Kari's other paintings lined the back wall and the wall to her left. Sienna vanished when they started moving about, but the offer of food drew her reluctantly back. She finally settled close enough to accept a morsel from Rafi and allowed Graham to stroke her ears.

"I can't believe Sienna has already forgotten us," Graham observed.

"She hasn't forgotten anything," Kari replied. "She's acting like a spoiled little kitty."

Conversation during the meal remained disjointed. Her two friends seemed distracted, even anxious. Twice she started to tell them about Ian. But their oddly distanced air kept her quiet.

Finally, she demanded, "Will somebody please tell me what is going on?"

"You might as well," Rafi said, lifting the kitten into his lap. "It's not like it's going to get easier with time."

Graham showed irritation. "Me? Why on earth should I be the one?"

"Because you know I'll mess things up. Then you'll spend the entire trip back telling me how you could have done it better."

"Oh, all right." Graham turned to her. "Kari, dear, there's more."

"The gala. I know. We need to go shopping tomorrow."

"No. Well, yes. Of course the gala."

"And you definitely need a dress," Rafi said. "I've already picked out the perfect—"

He was stopped by Graham's upraised hand. "May I?"

"Actually," Kari said, "there's something I need to explain—"

"Best let him get it over with," Rafi said. "He may never start again. Then I'll have to tell you. And that way leads to ruin."

"Tell me *what*?"

"Your retrospective is not in the exhibition hall."

"You already told me that."

"I did? When?"

"Last night." She saw how nervous Graham was. Kari reached over and took his hand. "Graham." She held her other hand across the finished meal. "Rafi. You two dear men are why we're sitting here. In the studio of my new home. Whatever it is you need me to do . . ." Pause for a big breath. "I agree in advance. I'll do it."

A very different Rafi began, "The retrospective is all about you. We'll be shunted off to some drab corner and left to molder."

"I won't let that happen."

Graham said, "We've added another condition to your attending."

Rafi said, "One that really was just for us. We demanded a booth in the hall. And not just any booth. Ours is directly across from the hall's main entrance."

"There's a six-year waiting list for *any* booth," Graham said.

"The directors shrieked so loud, they set the dogs to howling in Barbados," Rafi said, smiling at the memory. "But in the end, they agreed."

"That's how much they want you to attend," Graham said.

"Our plan was to showcase your two recent works," Rafi said. "Justin's and Indrid's."

"Marked SOLD, of course," Graham said. "Then we'd use the rest of the space for other artists. But now . . ."

Kari said, "You want to sell my works. The ones I've held back."

The two men did not respond. If either breathed, she could not tell.

Kari released their hands and rose to her feet. "Come tell me which ones."

But as they walked with her along the rows of the paintings, she found the distance growing between herself and the work. She had brought the paintings as an anchor, a reassuring link to all she was, what she had accomplished, and who she wanted to become.

Now, though, she felt as if they belonged to a different era. What Indrid had said came back to her in a rush of clarity. She was entering a new phase of life.

It was time to let them go.

They selected five.

Kari said, "Take them all."

Rafi staggered over and leaned against the opposite wall.

Graham said, "*All* of them?"

She pointed to the three easels. "Those too. Take them. They're yours."

"Kari, I don't know what to say," Graham told her.

"Well, I certainly do." Rafi pointed at the easels. "Hurry up, finish those, and we'll hang them where everyone will see them when they walk through the exhibition doors."

Graham smiled. "That will put the other exhibitors' teeth on edge."

"Put a knot in their bowels, more like," Rafi said.

"Rafi."

"Well, it's true. And I'm going to love every minute."

"Enough of that." Graham asked Kari, "Did you have something you wanted to tell us?"

"It's better if I show you." She pulled out her phone, checked the time, and added, "We need to hurry."

CHAPTER 25

They decided to take Kari's car into town, as Rafi and Graham's van was filled with items for the guesthouse. Or so they claimed. But as they pulled out their overnight cases, Kari spotted three wooden crates with LIMOGES stamped on the sides.

Fifteen minutes later they met on the front porch, showered and dressed and ready. Thus far, Kari had managed to explain only that there was a special event, one the entire town had become involved in. To say anything more would have been like pulling on a thread and unraveling the entire garment. As she locked her front door, Kari decided she had to at least make a start on the way into town. Tell them the basics. About Ian. Graham's favorite classical musician. Whose music formed a backdrop to any number of gallery events. Here. Playing at Castaways. Oh, and he was being accompanied by Connor Larkin. The movie star. Give them a chance to pepper her with questions. Which they would. For hours.

But as she left the porch, Sienna raced up to the screen

door and started yowling. Which meant they spent the entire drive into Miramar debating whether Kari should take the kitten to Miami. The only alternative, Graham insisted, was to leave Sienna in a cattery. "No way are you leaving that poor beast in the care of a child."

"Liam's mother is a detective," Kari pointed out. "She's promised to help."

"Say she does. Say they stop by to feed Sienna. And the kitten slips by them and escapes into the wild. What would you do then?"

Kari started to say she wouldn't go. The kitten was such a perfect reason not to travel. She was suddenly flooded with a desire to call it all off. Never leave behind her safe little Central Coast haven.

Indrid might as well have been seated in the rear seat beside Rafi. Watching her, solemn and silent.

In the end, all Kari said was, "I wish I knew what to do."

"You have another couple of days to decide," Rafi said.

Graham nodded. "Right now we need to talk about your brother."

"He's stopped by," Rafi said. "Twice. Limo idling at the curb."

"When I called last night, we were borderline frantic," Graham said.

"Our first stall in the Miami exhibition hall," Rafi said. "Across from the entrance. All those sad, empty walls."

"Your brother is desperate to attend the gala," Graham said. "It was the only way he'd even consider letting us show your painting."

"Which we simply had to have," Rafi said.

"Your brother can be very insistent," Graham said.

"Aggressive," Rafi added. "Demanding. Loud."

"When we refused to tell him where you were or pass on your phone number, he became quite rude."

"That sounds like Justin." For the first time since her arrival, Kari's family crowded in. Her mind felt split in two. The lovely California countryside basked in another gathering dusk. The breeze through her open window carried the Pacific spice she had come to love. Yet battling for her attention was the coldly avaricious flavor of her former home. The shrieking battles leading to divorce. Her mother's frigid disdain. Her brother's ability to pretend at momentary affection whenever a young lady captured his attention. Her father . . .

Graham broke into her reverie. "The gala is one of the city's biggest annual fundraisers. Tickets run several thousand apiece."

"Numbers are strictly limited," Rafi said. "It sells out in days. Hours."

"When I tried to put him off, he flew into such a rage," Graham said. He added in a smaller voice, "He frightened me."

Kari nodded, remembering. Her father's fury shook the earth. There was no telling what would set him off, so Kari had learned early on to avoid the man and flee his sudden eruptions. Justin's anger was more predictable and his outbursts far less common. He went weeks without revealing his darker side. Then something would stand between him and whatever goal he had in his sights. And he plowed his own furrow with molten wrath.

"I don't understand. What is so important about this gala? Justin doesn't care about Miami society," she said.

"The Miami show has become the largest contemporary art fair in the entire country," Rafi said. "The opening gala is a major event on the annual society calendar. Big names fly in from all over."

When she stopped at a light, Graham observed, "You're upset."

"A little."

"Soon as this is over, I'll put on my fire-retardant gear and call him back. Tell Justin—"

She pulled into a parking space and cut the motor. "No. Don't."

"Kari, I know you're under so much pressure. The last thing I want, the very last, is to add—"

"Tell Justin he's welcome." She watched a group of chattering people walk past their car. "I can't tell how much of what I feel is real. How much is an echo from the past."

Despite his fluttering nerves, Rafi had often struck her as the wiser and more observant of the two. Like now. "You're not just talking about your brother."

"No."

"It's everything. The trip, Miami, the showcase, the gala. All of it."

Kari breathed around the enormity of what lay ahead. She could almost hear Indrid's voice. Telling Ian that his confusion and uncertainty were no reasons to stop moving forward. Kari had suspected the woman had meant her words for her, as well. Now she was certain.

She opened her door. "Let's go inside."

The bartender, Marcela, spotted them at the entrance and came rushing over. "Ian's been asking for you. I think he was worried you couldn't make it." She led them up front, to a coveted table by the side wall. A sweating ice bucket held an unopened bottle of champagne and two glasses. Marcela pulled a third chair from several stacked beside the stage and said, "I'll snag you another glass."

Once they were seated, Graham asked, "And just who is this Ian?"

The bartender's smile widened as she started away.

"Marcela, wait." Kari pointed to an oil painting on the wall above their table. It showed a cove very much like Miramar's, sheltered in two cupped hands fashioned from a starlit night. "Whose work is this?"

Marcela's expression softened. "Sylvie's father."

"Really? It's beautiful."

"Isn't it?" Marcela studied the work. "I see it so often, I forget."

"Is he here?"

"Who? John? No, he passed years ago. Have Sylvie tell you about growing up on the road, traveling from Alaska to Baja, selling his works as they went." Someone called Marcela's name. She started away, adding, "Only don't ask her tonight."

The room was beyond full. Most of the tables were crammed so tightly, the patrons rubbed shoulders with those seated nearby. Kari's was positioned in an island of its own, separated by a channel holding thick electric cables. A small stepladder was positioned by the stage's left corner, with a video camera resting on top. A control board now dominated the bar.

Rafi asked, "What on earth is going on?"

"I've been meaning to tell you—" She stopped at the sight of Ian rushing toward them.

"Kari, I'm so glad you made it." Ian leaned over, kissed her cheek, set down a third glass, then said to the two astonished men, "Hi. Welcome to bedlam."

Rafi said, "You're Ian Hart."

"Am I? Oh, good. I was worried." Ian snagged his stool from the stage and settled on it with his back to the room.

Kari asked, "What's the matter?"

"Oh, you know. Last-minute issues."

But the parchment-tight lines around his eyes, the worried expression, said otherwise. "No, I don't know. Do you want to tell me?"

"Actually, I could use your advice." Ian glanced at the two men. "If it's okay."

"Rafi and Graham are my managers. And two of my oldest friends. Tell me what's troubling you."

"We could leave," Graham offered.

"And go where?" Rafi waved at the room. To Ian, he explained, "We run an art gallery two blocks off Rodeo. What we know, what we never talk about, would topple regimes."

"Rafi."

"Well, it's true."

Swiftly, Ian recounted Connor's early years as a struggling musician, his acceptance that he might never make it, his rise to stardom as an actor. And his occasional nights playing on the stage. Here. In Castaways.

Rafi said, "You're talking about Connor Larkin."

"Of course he is," Graham said. "Now let's both play mute."

"Go on," Kari said. "What's happened tonight?"

"He's scared," Ian replied. "It's been building since he learned about Miami."

Rafi sat up straight. "Wait, what?"

"Later," Kari said. To Ian, she urged, "Go on."

"I thought, you know, Connor is a highly trained actor. He's a pro at dealing with stress and performing when the cameras start shooting. But it's started to infect the band. Danny's crew. Everybody. They've lost the spark, the joy. I feel like I should . . ."

"What?"

"Take over. Become lead."

"Why don't you?"

"It's his band, Kari. They've been playing together for years." Ian nodded at the stage. "We're playing tonight in his *restaurant*."

Graham asked, "And precisely what difference does all that make?"

"A lot. It makes a huge—"

"Ian, I'm sorry. But your perspective is skewed. The points you're making, they *don't matter*," Graham said. "Right now, in this moment, it's all about the *performance*."

Ian opened his mouth. Started to speak. Leaned back. Silent.

Graham asked, "I take it from all the equipment that tonight is being filmed?"

"The main event is Miami. Danny Byrd has us playing part of his current film's soundtrack. Now he's putting together a documentary. That is, assuming everyone performs up to grade."

"And that is precisely the point, isn't it?" Graham said. "Making sure everyone gives their absolute best."

Rafi said, "Danny Byrd, the producer?"

"Right. How do you know Danny?"

"We're a Beverly Hills art gallery," Rafi replied. "We survive by knowing everyone who matters."

Graham rested his hand on Rafi's arm. *Settle.* He asked, "Where are Connor and the band now?"

"Upstairs."

"Your actor-musician friend sees this as a step toward his oldest dreams coming true. And he is terrified. How can you possibly worry about taking control of this situation?"

Ian remained silent.

"Your friend needs you. The band needs you. How do you normally prepare for a gig?"

Ian did not reply.

Graham nodded, as if silence was the proper response. "You make the world go away, correct? Fine. Now, you march right upstairs and do what's necessary."

Ian rose slowly, his gaze steady on Graham. Stared down at the three of them for a long moment. Then turned and walked away.

Soon as they were alone, Rafi said, "That was Ian Hart."

"Yes," Kari said. "It was."

Graham dropped his head into his hands and groaned.

Rafi's smile held a mischievous edge. "Feeling a bit under the weather, are we?"

Graham moaned a second time. "I can't believe I just told him how to do his music."

"You most certainly did," Rafi said. Not quite laughing. "That and a great deal more."

"I feel like the world's number one dodo," Graham said.

Rafi chuckled.

Kari said, "Graham, you just told Ian what I couldn't."

A long moment passed before Graham managed to lift his gaze.

Kari went on, "I didn't have any idea what Ian needed to hear until you said it."

"Really?"

"Yes. Really."

"Oh, do let him suffer just a little bit longer," Rafi said. "He never lets me off that easy."

"You two have always been there for me," Kari said. "Just like now."

CHAPTER 26

Ian paused long enough to tell the lighting, sound, and camera crews gathered behind the bar that they would be starting a few minutes late. Then he slipped through the crowd and climbed the stairs and entered the apartment occupying the old building's upper two floors. Marcela and her husband lived there now. But Ian suspected Sylvie Cassick still considered it at least partly hers. She and Connor were sprawled on the living room floor with their twins. The sunset's final glow illuminated Connor's drawn and weary features. His eyes looked haunted to Ian. Sylvie made the twins laugh in a vain attempt to engage her husband and lighten his mood. Ian doubted Connor saw anything at all. The three backup singers were gathered in the kitchen alcove, casting glances at Connor and talking quietly. The other band members and Danny and Arthur were scattered about the room. Watching Connor. Silent. Stressed. Worried.

When Ian appeared, Danny pointedly glanced at his watch. But before the producer could speak, Ian declared, "I need a minute."

To his surprise, Arthur smiled and nodded. The uncommon expression rearranged every line on the old man's face. Danny saw it, too, and whatever he was about to say went unspoken.

Ian asked Sylvie, "Could you excuse us for a moment?"

Sylvie looked at her husband. When Connor nodded, she gathered up the kids and climbed to the upper floor.

Ian asked the backup singers to join them. He then glanced at Arthur, who smiled a second time and said, "Danny, how about a cuppa?"

"I'm good. And we really need—"

"Danny." Arthur stood and gripped the producer's arm. "In the kitchen with you."

Ian opened his case and drew out his guitar. He gave the ladies time to find places with the band, then said, "This evening is a dry run. It's important, but it's mostly a practice session. We know what to do and when. We're all professionals. We go downstairs, and we play straight through our entire set. Any mistake or offbeat—and there are bound to be some—we make a mental note. Tomorrow morning we meet at Arthur's studio and break things down. Song by song. Any ideas about how to make things better, we try them out. Then we run through the set a final time. I think Danny should film our studio work, but that's up to him. Again, no breaks, no talk. A full run straight through."

He gave that a beat, then went on, "After that, I leave for Miami. I would advise you to take a break and not work on anything. Discussions, changes, all that is behind us. Give yourselves a couple of days off. Then we meet up. Anybody who likes is welcome to come see me perform with the orchestra. Kiki, the festival director, has promised me the hall's largest box. The next night is our night. The next time we perform will be on the festival stage."

Connor asked, "They're really moving us to the main hall?"

"That doesn't matter. It has no place in our conversation." Ian met his gaze. His voice hard now. Firm and totally in control. Doing his best to dominate the room and the crew's mood. "From this point on, it's all about the music. What venue, the lights, the shoot, we leave that to the *other* professionals."

Connor gathered his legs and sat up. Opened his mouth. Shut it again.

Now that Ian was committed, he had rarely felt more certain about anything. He lifted the guitar into position and swiftly checked the tuning. He knew an instant's lancing regret for the lonely absence at the center of his being. He wondered if this was how an amputee felt when the missing limb pretended to ache. Then he pushed it all away. This was not about him.

He refocused on the group. Bringing them together.

He played a quick introductory riff, three minutes of fire and brimstone. Enough to bring the ladies to their feet. Push the band members off the wall. Then he stopped. Looked around the room. Met each gaze in turn. Connor's last of all.

"Everybody with me now," Ian said. "You give me fever."

Lilliana said, "Honey, you take the words right out of my mouth."

He liked how the crew laughed in unison. All but Connor. But even he showed a spark to his gaze. "On three," Ian said. "One, two . . ."

They went downstairs. They climbed onstage. They counted down. They played.

The set's first two songs had been selected by Danny, then approved by Connor and, more importantly, Arthur. Ian thought the choices made sense. They were both renditions of music from the film and had been taped during multiple sessions in the studio. By this point, Connor and his band could play them by rote.

Ian thought Connor's voice lacked resonance and his playing was somewhat mechanical. But the actor hit the right notes, and in the final refrain, he showed a trace of his customary strength.

The applause after that second song seemed to startle Connor. Ian watched as he stared out over the gathering as many stood and shouted. He did not smile. Nor did he offer one of his customary jokes. But when he launched them into the third song, Ian heard the man's fire come back to the surface.

In a conversation following one of their multiple sessions, Connor had asked if his band had a personal favorite they might like to include. It had been an almost idle question, and clearly, the actor had expected them to come back with one of the melodies they included in their regular evening sessions. Instead, their response had been unanimous and had come so swiftly, Ian suspected they had long wished for this chance.

The song they'd wanted was Steve Winwood's "Higher Love."

Connor had initially balked at their request, for the song had a sharper edge than the sort of music he preferred. But Danny and Arthur both leapt at the idea. They felt the performance would have a far stronger appeal if the pace was varied. Reluctantly, Connor agreed to give it a try.

Within minutes of starting that first trial run, it was clear the idea held real potential. They played it in the original manner, but unplugged—a term that had become popular with any number of rock-jazz bands, who did sessions where all electric instruments were set aside. When the trio started singing their backup, Ian felt chills.

The same thing happened now onstage.

The song was introduced by a powerful punching drum solo, only this time it was played with brushes. The three ladies were squeezed between the piano and the rear wall.

Despite the lack of space, they managed to put some real rhythm into their dance. "Bring me a higher love," they sang. The audience responded with shouts of approval.

Initially, Connor and the ladies sang while Ian carried the melody on his own and the drummer beat out the strident tempo. Then the sax player added a tambourine, and the bass player lifted a steel-beaded swivel called a cabasa. Midway through the first verse, the ladies added castanets and maracas.

By the time they reached the first refrain, Connor and the bassist and the sax player could easily drop their percussion instruments and start playing, because the audience was clapping and beating time. Gradually, tables rose to their feet and danced in place. They shouted in time to the ladies. *Bring me a higher love.*

Danny's two cameramen stood on short stepladders, swaying in time as they shot the band, the crowd, the night. The producer and Arthur and the techies stood behind the bar, grinning and singing with the crowd.

Which was when it all came together for Ian. This sort of experience had once been a given, reaching a point in every session where he took a giant step away from the event and melded with his music. Only this was the first such experience he had known in over a year, and the impact was monumental. There was no crowd, no cameras, not even the band or the singers as individuals. It was just the one entity, totally unified, utterly focused. "Bring me a higher love," the ladies sang, and Ian never wanted the song to end.

And yet end it did. The crowd stood and shouted and applauded and whistled. Ian brought the night back into focus, in time to catch Connor's eye and share the night's first smile.

CHAPTER 27

That night Kari dreamed she was a ghost.

Such dreams, and the reality behind them, had framed much of her childhood. For years she had viewed herself as a slender wraith, one who drifted beyond the reach of her family's sudden rages. Her father's molten fury, her mother's icy venom, she had done her utmost to avoid both. The young Kari had had no idea what brought them on. Everything she did had seemed at least partly wrong.

Her brother shared their parents' dual nature, but at least with Justin, there were clear signals as to when he might erupt. What was more, Justin possessed a rock-hard solidity, or so it seemed to his young sister. He was able to endure their father's ire, remain intact, and then move on. Unlike Kari, who feared any such outburst might destroy her entirely. Even the slightest hint of another tempest left Kari withered. Utterly defeated. Weeping in terror.

It was far safer simply to vanish in plain sight.

In those dark early years, she often dreamed of being a ghost. Sometimes it was fun, slipping safely from place to place, watching and listening and moving on. Shielded even when their shouting matches took aim at her shadow form.

When she thought back on those fragile dreamscapes, Kari occasionally found herself frozen in place, captured by the thought of what might have happened if there had not been the two lifelines cast her way by the vagueness of fate. Her painting and Indrid, two reasons to grow beyond her wraithlike days and take on a real form. Have a purpose and a friendship, both strong enough to help her. Not to grow wings—that would have been too much to ask—but to find strength to walk forward. Face the new day. Build her own definition of a good life.

Tonight, in this dream, Kari merely drifted. She could not see clearly where she was. But she had the distinct impression of having entered a childhood space, one where she could pretend at safety. And yet the dream filled her with a restless disquiet. As if she risked missing something vital. Kari tried to run, to press through shadow walls and connect with a more distinct version of reality. And yet there were other wraiths, fragments of a life she had left behind, doing their best to hold her in place, keep her trapped. . . .

She woke up.

Kari opened her eyes to the pastel wash of another dawn. The only sound was Sienna's gentle breath by her left ear. She rose from her pallet, dressed, then lifted the slumbering kitten and left the bedroom. Her movements were deliberate, not slow or fast. There was no rush to the morning, though she was desperate to try to make sense of her dream. Gather some clear image from the internal tempest the night had left behind.

She entered the atelier, settled the kitten in her basket, grabbed a sketchbook and pencil, then returned to the kitchen. She put on a pot of coffee and began to draw. Page after page became filled while she drank two mugs and ate a bowl of granola. But the sketches remained amorphous, indistinct. As if the images in her head defied proper form.

Kari refilled the pot, set out fresh cups, and left them for Graham and Rafi when they woke. She carried her sketchbook and phone and mug back into the atelier, set up a blank canvas, and stood there. Taking cautious sips. Waiting to see if the swirl of images and emotions might finally . . .

Then it struck her.

She tore all the pages from her sketchbook and dumped them in the trash. Kari then took the same pencil and approached the canvas.

She drew a wraith standing before a mirror. Even before this initial figure was completed, she tossed the pencil away and began mixing oils. Every action seemed to take forever. Her impatience grew to a fire that threatened to consume her. Finally, at long last, she began to paint.

The very indistinct central figure was painted in pearl and white-gold. She surrounded it with a myriad of other indistinct figures painted in shades of blue-gray. They sprawled in languorous ease around three sides of the canvas, like ballerinas on break. Their oddly disjointed forms all faced the central figure, who stared straight ahead, facing the empty white expanse.

Kari stopped then. She took a step back and collided with Graham. Rafi stood beside him, both men gazing at the canvas. Their expressions were blank. Confused. She turned away. She didn't want to hear whatever it was they might wish to say. It was vital she remain focused on the work at hand.

She liked the quality of the half-seen wraiths. They added a vibrant intensity to how the central figure stared at nothing. That ghost, fashioned from the colors of honey and lemon, hovered at the canvas's heart. All the other apparitions took aim, their faces pointed at the main figure. And yet they did so without eyes.

Kari was tempted to leave the final space empty. A wraith staring into the cloud of unknowing.

Then she decided it would be an easy way out. The painting would remain less than it needed to be. Her inner turmoil unresolved.

Kari resumed work.

She was vaguely aware of quiet movements behind her. The men came and went. While the men were away, Sienna padded into the atelier's bathroom, where her litter box was stashed. The men returned, and she scampered back to her hiding place beneath the canvas tarp. The door opened, permitting a dry desert wind spiced with sorrel and heat to enter. The door closed. The men seated themselves. Spoons clinked against bowls. Kari felt a pang of hunger, but she pushed it away.

She painted a mirror in an ornate gilded frame. But what the mirror revealed was no reflection. Instead, a face struggled to break from the surface. Fractured, stretched, nearly torn apart by the effort required to emerge fully. The face was far clearer than the central wraith, who watched the reflection take form. Just the same, her features were incomplete. Or perhaps the features were fragmented by her battle. Only the eyes were painted in vivid clarity. Wide and desperate and frantic with the urgent desire to break free.

Kari was not finished, but she could not paint more. As she set down the palette and began cleaning the brushes, Kari glanced back. The two men sat on the blanket they had spread out the previous afternoon. Some distance away, Sienna had found a dash of sunlight by the side wall and sat observing the men and cleaning one paw. With a mild start, Kari realized in all the time they had known each other, the men had never before watched her paint. Rafi studied the painting with a furrowed brow, as if struggling to understand the work's deeper purpose. Graham, the normally calm and stoic partner, was having difficulty controlling his emotions. His face was creased with what could have been mistaken for genuine pain.

Graham's emotions left Kari unsettled, as if she had glimpsed a forbidden element from a locked and lonely room. She finished cleaning the brushes, then pulled the drop cloth away from her other two unfinished oils. Both had been started upon her arrival in Miramar, then set aside in her impatient need to work on these others. She set up two more easels, with her current work in the center position. On the left easel she placed the happy family walking the desultory city street. Only now they seemed to frolic blindly down a concrete canyon. On the right-hand easel, she set the woman staring through the glass door at two men raging into their phones. Kari had assumed these secondary figures required a great deal more work. Now she wasn't so sure. She actually liked how their vague images were threatened by unseen winds. Only the pair were too busy with their phones, too immersed in their angry tirades, to notice.

She walked back and settled between the two men. Sienna trotted over and climbed into her lap. She gave the silence a long moment, then pointed to the canvas depicting the two men and said, "I'm wondering if this one is actually finished."

"Not another brushstroke," Graham said. "Neither a jot nor a tittle."

"I suppose . . . if you like, you can have it for Miami."

"We like," Rafi said. "We like a lot." He hesitated, glanced at Graham, then added, "It's probably not my place to say so, but I think your new one is ready, as well."

She tried to distance herself from the new canvas. View it as, well, another work. But the emotions and the potent hours still held her. "Are you absolutely certain?"

Graham nodded, his gaze still on the canvas. "It should be front and center in Miami." He looked at her, his features solemn. "It is that good."

She had never given up a painting so soon after completion. Days and sometimes weeks of living with the work, touching up small elements, hours spent examining and in many cases wishing she could have done it better. This time, though, she heard herself say, "Then it's settled."

She was so drained from the hours of work, she could have remained there for hours. But Rafi rose to his feet and announced, "It's time to go see what this little frontier town has in the way of high fashion."

"There's a lovely shopping street, with some beautiful things in the windows," Kari said. Giving the new canvas a final look. Saying farewell. "I'll be ready in ten minutes."

CHAPTER 28

The morning following their concert, Ian approached Arthur's studio with a degree of concern. The heady lift of a successful performance was behind them. Now was the point when everyone needed to be drawn together and to focus on the main act. Miami.

Ian's main worry was Connor. The man whom Ian had effectively replaced as bandleader the previous evening. Which he needed to do again. Now. Today. In order to prepare the group for what would soon happen. The main event.

But when he entered the front room, Arthur greeted him with customary gruffness and ordered Ian to put on a fresh pot. When Ian realized Connor and the band members were already in the recording studio, he asked, "Shouldn't I go in?"

"Coffee first." Then Arthur rose and followed him into the kitchenette. "What you did last night carries the mark of greatness in my book."

Ian almost dropped the coffeepot.

"Here, give me that." Arthur filled it from the tap, set it in place, and began spooning coffee into a fresh filter. Anything but meet Ian's astonished gaze. "No one else could have accomplished it. Not Danny. Not me. Certainly not Connor. You took a clutch of frightened musicians and turned them into a unit. One with purpose. Well done."

"Arthur . . . I don't know what to say."

"Danny rang. He's checked the footage they shot. Claims they captured pure gold. His words."

Ian kept his back to the recording studio. "What about Connor?"

"I had him and the band come in a few minutes early. Read them the riot act. You are hereby appointed boss and chief bottle washer. Chairman of the ruddy board. For the duration. If anybody dares voice an objection, I promised to personally pluck their feathers."

"So Connor . . . He's okay?"

"Don't you worry about him, lad. Thanks to you, they all delivered. Connor is a pro at heart. He'll adjust to the new reality because it's best for everyone concerned."

"The *temporary* new reality," Ian corrected.

Arthur actually smiled. "Ah, lad. You do my heart good."

"What's that supposed to mean?"

The door opened, and three cheerful ladies piled into the front room.

"Right on time," Arthur said. "Pour yourself a mug and go get stuck in. That's a good little bandleader."

They began what for Ian was a standard sort of postmortem. Together they broke down the songs, discussed possible changes, emphasized new elements, moved on. The same yet different. The band's erstwhile leader remained remote. When addressed directly, Connor spoke in a soft monotone, then retreated to his dark silence. Ian had no choice, really. He did what Arthur said and maintained control. He was firm and handled the process in a swift and professional manner. Ian hid the way Connor's moroseness impacted him. He didn't show how Connor's distant gaze resonated at his own deep level. As if there in the actor's expression, he found a reflection of his own internal state. The same vague emptiness where passion once resided. The flame that now was reduced to ashes. It hurt Ian to look at Connor. He treated the actor with utmost care. Respecting every softly spoken word. Listening carefully, applying every suggestion without discussion or argument.

Two and a half hours later, they were done.

Ian walked around both rooms, shaking hands and thanking each person in turn, including the sound and lighting techs, Arthur, Danny, the cameraman. Taking his time, speaking about how they had come together in such a great way, and now they were ready. He followed the almost formal pattern used by the conductors he most admired. Making each person feel important. Like they were all standout performers.

He treated Connor like a valued soloist. Ian stressed how the actor needed to guard his voice, stay hydrated during the long flight, practice a few scales each day, nothing more. Connor had the music down cold. He would do fine.

Ian carried his phone out of the studio and along the graveled path to the rear wall. The stone was covered with some flowering vine he did not recognize. The blossoms' scent carried a fragrant welcome. He stood looking out over the rooftops and the tree line, down to where Miramar met the sea. He remembered standing there with Connor, returning with the actor to the studio, making the call to Kiki. Which had brought them here. To the point where he was the man with strength enough to walk forward, while his new friend crouched inside the ready room. Ian hurt for him and, in a most illogical manner, hurt for himself. He hoped desperately he had done the right thing by suggesting to Kiki that they perform together in Miami.

He phoned Kari. She answered by saying, "Just a moment, Ian." A pause, voices, sounds, and then a door dinged and Kari came back. "Thank you for last night. It was wonderful hearing you perform."

"Where are you?"

"Standing outside some fancy store. Graham and Rafi have taken me shopping. Dresses and outfits. I hate shopping."

"For the gala." Drawing out the last word.

"You're only making it worse, saying it like that. I started painting before dawn. I'm exhausted. No, *drained* is a better word. I want to be in a rocker on my porch, Sienna in my lap. Instead, I'm trapped inside their idea of a good time."

"Can I see you before I take off?"

Her voice sharpened. "You're going?"

"I told you. I'm leaving for Miami. Overnight in Los Angeles. Fly tomorrow. I always try to travel nonstop when heading to a performance. It cuts down on the risk." When Kari did not respond, he said, "Hello?"

"You're leaving." Her voice had gone very soft.

"Rehearsal is the next morning. Concert that night. Remember? You're invited."

"Ian, I must absolutely see you. I need this so much." A pause. "Does that sound awful?"

"No, Kari. It's beautiful."

"I have these moments of sheer terror. I think that's partly why I've been so involved in this new work. Then I stop, and it's like an avalanche hits me."

He liked saying it again. "How can I help?"

"Be my friend."

"Okey dokey."

"Look at what you've done. The day's first smile. Just a second." He listened as a door chimed, voices spoke. Then she said, "We're having lunch at a diner on the main street, just up from Castaways. Come join us."

"I'd love that."

"Graham says we need another forty-five minutes. I'm done now. I was done before we got here."

When Ian returned to the studio for his guitar, he was met by happy chatter and numerous smiles. The crew treated him as one of their own. All of them save Connor.

Arthur walked him out. "You handled that like a seasoned pro. Again."

"You notice Connor didn't have much to say?"

"What everybody saw was how you responded, lad. Sooner or later, Connor will recognize everything you've done. And are doing."

"I wish I could be so certain."

Arthur waited until they had rounded the side of the house, cutting them off from the view of all the others. "Danny is starting work on a new film next week. A feature. He's already sold the project to Apple Plus. It's a big step for him. Good mid-level budget. Three solid stars."

"I'm glad for him."

"He wants you to do the score."

Ian took his time settling his guitar case in the rear hold, shutting the liftgate, straightening. "Why am I hearing this from you?"

"Because I asked. Lad, I know you're going through a rough patch. And having this kerfuffle with Connor has only made things worse. The temptation is to doubt every step. Question. Hesitate. I've had fifty-two years' experience in this trade. And I'm telling you the best thing you can do just now is forge straight on."

Ian stared at the closed front gate, reflecting on how

closely Arthur's words aligned with what Indrid had said. "All right."

"All right, you'll think about it?"

"No. Tell Danny I'm in."

Arthur squinted at him. "Don't think for an instant this means I'll go easy on you. You give me one ounce less than your best, I'll toss you on the bug zapper."

"Understood."

Arthur offered his hand. "In that case, I'll see you in Miami."

CHAPTER 29

Ian went straight to Amelia's, where he showered and packed in record time. Everything should have been by rote, the standard preparations for just another journey, another city, another two performances. He didn't have the right clothes, of course. But suiting up for the gigs would be simple enough in Miami. Ian made a mental note to contact Danny or Arthur, ask what they would be wearing that second evening. It was a decision that should have been made by Connor, of course. No matter what Arthur might say, the man's emotional distance worried Ian. A lot.

As he descended the ridge and drove into town, Ian felt himself slowly winding down. Like a spinning top left to waver and fall. During the session, he'd had no real idea about how much he was giving, the energy required to lead the group. For the first time in his life, he had not merely performed. He had directed. Kept the crew focused and moving forward. Now, though, all the resulting tension drained away, leaving him adrift. He parked in the public lot a couple of blocks from the diner and sat there.

The car was filled with sunlight and a gentle drifting wind. He could still feel the music resonating inside him. He wondered if this was how it would be from now on. No fire, but instead a sense of quiet satisfaction. It left him feeling both sad and resigned, that he had lost something he had never fully appreciated. How often did someone stop and be thankful because they had hands? That was how it felt now. A part was gone, and yet he was finding a way to make peace with the new reality.

The Honda's seats were creased and wrinkled with years of use, yet as perfectly clean as Amelia's little apartment. And suddenly their former owner was seated in the seat next to him. A presence as gentle as the breeze.

He spoke the words aloud, addressing the woman who was no more. "I've had a good day."

Then she was gone. Ian patted the empty seat, rolled up the windows, and walked the street. Happy with the music that accompanied him. And the prospect of a new life taking hold, one that extended beyond Miami and the troubles he had left behind in Annapolis.

He entered the diner, saw he was the first to have arrived, and chose a booth by the rear wall. As Ian seated himself, he had the distinct impression this was why Amelia had wanted him to visit Miramar. What she meant by the midnight harbor. Sheltered in a way that left him able to talk about a new compass heading. Once the storms faded, and he was ready to get on with life.

He ordered a coffee and savored the weightless feeling. Everything about this town seemed incredibly fresh. A few of the other patrons looked his way and complimented him on the performance. Then they went back to their own meals and conversations. He wondered if such low-key respect for a person's privacy was a trait common to small-town California.

When they entered the diner, Graham came first. Then

Kari, with Rafi in the rear. Ian could see Kari was pale, her gaze scattered. He liked how the two friends were there to support her, a natural acceptance of her fragile state. And that was definitely the way to describe her today. Kari appeared scarcely connected to the diner's floor.

He rose and kissed her cheek and settled back down. Rafi slid in beside him; Kari directly across; Graham beside her. The waitress appeared, and they ordered. Ian found himself recalling days spent with Amelia in the Philadelphia hospital, seated on uncomfortable chairs in the waiting area, while her partner went through another test or treatment. He had seen patients whose state resembled Kari's, who were not fully connected to the material world. But there was a difference to this lovely young woman, an illumination that shone upon the three of them. The strain of exhaustion was evident, as well. But it could not extinguish this ethereal glow. Ian realized he was sensing the woman's creative fire. So strong, it actually seemed visible.

When the waitress departed, Kari told him, "I was having a really nice day. Until these two awful men dragged me away."

"And took you shopping," Ian supplied. "Which you hate."

"Let's not forget why this was happening," she said.

"The gala. Miami."

"Double yuck."

Ian wanted to tell her it was going to be okay. Wishing it was within his power to make it all fine. In the end, he decided to remain silent.

Graham cleared his throat and addressed Ian, "Changing the subject. I really must apologize."

"Sorry, I don't follow," Ian said. "Apologize for what?"

Kari said, "Told you."

Graham said, "For being an opinionated busybody."

Rafi offered, "He's talking about last night."

Ian took his time, studying these two men. He had the impression they had done their best to dress down, blend in with the small-town California vibe. But their knit shirts and gabardine trousers and sockless loafers and gold watches and perfect hair all spoke of a distinctly different world. Graham was the sharper edged of the two; Ian had to assume he was the one who negotiated and contracted and counted. Rafi was smoother and sleeker. But equally intelligent. And clearly enjoying Graham's discomfort.

Ian said, "Graham, you told me exactly what I needed to hear."

Kari nudged Graham. "See?"

Ian went on, "Did you hear how we played?"

Graham nodded. "It was wonderful."

Ian described going back upstairs and doing what Graham had advised. Bringing the group together in the process. "So, thank you."

Graham said to Kari, "Okay. So you were right."

"Of course I was."

"I can breathe again." To Ian, Graham said, "We love your work."

"We play it all the time in the studio," Rafi added. "And at home."

Kari said, "My introduction to you was at the Hollywood Bowl, thanks to these two. Which was almost as expensive as the outfit we just bought."

"Correction," Rafi said. "Two outfits. Both of which are simply gorgeous."

While they ate, Ian listened as the three of them discussed what Kari should do with Sienna. He ate his late, late breakfast of a spinach-and-avocado omelet and savored the chance to observe them. The patient care the two men showed Kari was genuinely moving. This was not just about a kitten. It was an important decision that Kari needed help with. They were there for her. Ian loved that most of all.

He watched as Kari's otherworldly glow gradually faded. He wondered if this was Graham and Rafi's normal pattern of behavior, gently helping their artist friend reattach herself to earth. Old friends, trusted allies, talking for almost an hour over what should be done with her kitten.

Finally, Ian pushed his empty plate to one side and asked, "Am I allowed to offer a different opinion?"

"About last night?" Rafi smiled at his partner. "Graham was worried you were going to make him go sit at the bar."

"Observe," Ian said, and swept his hand around the room. "This is a diner. No bar."

"I meant the one down the street."

Kari said, "Don't be mean."

"You should see how he is with me when I mess up," Rafi replied.

"Nobody messed up," Ian said.

"Thank you so very much," Graham said. To Rafi, he added, "I believe the gentleman was actually going to make a point."

Ian told them, "Everything I've heard has been about the cat."

The three of them exchanged a look.

Rafi said, "And?"

"I don't hear anyone asking what would be best for Kari." Ian asked her, "How do you feel about Miami?"

"I told you already. It fills me with a very real dread."

"How do you feel around Sienna when times are less than great?"

She studied him a long moment. Then, "Better."

Ian showed them open palms. "Case closed."

There followed a moment's silence. Then Rafi told his partner, "Go ahead. Ask him."

"Me? Why should I be the one to stick my foot in again?"

"Because you look so good doing it." Rafi smiled. "And you know if I try, I'll make a total mess."

Ian asked, "Mess of what?"

Rafi said, "Ask him, Graham."

The man seated across from Ian said, "It's about Miami."

"Quadruple yuck," Kari offered.

"Day after tomorrow we begin setting up our stand."

"The hall opens at noon," Rafi said. "It's a madhouse. Everything has to be vetted before it's admitted. Security is *so* tight."

Graham went on, "For the first time in years, we are going to be showing unsold paintings by Kariel."

"We're going to be inundated with clients and jealous owners of other galleries," Rafi said. "It's going to be heaven."

Graham asked, "Who's telling this?"

Rafi replied, "You are. I'm just filling in the gaps."

Ian said, "You're super busy. I understand. I already told Kari I wanted to help her get through this. I meant what I said."

The two men just exchanged a long look across the table. Only this time, Kari shared their expression. Solemn. Nervous.

Ian said, "Look. I have no idea what's going on here. But I'll do whatever it is that you're not asking."

Kari said, "Ask."

Graham said, "Kari's been given a penthouse suite. Two bedrooms separated by the main parlor."

Ian leaned back. "Whoa."

Kari said, "It's silly. I know—"

"Kari, no." Ian addressed the men as much as her. "We only just met. I'm amazed you trust me enough to ask."

Kari asked, "You'll do it?"

"If you think it would help . . ."

"I don't think. I know. Especially if I enter total meltdown."

"We won't let that happen," Ian said. "Guys, tell the lady."

It was Kari who said, "We're not done with the asking."

Graham said, "The showcase includes an invitation to travel by private jet."

"You're kidding."

"Oh, sorry. Didn't you know?" Rafi did a ta-da motion with his hand. "Allow me to introduce Kariel, the star artist of the Miami Art Fair."

Graham went on, "We're now transporting seventeen new paintings on that jet. Which we didn't know existed until yesterday. All this will require a huge amount of unexpected work. And logistics."

"All our other works have been in Miami for days," Rafi said. "Vetted and waiting. The security issues I mentioned are all about these new paintings, which we intend to hang in our temporary gallery. And that is going to make such a fuss. You wouldn't believe just how bent out of shape our fellow exhibitors are going to be when they hear." He beamed. "Like I said. Heaven."

"We have to get home and pack," Graham said. "Then it's cram the jet full of our new goodies, off to the exhibition, and straight to work. Pushing the security to vet and approve and let us get on with the real work. Redesigning our layout. Begging for extra room."

Kari said, "What they're dancing around is, can I fly with you? Please?"

CHAPTER 30

But there were no last-minute seats to be had on any direct flight, at any price.

Graham stayed busy on the phone while Kari packed.

Ian helped Rafi unload the van, which held an astonishing amount of gear. Boxes of kitchen utensils, crates of bed linens and towels. An art deco chest of drawers. Matching table and two chairs. Standing lamp and a modern version of an Eames chair with its stool. The three wooden crates stamped LIMOGES they left on the guesthouse kitchen's narrow counter.

"She can find them later," Rafi said. "Or the next time we're up."

Ian nodded agreement. Today was not made for exchanging gifts.

The van emptied, they settled the paintings going to Miami back into the crates, sealed the tops, and took them to the van. Sienna sat by the main house's rear door, mewing through the screen as Ian passed, then vanishing whenever Rafi or Graham came into view. Each painting they lifted and settled into place had Ian wanting to freeze-frame, step back, lose himself in Kari's work. But Rafi granted him only moments before insisting they resume work. Just the same, Ian was certain the man approved of his responses.

Ninety minutes after their arrival, they were ready to leave. Graham had booked two seats on the early-morning flight out of Santa Barbara, connecting through Dallas. Ian thought their accelerated pace actually helped Kari stay in balance. They all waited while she locked the doors to her house and settled in the Mercedes's passenger seat. Ian drove because she had asked that he do so. They followed Graham's van down the valley lane, through the main gates, and off they went.

Sienna's response to yet more travel proved a pleasant surprise. Ten minutes down the county highway, she mewed to be released from her carrier. She endured a time in Kari's lap, then clambered onto the central console and sat with her head cocked high. As they passed through San Luis Obispo, she climbed Ian's right arm and settled on the back of his seat. She nuzzled his neck from time to time, but when they joined the freeway, she sat with her head up and watched the road unwind. The kitten's calmness helped Kari enter a repose that he had not seen before. Legs tucked up under her, shoes left in the footwell, head back, and auburn-gold hair spilling everywhere. He wished she would take off her sunglasses so he could see those amazing eyes.

As they passed the Lompoc exit, Ian recalled his arrival. The dreadful flight, the awful rental car, the motel, the family in the next room shouting through the night. How long ago it all seemed.

Where the hills rose and tightened, the sky overhead blackened with a sudden Pacific storm. The car was buffeted with winds as strong as fists, causing the truck directly ahead of them to veer suddenly into the next lane, almost clipping Graham's van. Sienna fled into Kari's lap and huddled as the rain struck, reducing Ian's visibility to the vehicle up ahead and little else.

As the world closed in around them, Kari said quietly, "I've been thinking about my family."

In that windswept moment, Kari went from utterly silent to talking nonstop. Ian had no idea how to respond. He was filled with a sense that her words were an intimate gift, a rare glimpse into what she had spent a lifetime hiding away.

Kari stopped speaking only when they followed Graham off the freeway and entered the Santa Barbara resort's front drive. She stood silently as Graham and Rafi checked them in, and then she walked down the hillside lane holding Sienna's carrier. The hotel was composed of smallish villas built in the Spanish style, with broad balconies. The wind clutched at them, carrying the scent of more rain to come. It hastened their farewells, and soon enough Ian deposited his cases in his own room, then went next door. Kari's room had a fireplace and a broad ocean-facing balcony with French doors, already wet from another incoming squall. Ian lit the gas fireplace, waited while Kari selected a meal from the room-service menu, called in their orders, then settled into the chair across from hers. Sienna climbed into his lap.

Kari picked up where she had left off.

Word by word, she painted a new series of images. The child lost to a trio of people who equated rage with strength. Who fought their way through a harsh realm, until eventually the two parents turned on each other. The young girl who did not share either their rage or their attitude toward the world. Who grew to despise everything their fury represented, the flash and clamor of a life lived in the public eye. Who retreated into a secret realm, where silence meant safety. Who lived a ghostlike existence on the periphery of her family's world. Whose creative gift was sheltered within a lonely life.

Ian suspected she was not even aware of her own tears.

At a knock on the door, Ian walked over and insisted on taking their trays. They ate in silence at the fireside table, watching the storm lash the night-clad windows. The kitten climbed into Ian's lap, allowed him to feed her for the very first time, and in so doing, she drew out Kari's first and only smile.

Ian settled the trays outside the door, returned to the fireside table, and stood behind his chair. He had a sudden awareness of the king-size bed, Kari's openness to his staying, the sudden burning temptation that took him totally unawares. As if he had been too busy listening and absorbing to realize where this was taking them both.

If he wanted.

A sudden blast of wind and rain pelted the balcony doors, as if the storm was actually trying to speak with him. What he heard was a reminder of his own wrong moves. The man he was trying so hard to leave behind.

Kari chose that moment to speak for the first time since their dinner had arrived. "I feel as if this is the destiny I'm forced to accept. All that's changed is my location."

That was all it took. The burning urge was transformed into nothing save more ashes, which Ian could actually taste.

She went on, "I'm so happy in Miramar. But there's this whisper in the background. That I'm still fated to drift my way through a lifetime of lonely days."

"Kari." He remained standing behind his chair, waiting until she lifted her gaze. "You're not drifting now. And you're not alone."

She blinked, dislodging a tear, which fell upon the purring kitten.

When she did not speak, Ian told her, "Get some rest. We leave early."

She was still seated and staring at the fire when he left.

CHAPTER 31

Ian arranged to leave Kari's ride in the hotel lot. He loaded his suitcase and two guitars into the hotel limo, discovered Graham had taken care of his bill as well as Kari's, and stood waiting out front. The morning sky was scrubbed clean by the storm, which had passed just before daybreak. The air was Pacific fresh. A perfect day to fly.

Kari did not show.

He was about to go back inside and call her room when she appeared. She had resumed the same distant fragility he had last seen at the diner, only this was much more severe. He eased her into the limo, helped load her suitcases, tipped the bellhop, slipped in beside her. Tried to find something that might make the moment better, decided he was better off staying silent.

The Santa Barbara airport was a little gem, with hacienda-style buildings framed by a garden of blooming shrubs and imperial palms. The airport staff were cheerful, friendly, efficient. Ian thought several people eyeballed him. Certainly the woman checking them in recognized his name. But he had been out of the media's eye for over a week. A week was almost an eternity in the whirlwind of celebrity gossip.

As Ian handled the check-in process, he gradually became more comfortable with his silent-support role. Being with Kari, even in a situation like this, when she remained both distant and disconnected, was truly pleasant. He marveled at his response to her needing his strength. Guiding her into the waiting room, finding spots by the front windows, enjoying the small-town vibe drew his past travels into clear focus. And not just the journeys. The tight insistence that had grown around his stardom. Traveling to a new gig had always meant going direct. Always. He had refused to connect because he had wanted control over his timing. On the few occasions when a connecting flight had been unavoidable, usually with international gigs, he had always insisted on spending the night somewhere between flights. It used to drive his manager nuts.

Upon boarding the plane, they settled into the front row. Kari took the seat by the window, Sienna's case tucked neatly behind her feet. Once they were airborne, Kari reached over, took hold of his hand, shut her eyes, and drifted away. When the kitten mewed, Kari gave no sign of having heard. Ian reached down with his free hand, lifted the kitten's carryall, and settled it in his lap. He unzipped the flap a trifle, enough to reach one finger inside and stroke the little head.

His clarity of memory, his determined walk through the recent past, continued as they flew. He felt as if he was talking to the purring kitten, sharing secrets, in keeping with the confidences Kari had offered the previous day.

He used to call it *la vida loca*. The crazy life. Ian had always meant it as a half joke. Classical music was bound by traditions and strictures that went far beyond the music itself. He knew the tales of modern music stars and their excesses. The truly wild life had never much appealed to him. The music had been enough, at least until that point when his interior world began to crumble.

Ian had been almost living with his almost fiancée at the time. Andrea was a Bulgarian model with impeccable style and the smoothest skin he had ever known. Her face had a sprinkling of golden freckles, which she despised and he thought beautiful. She claimed to love him, and in their rare moments of solitude, he often wondered if she was the one. But part of what drove him to an awareness of his empty void was the subtle knowledge that their relationship was a lie. She loved the high-speed high life. The cameras, the endless new vistas, the palatial receptions, the attention they garnered as the star couple of the classical world. And he . . . It took him months to accept that he was simply going along for the ride.

Now it was hard to face the resulting questions. If their breakup was actually when he began sensing the change. If it was really his response to helplessness. If he had become aware at some deeper level that his creative and professional lives were undergoing a seismic shift. If that was why he so quietly accepted the inevitable farewell from this woman he did not love.

When they landed at Dallas–Fort Worth, Ian resumed his role as guide. Together they walked the long concourse, entered the first-class lounge, and he settled Kari into a seat by the window.

"Can I get you something?" he asked.

She spoke for the first time that morning. "I'm so sorry."

"There's no need—"

"I don't know what to do."

Ian pulled his chair in close enough to her to block out the other passengers. Repeated the same words, only with salsa. "Tell me how I can help."

Sienna mewed. Kari lifted the case, unzipped the flap, settled the kitten in her lap. "I was having breakfast. Everything was fine. Then Graham texted me the itinerary. I threw all the food back up. Now . . ."

"Can I see?"

She rummaged through her purse, found her phone, scrolled, handed it over.

Ian needed ninety seconds to declare, "This is nuts. They have you running flat out for two days, from seven in the morning to . . . Kari, they don't even have you attending my concert."

"Graham called. He said the same thing. But with fire. I've never heard him angry before. It's always Rafi who goes off the rails." She stroked the kitten. "He says he's going to cancel everything. Neither he nor Rafi agreed to any of it, and they're telling them no."

Ian hesitated, then decided it needed to be said. "I don't think that's a good idea. The people who put this together, they can't do anything to you. But they'll go after Graham and Rafi."

She focused on him fully now. "I can't let that happen."

"I agree."

"So I have to do what they're saying?"

"No. Absolutely not. But there needs to be some form of compromise. A face-saving measure."

"Call them."

"Maybe you should be the one to do that. You're their client. They hardly know—"

"Don't even start." She retrieved her phone, scrolled through the contact list, touched a number, handed it back. "Besides, Rafi thinks you're a dish. He wants to take you home to Mama."

Ian accepted the phone. "Graham must have loved that."

"He told Rafi to get in line." When Ian did not lift the phone, she added, "You said you wanted to help. So help."

It was Rafi who answered. The man sounded almost cheerful. "How's our incredible hunk doing this morning?"

"Soon as he shows up, I'll ask."

A pause. Then, "Excuse me while I go drown myself in the tar pits."

"Is that Graham I hear shouting?"

"He's busy roasting Miami officialdom. Which is why I have the opportunity to embarrass myself totally."

"Can you ask him to give me a minute? Now?"

There was a pause, a final blast in the distance, and then Graham huffed, "I truly loathe losing my temper."

"Let me tell you what I think happened," Ian said. "They assigned Kari's schedule to some high-class outside PR group they use for the entire art thing."

"Art fair, not thing."

"Whatever. Soon as the PR team heard Kari was using this as her coming-out party, they freaked. It was their chance to parade on the global PR stage."

Graham was silent. Then, "Have you been speaking with those awful people in charge?"

"You know I haven't."

"Because you're basically echoing everything they just told me."

"The question," Ian said, "comes down to whether you ever want anything to do with the Miami show ever again."

"Wait, wait, let me put you on speaker. All right. Rafi is listening. Is Kari there?"

"Right here beside me." Ian started to hit speaker on her phone as well, then decided it might work best if Kari remained slightly apart.

At Graham's request, Ian repeated his impressions for Rafi. Then he said, "There should be some room for compromise. Right now they have her running flat out for two days."

"I insisted they go back to the original agreement," Graham replied. "Kari arrives at the gala after your concert. She gives one interview on-site. Nothing more."

"Hold that thought. What if we could work with what they clearly want to see happen? Offer a concept that satisfies the PR group? Only shape it into something Kari might actually enjoy?"

"Not possible," Kari said. "Not in a million billion years."

"What did she just say?"

"She has reservations."

"Ha," Kari said. "Joking at a time like this. Double ha."

Graham asked, "What did you have in mind?"

"Anything that happens at the gala is going to be rushed and noisy." Ian pondered. Then, "Kari's had her share of bad experiences with the art critics."

"They've been awful," Kari said.

"But what if the Miami interviews aren't done by critics at all?" Ian talked as much to her as to Graham. "Her world, her fans, these are people who defy the critics. Fine. So restrict the interviews to journalists who are truly fans of her work. People who have written and talked about her before. Who can show they are on her side."

Kari was watching him now. Fully there.

Graham remained silent.

Ian felt as if his idea took form in Kari's crystal gaze. "Say she limits herself to two interviews. Tight restriction on who attends both. In one, she walks around the exhibition. Talking about how her art took form. Her beginnings."

Another silence. Then Rafi asked, "The second?"

"Same structure, only this one takes place inside your gallery at the art fair. She talks about what she's doing now. The new pieces. How she feels herself growing. Where she is headed. Who she is becoming."

Graham asked, "What do you think?"

Rafi responded, "What do *I* think? I'm back in heaven again."

Graham had resumed his calm, thoughtful air. "This is a wonderful idea, Ian. How does Kari feel about it?"

By this point she had shifted over so as to lean her head on Ian's shoulder.

"She seems agreeable." Ian asked her as much as them, "Can I make one more suggestion?"

Graham said, "By all means."

Kari nodded against his shoulder.

"Is there a top-tier art school in Miami?"

"There are several," Graham said. "My favorites are the School of Fine Arts and the University of Art and Design."

"Why not see if they'll do a joint session, open only to students, to be televised after the fact? And it's not handled by some snotty professor. The interview needs to be performed by the biggest television personality they can arrange. Aim for a structure they could offer to the Arts Channel as a special. At least, that's how you should pitch it."

Another silence. Then Rafi said, "Shivers."

Graham asked, "Kari is open to this?"

As if in response, Kari slipped the kitten into Ian's lap. But only so she could wrap both arms around his neck.

Ian said, "Kari thinks it might work."

CHAPTER 32

They landed in Miami as evening's final glow painted the tropical sky. Kari followed Ian down the tunnel and into the airport proper, marveling at her state. She had expected to be approaching a total meltdown. Seeing herself enter a big city's airport terminal, surrounded by the crowds and lights and cold indifference of people too busy to care about others. Inserting herself back into the world she had struggled and yearned to leave behind. For good and forever.

Instead, all she felt was calm. She did not like the place. She did not like the crowds. But neither the clamor nor the throngs nor the alienness seemed able to touch her. She glanced down at the hand holding hers and wondered if this was what it meant to be in love.

When they passed the terminal shops and approached baggage claim, Ian drew her over to a side window. "Are you all right?"

"Yes, Ian."

"Would it be okay if I took the lead out there? I know what to expect, is all."

She resisted the urge to kiss him. Silly. Stupid, in fact. But still. "Of course."

"Can I have your luggage tickets?"

She handed him the kitten's carryall and rummaged through her purse. When she looked up again, she caught Ian staring out the side window, his expression somber. Grave. "What's wrong?"

"Nothing." He did his best to smile. "An unwelcome memory, is all."

"Ian, tell me."

He pointed at the gathering night. "When I arrived in California, I stood in a place just like this. My world had basically collapsed. I was the headliner for every bad-news entertainment blog. I thought my life was over. I was too crushed to feel it totally. I know that sounds crazy. But I was basically numb. And now . . ."

"And now it's all so close," she said.

"Yes." He stroked the kitten through the soft mesh. "Right here. With me. Again."

Kari breathed around the enormity of what she was thinking. "I spent the flight from Dallas reflecting on what isn't happening. I mean, happening to me. Since you and Graham and Rafi took my side over this itinerary. It's not that I've stopped being afraid. I am. And in a way, I regret taking this on. And I don't like being here. Just the same, though, I'm increasingly certain this is the right thing to do."

Ian continued nudging the little head with one finger, stroking Sienna through the soft screen. "That's how I feel. Exactly."

She loved finding the strength to be open about all her desolate secrets. With him. In this alien place. Being able to say, "It's like Indrid said. Moving forward one step at a time."

* * *

The Miami airport was old and in desperate need of renovation. But the general air of tired seediness was brightened considerably by the fragrances emanating from the Cuban restaurants lining the terminal corridor. Not to mention the salsa playing over a café's intercom. Ian walked through the concourse with Sienna's carryall slung from one shoulder, one hand holding Kari's hand, the other gripping the one guitar case he had carried on board. Like he belonged. Like he had earned the right to feel this good.

He approached the uniformed lady driver with his name on the electronic board. Ian did his best to ignore the multiple stares pointed his way. If Kari even noticed the looks, she gave no sign. Ian shook the driver's hand, passed over the luggage tickets, said, "I need to get my companion settled in the limo. Where are you parked?"

She handed Ian the keys. "Straight out the exit, sir. Cadillac Escalade with the hotel insignia on the door."

They left the terminal, walking beneath a Miami Music Festival banner bearing his name and photograph. He could almost feel the city's tension and energy trying to drive a wedge between them. Because he needed her. It brought an intense flood of pleasure, admitting this to himself. Once they were settled in the limo's rear seat, he started in. "I need your advice, and I need to lay it out while we're alone. You can't ever say anything important in front of a driver—"

"I know all that," she said. "My family. Remember?"

"Right. Of course. Sorry. It's Connor. I am really, really worried—" He stopped because she began rummaging through her purse. "What is it?"

"I want Graham to hear. He's the best I know at handling situations like this." She pulled out her phone, dialed, said, "Let Sienna out of her case."

He unzipped the flap and lifted the kitten onto the console between them. Sienna instantly padded over and settled into Kari's lap. She placed the phone on the center console and pressed the speaker button. When Graham answered, they heard a sibilant rush so loud it almost drowned out him saying, "Just a minute!" Gradually, the noise diminished, to where they could hear him clearly. "Can this wait?"

"Not for an instant," Kari replied. "What's that noise?"

"They insisted on starting the engines while the crew was still loading your paintings. Something about losing their position for takeoff." A door thumped shut, and the jet went quiet. "All right, dear. What is it?"

"Ian has something you need to hear." Kari said to Ian, "Tell him."

"Connor hasn't recovered like I've hoped." Ian swiftly recounted how the post-concert session had gone down. Connor's utter lack of connection. The mechanical way he had responded, almost by rote. Ian finished by saying, "I tried to talk with Arthur about it—"

Graham broke in. "I'm sorry. Who is Arthur?"

"Film editor," Kari said. "Not important."

"Well, it is, but . . ." Ian actually smiled at how Kari rolled her finger. *Get on with it.* "I thought I needed help in handling the situation. Arthur obviously thought differently."

Rafi asked, "This Arthur, he's the older gentleman who handled the recording?"

"Right. Arthur Rowe. Two Oscars. He's also editing Danny's film." Ian started to add Arthur's news about the next gig, then decided that needed to wait. "Arthur keeps telling me I shouldn't concern myself, that Connor's a pro and he'll come around. But landing here, it hit me all over again. I'm worried, and I don't know what to do."

"Arthur's right," Rafi declared.

"For once, I agree with my friend," Graham said.

"Well, I never," Rafi responded.

"Don't get used to it," Graham said.

Kari was almost cross. "Guys. Let's focus here."

Then Ian spotted the lady with their luggage. "We're in a

limo, and our driver is on approach. We can keep talking, but it needs to be circumspect."

"My middle name," Rafi said.

Graham said, "We're taxiing for takeoff. Let me discuss the situation with Mr. Circumspecter here. We'll call you back."

Ian cut the connection, said to Kari, "You were right to call."

She watched the driver settle behind the wheel. "You should talk with Indrid."

"I don't want to disturb her."

"You heard what she said. She would be *honored* to talk." Kari flicked through speed dial. "There it is. Indrid."

"Will you ask?"

Kari nodded.

Ian held her gaze as she greeted the good doctor, said Ian needed to speak with her, set up an appointment for them to chat in a couple of hours.

Kari cut the connection and said, "See how easy that was?"

"Thank you." He pointed to the phone. "For both of these connections. I owe you."

She actually smiled. "That's a new one. For me, anyway."

"It's true."

When her only response was to reach across the kitten and take his hand, Ian leaned forward and asked the driver, "What are your instructions about our arrival?"

"Let the front desk know when we're on approach, sir. That's pretty much it."

"Call them back. Ask the manager or their representative to meet us out front. We want to go straight to Ms. Langham's suite. No stopping for registration. No slowing down for an elevator or any other reason. No photographs." Ian settled back. "If you face any issue, pass me the phone."

Kari studied him. "So that's how it's done."

* * *

Graham phoned back while Kari and Ian were trapped in slow-moving bridge traffic. When Kari answered and put them on speaker, Graham announced, "Rafi agrees with me. You're worrying about issues that need to wait."

There were worse places to get stuck, Ian decided, than in the back of a limo on the way to Miami Beach. Even Sienna seemed interested in the vista of sunset waters and, up ahead, an island filled with high-rises that glistened in the golden dusk. "What if the issue we're discussing impacts our concert?"

"It won't." Rafi assured him. "It can't. You won't let it."

"You're sure about that, are you?"

"You handled it at the restaurant," Rafi reminded him. "You'll handle it again now."

Graham said, "Connor is one of the team. You bring the others along. He will follow."

"He needs to wake up, is all," Rafi said.

Graham said, "Connor's played with this group for years. Isn't that what you said? He trusts them. He *likes* them. If Connor sees the others responding to you in a happy and positive manner, he will *want* to follow their lead. And yours."

"Let's not forget, he is also a highly successful actor," Rafi added. "Hard as it may be for him to accept, he is being given his role. By you."

"Mark my words," Graham said. "He is a trained professional. He'll come around."

"Kicking and screaming, most likely," Rafi said.

"Tantrums are part of working with artists," Graham added. "It's in all our contracts."

The Ritz Carlton was a bastion of South Beach. The high-rise towered like a gleaming marble pinnacle above its older, more tawdry neighbors. As Ian had requested, an assistant manager was there to greet them and personally open Kari's limo door. They were ushered straight through a lobby filled with families and the clamor of half a dozen languages. A smiling bellhop held the elevator door open for them, pressed the top button with a gloved finger, and waved other guests to a different lift.

When it was just the three of them, the hotel director ventured, "Was your manager correct when he said Mr. Hart intends to take the Royal Suite's second bedroom?"

"Yes," Kari replied. "He does. Absolutely."

"I must tell you, that comes as a great relief. Ms. Kerkorian was adamant that we also find space for Connor Larkin and a Mr. Daniel Byrd."

"Good for Kiki," Ian said.

"Yes. Well. Ms. Kerkorian actually insisted that we take in your entire group. Including the film crew. Eleven rooms in total." The manager sniffed. "I had such a difficult time trying to explain that we have been booked solid for months. But you know Ms. Kerkorian."

"So Connor and Danny have arrived?" Ian asked.

"Seventh floor. The family we were forced to relocate is now, thankfully, in the suite originally reserved for you, Mr. Hart. If you had insisted on taking that, as well, I don't know what we would have done." He smiled nervously at Kari. "The call from your manager, Ms. Langham, truly made my day."

The suite was, in a word, stunning. High ceilinged and flowing in lyrical majesty, one grand chamber after another, out to where the trio of balconies overlooked the Atlantic. Parlor large enough to contain a grand piano resting under one of four chandeliers. Full kitchen. Dining room.

The master bedroom was only slightly smaller than the downstairs lobby.

Kari took one look and told Ian, "You can definitely sleep in here."

"Not on your life."

"Ian, I can't . . ." She stopped because he had already turned away and was headed for the double doors on the parlor's opposite side. "Please."

"Sorry. Not happening." He slid back the doors and discovered a Canali suit bag on the bed. "What's this?"

"Compliments of Ms. Kerkorian," the hotel director informed him. "I believe there's a note."

Ian opened the envelope and read.

For my newly favorite bad boy. In case my attorneys still have your clothes under lock and key. Consider this a bribe to have you continue this spate of good behavior. Please. For all our sakes.

Once the bellhop had deposited his cases in his bedroom, Ian called Arthur. "I forgot to ask about our dress for the concert."

"Then it's a good thing you have me and Danny to watch your back."

Ian stared down at Kiki's clothes, now spread over one of the room's two double beds. The Canali tux came with two identical pairs of pants. And three formal shirts. Ian had tried on the jacket. It fit perfectly. "And?"

"Danny wants to go formal. He thinks it will contrast well with the restaurant's casual air when we cut and paste for the documentary."

"Connor agrees?"

A pause. Then, "Lad, you've got to stop worrying so over Connor."

"Arthur . . ."

"I know, I know. He's the bandleader. He's the lead vocals, yada yada. You're sounding like a broken record."

"That's no answer."

"It's all the answer you're going to get. Now, be a good lad and go do whatever it is stars do in Miami."

"Pace the floor," Ian replied. "Worry about not getting answers to questions that really matter."

"I'm hanging up now," Arthur said. And he did.

CHAPTER 33

Kari heard Ian's conversation because he kept his bedroom doors open. She pretended not to watch him as he stood by the bed, talking with the old man, who clearly did not give Ian what he thought he needed. When he cut the connection and remained where he was, she used her own phone to call Indrid.

"I'm a little early, I know," she said when her friend picked up.

"Now is fine. How are you, dear?"

"Sitting in the living room of my suite. So high up, all I can see are evening shades of blue."

"What a lovely impression. But it doesn't answer my question. How are you?"

"Coping. For the moment. Thanks to Ian." She called out, "It's Indrid." Back on the phone, she added, "No telling about tomorrow, though."

"Let's see. I know there is something happening tomorrow. What was it . . . ?"

Kari slid over a touch and patted the sofa next to her. As Ian settled, she told Indrid, "You're making fun of me."

"Only a trifle. And only with love. Now tell me. What happens tomorrow?"

"Just Ian's big concert. I may have an interview. We haven't received the revamped schedule yet. And the gala." She dragged out the last word, *gala*. Added a touch of genuine dread.

"You know what I just heard?"

"What?"

"How you put the young man's event first."

"Did I? I wasn't listening to myself."

"I wish you were close enough to hug."

"You just did. Here's Ian." She passed him the phone. "Want me to leave?"

"Don't you dare." He turned on the speaker and placed the phone on the coffee table. "Indrid, can you hear me?"

She asked a second time, "How are you, dear?"

"Worried. About everything. Right now, though, my biggest concern is one of my bandmates." Swiftly, Ian recounted the situation with Connor. Kept rubbing his forehead, dragging hair back from his face.

When he went quiet, Indrid asked, "How are you handling it?"

They both listened as Ian described his tactic at the restaurant, a quick and intense run-through of the first song.

Indrid responded, "That sounds like an excellent plan."

"Really?"

"Yes, Ian. You are drawing them together, helping them to focus on the crucial moment. May I make one suggestion?"

"Absolutely. It's why I called."

"Connor needs a friend. Someone who can help him face his own wall. Do you understand what I'm saying?"

Kari felt him shudder. Ian replied, "All too well."

"He may not see it as that. Whether you tell him or not depends on the moment. Trust your instinct." A pause. Then, "I find it remarkable how all three of you seem to be facing the same crisis moment just now."

"*Remarkable* is not the word I would use," Ian said.

"Remarkable and beautiful both," Indrid replied.

"I thought . . ." Ian straightened. "All this time I've been worried he's angry because I've usurped his position as bandleader."

"That may be what he sees as well. If so, being open about your own struggle may help clarify things for him."

He nodded slowly, gaze resting on the phone. "Can I ask you about something else?"

"Of course."

"Coming here feels like a terrible mistake. It was so hard to escape this world. And it cost me so much. Now I'm diving right back in."

"I'm not sure that's actually what frightens you. Or rather, it doesn't frighten you as much as something else. Shall I tell you what that other thing might be?"

"I suppose . . ."

"Who you are now is not the same young man who struggled so hard and finally broke free. What frightens you is coming face-to-face with the man you are no longer."

Ian slid off the sofa. Knelt on the floor. Planted his elbows on the coffee table. Placed his face in his hands. Stared at the phone.

"These few days at such a crucial juncture have brought considerable changes. That is what I heard most in our time together. That you are changing, and rapidly. Which is why I am so confident about your situation now. And why I trust you to do the right thing. With your friend Connor. And with my dear Kari. And to confront yourself, young man, with honesty."

"I don't—" Ian was halted by the ringing of his phone in the other room. "Excuse me. I should probably answer that."

Kari watched him enter the bedroom, lifted the phone, said, "Thank you, Indrid. So much."

"I cannot tell you how glad I am you two have found each other," she replied.

Indrid might have said something more, but Kari's ability to hear was abruptly ended by Ian returning to the doorway, his phone in one hand, and saying, "It's Connor."

CHAPTER 34

When Kari ended the call with Indrid, Ian walked back into the parlor, seated himself beside Kari, and asked Connor, "Where are you?"

"Room seven-oh-one. Danny and Arthur came out a day early to scope the scene. Sylvie got fed up with me moping around the house and ordered me to go with them."

"I know that's not true."

"She might have said it differently. Something about my needing to come early and take time to settle. But that's what she meant." A pause. "Buy you a drink?"

"Hang on a second." He told Kari, "Connor is downstairs. He wants to meet in the bar."

"Ask him up."

"I don't want to bother—"

"Ian. Really. You heard what Indrid said."

"She didn't say a word about my bothering you with my problems."

She just looked at him. With those eyes of blue crystal and

smoke. "He's here because he needs you. This is your place as much as mine."

"Kari—"

"Hush now and ask him up."

The suite shared a butler with the other top-floor residences. Ian learned that when he called down for coffee, which arrived just as he opened the door for Connor. They stood to one side as a dark-suited woman wearing white gloves carried in the service for three on a silver palaver. She set it on the front table, asked if there was anything else.

Ian asked Connor, "You hungry?"

"I could eat."

"Me too," Kari said. She waited as Ian asked the woman for a tray of sandwiches, and then she approached Connor with her hand outstretched. "Hi, Connor. I'm Kari."

"You were at the restaurant."

"Several times."

"I mean, for the show."

"Both of them." She smiled. "Lucky me."

Ian said, "Kari is a newcomer to Miramar."

"And now you're here." He glanced at Ian. "Lucky you."

"It's not like that. This is Kari's suite. She's . . ."

She liked how Ian hesitated over what to say. Honoring her confidences. Letting her decide. She told him, "It's all right."

Ian said, "This is Kariel."

Connor did a double take. "The artist."

"They're doing a retrospective as part of the art fair. Which happens the same time as the concerts."

"Kariel. Wow. My wife thinks you're the greatest thing since her dad."

"I saw the painting her father did of the midnight harbor," Kari said. "Ian used that expression when he was talking about his aunt. The midnight harbor. I liked it so much, I decided to try to paint it. Then I saw her father's work, and now I feel like he did it for me."

Connor studied her a long moment. "You say that to Sylvie, she'll probably break down and bawl. There's a lot of history to that painting. Tales on top of tales."

"I'd love to hear them."

"Maybe we should leave that for another time," Ian said. "Why don't we get comfortable on the balcony?"

Connor took a long moment to study the starlit Atlantic, savoring the tropical breeze. When the doorbell chimed, Kari went back inside, took the trolley from the butler, and rolled it in herself. As she approached the open balcony doors, she heard Connor say, "I should go. You need to get some rest."

"I never sleep before a live performance. It's one of life's defining traits. You'll keep me from another few hours of tossing and turning."

"Still, it looks to me like I'm interrupting."

"I told you, it's not like that." Ian was seated with his back to the parlor. "We met less than a week ago. She's dealing with her own set of personal issues. I offered to help. For the moment, that's all it is."

"For the moment."

"We'll get through these gigs, go home, see what happens. But I won't lie to you. A guy can hope."

Kari stepped through the doors, warmed by far more than the tropical breeze. "Come inside and help yourselves."

They made plates and filled cups and took them back out on the balcony. From where they were seated so high up, they saw just starlight and silvery clouds and inky-black sea. Music and laughter drifted up, but they were immune to the city and the swirling crowds far below.

Finally, Connor set his plate on the low table and said, "Ever since I moved to Miramar, I've had these two lives.

Home means the woman I love more than my own life. The twins. My music. You understand what I'm saying?"

Ian nodded. "I think so."

Kari asked, "Should I leave?"

"I feel comfortable with the two of you." A pause. Then Connor added, "Maybe it's good to have a lady's perspective here."

Ian reached for Kari's hand and said, "Stay."

Connor went on, "The way things were, I chose the songs I love. I made them my own. When there was time, I invited friends to join me. We played in a setting that suited us all. A place filled with *other* friends."

"A full house, or so it seems," Ian said. "Every time. They love your work."

"They should," Kari said. "You play beautifully."

"My songs," Connor repeated. "My renditions. My stage. My friends. When it's time, I go shoot my next picture. A hundred different people telling me what to do, how to stand. I speak the words they give me. I act. When it's done, I go home."

"Two worlds," Kari said.

"And then I come along and mess everything up," Ian said. "I'm so sorry."

"For what? Giving me a taste of a lifelong dream I thought would never come?" Connor rose and walked over to the railing. "Nights after I get back from a shoot, I'm hollowed out. A long time lost, that's how it feels. The chance to have those days with my wife and kids and home. It's *gone*. Then, after a while, things steady up. And I get back into the rhythm of Miramar life. That's how I think of it."

"Miramar life," Ian repeated. "A good place, a happy world."

"There you go."

Ian said it again. "Then here I come."

"You. Danny. Arthur." Connor gripped the railing, rocked

back and forth. "My friends giving me the dream I thought was lost and gone forever."

"I'd like to be that," Ian said. "Your friend."

"I don't have any reason to feel as bad as I have."

Kari surprised herself as much as the men when she was the one who said, "You have *every* reason."

Ian looked at her a long moment, his smile illuminated by the interior lights. Finally, he told Connor, "Come sit down. Please."

The actor walked back over, seated himself, and went on. "For a couple of days now, I've been surrounded by this huge looming shadow. This black nothingness. Thinking about here, Miami, leaves me feeling like it's about to swallow me whole."

Kari stared at the hand holding her own and felt the words rise up, a great hot balloon of emotions and memories and needs that forced itself out into the open. Finally. "I've spent my entire life in hiding. It's the only way I knew to protect my gift, my one reason for wanting to keep on living. When I came to Miramar, I thought I was making a new hiding place. One I could call my own. Instead . . ."

Connor shifted in his seat. Leaned forward. Watching her. "What's happened?"

"It's all so new, I don't know if I can put it in words. But I think . . . Maybe it's time I grow beyond my comfort zone. Not stop hiding. But make room for more. More people, more experiences, more life. The thought absolutely terrifies me. I'm afraid I'll lose my gift. That I'll open myself up to attack. Something I can't handle and still paint. The fears mostly strike in the middle of the night. Then I wake up, and I paint like I've never painted in my entire life. It just flows out, this huge torrent of colors and impressions and . . ."

Ian asked softly, "And now?"

She felt his power coursing through the hand holding hers, an electric current strong enough to help her say, "The fears and the joy. It's this huge tumbling mass. Then something strikes, like the gala and my itinerary, and I feel like it's all about to come crashing down around me."

Ian's gaze was as strong as his hold on her hand. "How can I help?"

"Be who you are. Do exactly what you're doing. Shielding me. Showing me a way through. Keeping me safe." She released his hand so as to wrap her arm around him. Leaned in close. "I'm such a mess, Ian. I'm this bundle of fragments that come together only when I paint."

"I think you are the most amazing woman I have ever known."

She hid her face for a time in the fold of his neck. Then, "Tell Connor about Indrid."

CHAPTER 35

The next morning Ian was dressed and downstairs at half past six, when the main restaurant opened. He was tired from the flight and the too-short night and the scattered dreams that he could not remember. But he was well accustomed to going without sleep before major performances. Despite all the reservations and concerns that had accompanied him, now that it was time, he felt ready. More than that. He actually felt excited.

Kiki had texted that transport had been arranged for nine. At seven he texted the festival director and canceled the ride. He went back upstairs, packed his music in with his primary guitar, then fit an extra tux shirt and trousers into the second case. He returned downstairs and asked for a taxi. The lobby staff must have been alerted to who he was, however. Three minutes later Ian settled into the hotel limo.

The orchestra's final rehearsal started at eight, but as was the norm, the star was not expected to be present for their initial run-through. Ian wanted to make an entrance, but not the one they probably anticipated.

The beachside roads and the main bridge were almost empty. Ian reveled in the breeze off the ocean, the early morning coolness. The air tasted almost sweet through his open windows. He asked the driver to drop him off a block from the concert hall, accepted his guitars, and set off on foot.

The Adrienne Arsht Center was the largest concert venue in Florida and home to MISO, the Miami Symphony Orchestra. Ian had never played with them but had heard good things. Israel Saban, the guest conductor brought in for this music festival, had a worldwide reputation. Despite the cool breeze, Ian found himself burning with shame as he recalled Saban's cold and dismissive scorn.

Which was why he was doing this. Arriving with the rest of the orchestra. An hour and a half before he was expected.

Several members of the orchestra were standing outside the main doors, instrument cases at their feet. Then a woman cellist noticed Ian's approach. Her eyes widened. She said something, enough to make her mates turn around. They watched in astonished silence as Ian crossed the front plaza, wished them a good morning, and entered the concert hall.

He followed the sound of instruments being tuned and playing certain passages, an all too familiar cacophony. He entered the main hall by way of the rear doors and walked along the central aisle, down the gentle slope, toward the stage. The hall was mostly dark, with just the stage in full illumination. Which meant he was not noticed until he reached the front row.

Only about a third of the orchestral chairs were taken. The actual rehearsal was still fifteen minutes from its start. As soon as Ian was noticed, those players who were already in place went silent.

Ian sketched a casual wave, slipped over a couple of seats, propped his guitars on the next chairs, and pulled out the two scores.

After a few long, silent minutes, the orchestra resumed its

routine. Scaled down a notch. He did not look up again, not even when arriving musicians passed his row, saw who was seated there, did a double take, then chattered their way on-stage.

Ian's appearance broke all the rules regarding the behavior of soloists. They were expected to give the conductor a full hour to bring the orchestra together. Sometimes much longer. They would then make a grand entrance. For a star to arrive early and work through the scores was unheard of.

His sheet music contained all the handwritten notes he had made while Saban had poured out his scornful instructions. They were clear enough. Ian did a mental run through places where his playing would need to be altered to suit the conductor's vision. He liked Saban's concepts and thought they added to the music's scope and flavor.

From time to time, he made a conscious effort to check his internal state. Ian was worried the acidic ashes might bite, fill him with the taste of defeat. But all he felt was calm. As if the absence of his customary fire was becoming the new norm. He knew it was probably strange, feeling a dual sense of relief and satisfaction over the lack. But given how it had been up to his departure from Annapolis, feeling nothing at all was a distinct improvement.

Ten minutes later, the conductor arrived.

Israel Saban was a squat rotund man in his midsixties. His remaining hair formed a silver-white wreath above his ears. He had been born in Romania, but his family had emigrated to Switzerland when he was still very young. He was a virtuoso pianist and had played with the Frankfurt and Zurich symphonies before dedicating himself fully to conducting. He currently served as senior conductor and concert master at La Scala in Milan.

He wore the pants to a nice suit, a crisp white shirt open at the neck, and carried a battered briefcase. He appeared from behind the right curtain and offered the orchestra a perfunctory greeting as he strode swiftly across the stage. He was in the process of opening his music when the lead flutist leaned forward and spoke softly. Saban froze in place, staring at the musician. The woman used her instrument to point in Ian's direction. Saban turned \slowly and spent a long moment staring.

Ian rose to his feet. "Good morning, Maestro."

"Mr. Hart."

"I wish to apologize for the uncertainty and distress caused by my behavior."

Saban took his time. He stepped away from his dais and moved closer to the stage's edge. He lifted his voice so the entire orchestra could hear. In his heavily accented English, he said, "I have been informed that you were actually not the culprit in this little drama."

Ian did not know what to say.

"In fact, what I've heard is your former manager signed contracts in your name, failed to inform you of these new commitments, stole your advances, and then fled the country. Is that not so?"

Ian remained silent.

"When you learned that we expected you to perform at the festival, you immediately contacted Ms. Kerkorian. Is that what actually happened, Mr. Hart?"

"Sir, Maestro, regardless of the specifics, I wish to apologize for the distress all this has caused."

The conductor regarded him a long moment, then said, "You will give us fifteen minutes and then join us, yes? Splendid." He turned to the orchestra. "Places, everyone. Let us do our best to shine for the artist, who has proven himself to be a true gentleman."

Two and a half hours later, Saban declared himself satisfied. He walked over and shook Ian's hand. As he escorted

Ian from the stage, some of the other musicians began applauding.

The sound was so unexpected, they both turned around. The strings sections clapped their bows upon the strings. The drummers and timpanists boomed a happy farewell. Someone shouted bravo.

Saban smiled at Ian and said, "We shall give the audience their money's worth, is what I am thinking." He shook Ian's hand a second time. "Until tonight."

CHAPTER 36

In the hour before dawn, Kari dreamed of her father.

Long before the image became clear, she felt his presence. When he finally appeared, she faced a beast of shadows and fire. A raging behemoth, a power that had always terrified her. He shouted her name. The force was enough to shrink her down, strip away her adulthood, leave her quivering and frightened and a child.

Then the music began. A faint melody, one without true form. Played by some stringed instrument, but not really. The music would one day become a song played by a man holding a guitar. In her dream, though, it was not yet fixed in its true and final form. Just a thought, really. Just a hope.

The unformed melody remained both soft and gentle, almost lost to the noise made by the raging beast. Even so, she heard it, and she knew she was safe. The melody and the man sheltered her in this hard moment.

She found herself able to take a giant step away from her father's wrath. Breathe herself back into full adult form. Still frightened, but safe. The word became part of the melody. *Safe.*

She woke up and instantly rose from her bed, padded across the overlarge bedroom, and entered the parlor. She knew Ian had left before she saw his note beside the coffee maker. The sunlit suite had a hollow, empty feel. She held the page with his words, and she caught a trace of his fragrance in the air. There in the silence she also caught the faintest hint of the half-formed melody.

She put on the coffee, used the bathroom, dressed, fed the kitten, and took her sketchbook from the suitcase. Then she went around opening all the sliding doors, reveling in the light and the humid heat, the sound of waves and laughter from down below. And the faint hint of Ian's melody still echoing through her world.

Kari became so caught up in her work, she did not hear the door to the suite open. She was unaware of Ian's presence until a pair of feet stepped into her field of vision. She jerked so hard she almost fell off her stool. Ian reached out a hand without taking his eyes off her sketches. Pages and pages scattered all over the parlor floor.

Ian made a slow circle. Another. Then, "Someone's been busy."

"How was your session?"

"Fine." He waved it aside. "Kari, this is incredible."

She followed his gaze. Standing up for the first time in hours required her to unkink her back. Sienna lay sprawled on the sunlit carpet between two sketches, cleaning her paws. From this higher perspective, it looked as though the kitten was stationed in the center of a paper whirlwind.

"When I get home, I'll tape them to the walls, try to sort through what I'm doing," Kari told him. "I think it's parts of maybe four paintings . . ."

He was already moving. "Back in a second."

The front door clicked shut. She was suddenly tempted to gather up everything. Sweep up the pages, hide them inside her suitcase. Do what she had always done whenever someone invaded her space.

Only Ian was not invading. And she *wanted* him to see. She *loved* the way he became so absorbed in her work. She shivered another time.

Then he was back. "I knew butlers were good for something." He held out a tape dispenser.

The lady butler stood in the doorway, smiling. Ian kicked off his shoes and walked around the parlor, careful not to step on Kari's sketches, taking down the suite's paintings, setting them on the floor, backs out.

That done, he asked the butler, "We're okay?"

"Oh, absolutely." She was studying the sketches, which came close to filling the center carpet. "I've already told security you're not making off with our goodies."

"Thanks so much."

She looked at Kari. "I've loved your work for years, Ms. Langham. It's nice to know you've been inspired here."

When the door shut, Ian said, "Tell me what goes where."

Kari stood where she was, marveling, "I've never let anyone see my sketches before. Not even Graham and Rafi. I was always afraid that if they didn't like what I'd done, I would never paint the canvas. At least that's what I told myself." She waved at Ian, the sketches, the closed front door. "Now . . ."

He waited with her through a long moment, the only sound Sienna's constant purr. Then, "How can I help?"

They used both side walls.

Kari stood in the center of the room while Ian did most of the actual work. He lifted the sketches one at a time, waited while she studied the work and decided where the particular concept was going to fit. Sienna padded around the pages still littering the floor, purring and generally getting in the way.

Five paintings gradually took shape, all of them tied in one way or another to her dream. Or her family. Or who she was now becoming. Perhaps. It was all too fresh and uncertain to actually name. Declarations needed to wait until after, when the canvases were complete, and she was able to look back and view this incredible time in hindsight.

Ian seemed genuinely happy, being part of her conceptual process. Twice she stepped over, pried the sketch and tape from his hands, insisted on being at the center of his arms. Sienna loved those moments most of all.

Forty-five minutes later, Ian confessed, "I'm beat. The practice, our flight, the night . . . It all feels like a weight I'm carrying."

"Go to bed."

"That's a futile gesture. I never sleep before live performances. Besides, I don't want to leave you." He paused. "Does that sound totally lame?"

"No, Ian. It sounds wonderful."

He walked into his bedroom, returned with two pillows and a blanket. Stretched out on the sofa, then stood back up and shifted the furniture around, moving the coffee table out of the way, positioning the sofa so he could see her and one wall. Kari stood where she was, watching him settle, smile her way.

The next time she looked over, Ian was fast asleep.

Sienna padded across the floor. She meowed twice, pacing around the sofa. When Ian did not respond, she climbed up by his feet. She walked his entire length, purring softly. Ian did not move. Sienna settled on the blanket, in the space where his hands did not quite meet his chin. Kari smiled, mostly because she was jealous of her kitten.

Half an hour later, Kari stopped working. Five sketches were still spread out over the bar's granite surface. Most of these she did not actually remember drawing. They were swift lines, the sort of churning half motions of unfinished dreams. Just the same, they held a special fascination for her, as if they challenged her to reach deeper, look further. She spaced these out over the bar's surface, then went into the master bedroom. She was scheduled to meet her managers in twenty minutes.

She showered and dressed in one of the Miramar outfits Rafi and Graham had helped her select. She liked how her newly styled hair could be blow-dried and shaped with her fingers. She did her face and eyes like the LA cosmetician had shown her. When she was done, she studied herself in the floor-length mirror. But it was not really her reflection that held her.

She reentered the parlor and stood there, staring down at the man asleep on the sofa. Sienna looked up, meowed quietly, then snuggled back and closed her eyes.

Kari had assumed Ian would be with her for all the interviews. Shielding her from the worst of it all by his presence and strength. She walked to the bar, opened the fridge, poured a glass of juice. Studied the mystery sketches and the man. Wondering if there was a connection she did not see.

There was a soft knock on her door. She set the glass on the dining table as she passed it. Opened the door, smiled at her two managers, accepted their compliments, said, "I'm ready."

Chapter 37

Ian woke to a golden light streaming through the windows. He rose to a seated position and sleepily surveyed the empty parlor. He did not notice the kitten until Sienna complained about being dumped on the floor.

He picked up the kitten, carried her into his bedroom, and deposited her on the bed. He checked the time, then stripped and entered the shower. The day was beyond astonishing. His professional life had held to a standing rule that shaped much of his routine.

Before any live performance, throughout his entire career, Ian had never slept either well or long. Solo guitar recitals, duets, concerts with full orchestras, it made no difference. Whenever he did manage to drift off, his dreams were dreadful. Broken strings, conductors shouting, audience booing and departing in mid-performance. Discovering he had forgotten his instrument or his pants. Worst of all were dreams where his first teacher, Monsieur Lachard, climbed onstage and publicly berated him for demolishing a perfectly good piece of music. Nervous exhaustion had simply become part of his playbook.

He took his time showering, reveling in the feeling of being so refreshed. Afterward, he wrapped a towel around his middle and stepped out onto his bedroom's balcony. Miami seemed at its most tropical in the late afternoon. A gentle sea breeze carried hints of blooming flowers and sounds of laughter from far below. Then he heard voices enter the parlor, and he retreated inside.

He dressed carefully, watched by a kitten who had taken up position on his pillow. She washed herself and observed him donning Kiki's finery. The festival director had thoughtfully supplied him with gold cuff links, two silk bow ties, black socks, and Italian slip-on loafers. All in his size. The lady was nothing if not comfortable with details.

Aromas of food wafted under his closed door as he knotted his tie, a talent he had mastered after much practice. Sienna mewed and padded across the bed toward him. She had smelled it, too.

Ian opened the connecting door and told the kitten, "I can't carry you. Not without showing up with cat hairs on my tux."

She sat on the bed's corner and mewed.

"It's not happening, Sienna. Use your own legs for once."

Kari said from the other room, "She's being shy because Graham and Rafi are here."

Ian told the kitten, "Normally, that would get you a pass. Not today."

Kari walked in. Ian needed only one look to declare, "Wow."

Graham's voice filtered in from the parlor. "Nothing beats the wow factor in my book."

Ian said, "You look stunning."

"It's by Fendi," Rafi called. "Soon as I pulled it from the rack, I knew she'd look fabulous."

Graham countered, "Actually, what you said was, she'd stop traffic. Which she did."

Rafi appeared in the doorway, looking so pleased he might as well have invented her. "Nobody does discreet elegance like Fendi. Single-breasted jacket with stand collar and fitted waistline. The sides and sleeves are silk, and the front is cashmere. Ditto for the skirt."

Kari appeared sheathed in a blue-gray cloud. One that clung to her form and accented everything while being conservative, an impossible combination.

Ian told her, "It's like it was made for you."

"Thank you, Ian."

Rafi said, "And look at you."

Kari smiled at him and asked, "Who are you, and what have you done with the man sharing my suite?"

"Oh, him. I forget."

She picked up the kitten, then used her free hand to pull Ian forward. "Let's eat."

Kari's two managers were dressed in gabardine slacks and jackets of woven silk. Rafi's outfit was blue and gray; Graham's autumnal russets. Graham stopped preparing a plate from the chafing dishes warming on the bar counter, inspected Ian, said, "Very nice indeed."

They dined on grilled flatiron chicken breasts and crisp vegetables and unadorned rice. No sauce, no bread, no butter. Lemonade or sparkling water to drink. Fresh fruit salad and green tea for dessert. Ian ate lightly and enjoyed every morsel. Through their meal, Sienna remained in Kari's lap, mostly hidden by the table's edge, mewing softly when it was time for more chicken. He thought the care they showed over his preconcert meal was a gift, and said so.

Graham said, "You're far from the first nervous Nellie we've coaxed and prodded toward a performance." He smiled at Kari. "Present company excepted."

"He doesn't look nervous to me," Rafi said.

"No," Kari agreed. "He looks divine."

"Speaking of performances," Ian said, "how did the interview go?"

"Kari stopped traffic, just like I said she would," Rafi replied.

Graham and Rafi turned their description of Kari's triumph into a pas de deux, a verbal ballet, embellishing her time in the publicity limelight until she shouted her protests and laughter. All of them pleased at how well she had done, how she still illuminated the moment.

For the first time in Ian's adult life, the time of his performance came too soon.

They swept through a hotel lobby crammed with two distinct groups. The Miami glitterati descended from limos and supercars and glided to the bar, while the international *turistas* clutched at children and gawked in clouds of salt and sunscreen. The manager spotted their approach and scurried over to escort them personally through the noisy crush. A phone camera flashed once, twice, three times as they passed. Ian actually enjoyed wondering whether they were taking pictures of him or Kari.

In the limo, Ian repeated what he had said upstairs. "You're in for a long wait."

"There's nothing like a bottle of champagne, wonderful companions, and a pretty bar to waste an hour," Graham said.

As they crossed the mainland bridge and joined the traffic streaming along Biscayne Boulevard, Ian said, "I forgot to call Connor."

"I spoke with him," Kari replied.

"You did?"

She nodded. "And Kiki."

"You spoke with the concert director?" Ian said.

"Twice. She's nice."

"Correction. She's nice to you. Where was I during all this?"

"Conked out on the sofa," Kari replied. She sat between him and Rafi. Graham was on the jump seat, smiling at everything and everyone. "Making all kinds of racket."

"I don't snore," Ian replied.

"Oh, really?"

"Never, never."

"Well, then, Sienna was sure loud for a beast her size."

"You're making this up."

"Whatever you say." To Graham, she said, "He honks like a goose, this one."

"Changing the subject," Ian said. "Why did Kiki call?"

"First time, just checking on you." Another smile. "Glad to hear you snoring away. She's assigned you two boxes so everybody can attend together."

"That's great."

"That's what I said. I asked if Connor and the others could also attend the gala. Her second call was to say that's in place."

"I should have handled that earlier," Graham said. "But I was too busy shouting at people."

It was then Ian made a decision and said, "You should be in the box tonight. With your friends."

She lost her smile. "You don't want me?"

Ian checked his immediate response, then replied, "I spoke with the stage manager. He'll set you up behind the side curtain. If you want."

"If *I* want?"

He nodded. "The stage is one of the largest I've ever played on. And it extends partly into the audience. You'll be almost as close in the box, if you'll sit by the railing."

"You know I will. Are you sure?"

"Yes. Plus, the rehearsal went well. Better than that."

She gave that a moment. "You'll be okay?"

"I really think I will."

And he was.

CHAPTER 38

The Arscht Center was actually two different structures situated on either side of Biscayne Boulevard and connected by a pedestrian bridge. The Knight Concert Hall was a true work of art, with its interior designed by world-renowned Artec Consultants. Every one of the twenty-two hundred seats had almost identical, nearly perfect acoustics. There were, in fact, no actual boxes in the traditional sense. Instead, the upper balconies extended all the way around both sides of the stage, like a pair of giant horseshoes set atop one another. Movable screens were used to provide a temporary air of exclusivity.

As Ian alighted from the limo, an usher appeared at the stage entrance. Ian bade the others farewell and allowed himself to be led past security and down the main corridor to the door bearing his name. The star's quarters were suitably grand. Ian shut the door, slipped off his jacket, and studied himself in the wall-sized mirror. Saban had instructed him to perform in his tux shirt and trousers, a method often used to isolate the soloist from the orchestra. Ian had left his instruments here after the practice. His primary guitar rested in its stand, and the backup was stationed in a cubby by the shower. Champagne glistened in an ice bucket, along with a glass container of fresh-pressed smoothie.

As he studied himself in the wall-sized mirror, Ian found it hard to consider what he felt was a mark of real change. That would come later, perhaps. When he had known more than one such instance of calm. Yes, of course, there was a taste of sadness. The lack of passion and fire remained in place. But in this moment of quiet readiness, Ian felt he actually might be doing what Indrid had said. Growing beyond his dark night.

The conductor or one of his aides had left the requisite tuning fork, identical to the one used by the lead violinist. He tuned both guitars, played through several of the sections where Israel Saban had insisted upon revisions. Drank a little water. Mostly, he savored the moment.

When the knock on his door came, he was ready.

CHAPTER 39

The Knight Concert Hall's stage stretched into the audience like a wooden hand. Ian loved the intense flavor such modern structures gave the music, both the nearly ideal acoustics and the audience's proximity. Many musicians, especially soloists, found it unnerving. He had heard them speak of how the audience was allowed to invade their private space. Ian could well understand the sentiment but did not agree.

He had always loved that first instant of coming into view onstage. All his senses were in overdrive as he entered from stage right. With a single step, he experienced a subtle shift to the air, from the compressed tension and dust and shadows backstage to the open volume and anticipation of a sold-out hall.

Tonight he thought the acoustics were particularly sharp. He had sensed the same element during rehearsal. It seemed as if the architects had designed the chamber for the benefit of the orchestra as well as the audience. He listened as the grand wash of applause echoed off distant walls. He stepped forward and bowed, the audience's faces like crinoline masks in the reflected light. He turned, acknowledged the conductor and symphonic orchestra, bowed once more to the solo violinist, settled on his chair, positioned his guitar, and waited.

The conductor raised his baton, checked his violinist, checked Ian, counted the time, and began.

Their first piece, Vivaldi's Concerto in D Major, was written in the 1730s and had originally been designed for the lute, two violins, and what historians believe was a harpsichord. There was some dispute over this, because according to the original score, the final line called for a *basso continuo*, an underlying series of lower notes that might also have been played by several instruments together. The lute was a stringed instrument with a bowed back, creating a soft and lovely sound. But its low volume meant other instruments had to be limited in number and played *piano, piano*. Quietly.

After the modern-day version of the guitar appeared in the mid-1800s, new renditions were made of the more popular Baroque concerts. Yet the problem remained the same: how to utilize the full breadth of a modern symphony and not drown out the solo guitar.

Their conductor, Israel Saban, did a masterful job of bringing out a rich and fluid sound, while carefully restraining the orchestra's overall volume. The result was a delicate and precise work of art, one that had the audience holding its breath to the very final note. Then . . .

Bravo!

When the applause finally quieted, the chamber remained filled with an electric joy. The audience was with them now, fully and utterly engaged. Joined together by a confidence that they were going to be not just entertained but also thrilled. The orchestra felt it as well. The players shared a smile with the conductor before he lifted his baton, received his nod from Ian, counted time, and began again.

The world of classical guitar underwent a seismic shift with this second piece. Ian had loved this music from the very first time he heard it, and the more he'd learned of the composer, the deeper this bond had grown. The composer, Joaquín Rodrigo, had been nearly blind since childhood. He had created his best work in the midst of the worst crisis Europe had ever known. This particular piece, the Concerto de Aranjuez, was written in 1939. The Spanish Civil War was at its bloody zenith. Rodrigo's work was to be premiered before the dictator Francisco Franco, who had recently signed a wartime pact with Adolf Hitler. Rodrigo's music was supposedly intended to celebrate the current political situation. It had to be grand in nature. It had to be relevant to Franco's aims of remaking Spain as a modern power. It had to bow to Spanish music and its historical roots. . . .

All this and not drown out the solo guitar.

There had been centuries of debate over how to include a guitar's resonant precision within a full orchestral arrangement. No guitar could be made loud enough to compete. If an entire orchestra ever struck a truly emphatic note, anything the guitar might do, no matter how lovely the sound, would be lost. The guitar, after all, was not a piano. There was no way to hammer out more volume. So the guitar was mainly restricted to chamber music. Played with just a few other instruments, never so many as to drown the poor fellow out. And so it remained until one remarkable man changed everything.

The nearly blind Rodrigo did not even play the guitar. His passion was piano. Yet with this concerto, Rodrigo utterly transformed the relationship between guitar and orchestra. Allowing the other instruments to perform along their full range, and yet enabling the guitar to stand out with its incredible beauty.

Rodrigo designed this concerto as a series of minuets. The orchestra and the guitar entered into a lyrical dance. When the guitar played, the orchestra almost held its breath. Then it leapt in volume, a huge crescendo that echoed and somehow even amplified what the guitar had to say. The effect was, in a word, magic. Crowds all over the world could not get enough of this remarkable new concept. A lyrical ballet featuring two completely different sounds.

The audience brought Ian and the conductor back five times. Even then, they refused to be seated. When Saban turned around and lifted the orchestra, Ian backed to one side and applauded with the hall. And there on the balcony's left side was Kari. She felt so close, it was as if she could reach across the hall and embrace him.

During the applause, two cellists and the timpanist drew out the grand piano that had been waiting patiently backstage. A discreet curve had been designed into the orchestra's second and third rows, unnoticed by the audience until the piano was fit into place.

During rehearsal, Saban had proposed that if indeed an encore was called for, he and Ian surprise the audience by performing a duet. The piece was another of Ian's favorites, the Sonatine in A Major, by Anton Diabelli. It was just the two of them now, Ian and the conductor, transforming the orchestra into another happy, perspiring, smiling audience.

Diabelli was a nineteenth-century composer and music publisher, and the first man to recognize Schubert's genius. Diabelli also conducted the first public performance of what became one of Schubert's most famous pieces, "Erlkönig." Two hundred years later, Segovia arranged this work for the guitar. And Segovia's rendition, a century or so after that, became the first serious piece Ian learned to play.

Diabelli's most famous compositions were his sonatinas, piano duets that constituted remarkable balancing acts between the guitar and a much more powerful piano. In these compositions, the instruments formed opposing forces that swirled and spun in magnetic tension.

Too soon it was over. For the first time in over a year, Ian greeted the music's conclusion with that impossible thought. *Too soon.*

As the audience rose to its feet and shouted its approval, Saban joined Ian at the front of the stage. He pretended to mock Ian's height and dragged him over to center stage. There he climbed onto the conductor's stubby dais, stood on his tiptoes, and drew Ian into a sweaty embrace.

CHAPTER 40

Back in his dressing room, Ian stripped and showered and dressed in the second shirt Kiki had thoughtfully supplied. The noise of a happy orchestra filtered through his closed door.

For almost a year now, these moments after the music and the applause, when the adrenaline rush faded and the lost hours of no sleep became an intolerable burden, these had been the hardest of all. The absence of his former passion and fire had formed a bitter, acrid taste that had rendered him physically ill, so nauseated he had often vomited. So he had banished everyone from his dressing room following concerts. Including his ex-manager. The thief.

He stood facing the wall-sized mirror now, his bow tie dangling from one hand. Ian's reflection served as a means to inspect his internal state. The emptiness was still there, but different. No ashes, no bitter flavor to the moment, no enduring agony over what was no more. Instead . . .

Ian could not name how he felt. Nor, he decided, was it necessary. Not tonight.

As he slipped the tie around his neck, there was a knock on the door. "Come in."

Israel Saban opened the door. "I am not disturbing?"

"Not at all, Maestro." When the conductor glanced around the empty room, Ian added, "I asked everyone to meet me upstairs."

"Ah. The quiet moment. So very necessary." He stepped inside. Saban wore a fresh shirt and formal wear, his hair gleaming damp. "A word?"

"Of course. Can I offer—"

"We are due upstairs. And I must fly to New York." He closed the door. "We should come together, you and I. There is a piece I have been arranging. Mozart's work begs for a Rodrigo-style dance. Full orchestra, the great booming noise, and in balance, the guitar. Mozart does the light ballet of sound better than anyone."

"Maestro, I don't know what to say." Ian fumbled for the stool, seated himself.

"But you will consider?" Saban looked genuinely worried. "I have been searching for the right partner. When I heard you tonight, I thought to myself, *Finally*."

Ian debated, then decided the man deserved honesty. "The reason my manager vanished was because I said I wanted to take a year off. I needed this. I've felt like the passion for music was gone."

"This need I very much understand." Saban leaned against the door. Crossed his arms. Frowned at the floor. "A year. Well, if I must wait a year, I must."

"Maestro . . . Thank you. So much."

"You will tell me if you become ready before the year is over?"

"Of course."

"Excellent." He opened the door. "In the meantime, you must come visit me in Milan. I will do my best to tempt you back into the arena. Good food, wonderful wine, beautiful Italian ladies, and my music. Who knows? Perhaps you may decide the year of freedom must wait."

After he departed, Ian remained where he was, staring at the empty space.

Chapter 41

The second building across the street contained a very large reception hall, which tonight was reserved for the music festival's opening night reception. Ian's companions made a happy crowd by the entrance, clustered out of the way so as not to block the incoming VIPs. Connor stood surrounded by his band, with the backup trio towering over them, their smiles competing with the chandeliers. Arthur and Danny and Megan and Graham and Rafi. And Kari. Ian slowed his movements for the cameras tracking his every step. He kissed Kari's cheek. Shook Connor's hand. Thanked them all for coming. Accepted their compliments in return. He leaned in close to Kari's ear and explained he needed to do a circuit alone. He then motioned Connor close, mostly so he could enjoy a moment of seeing the man's cloudless gaze. Asked him to serve as the lady's companion. Then together they entered the main room.

The din was so fierce he could not hear a word anyone said. Nor did he need to. The light in people's gazes, the smiles, the way they reached out. Wanting to connect. Wanting to share their own joy.

He did the requisite parade, twice meeting up with Saban so the journalists could shoot them together. He smiled for countless selfies.

Ian finally reached Kiki Kerkorian. The festival director stood on the bar's far side, allowing people to approach her as they would a ruling monarch. She lifted one cheek for him to kiss, drew him around so they could smile for the cameras, then pulled him back two paces into a storage alcove.

In the relative quiet, she said, "Israel is over the moon."

"I think it went well."

"It did more than that. Wherever did your encore come from?"

"Israel suggested it. I jumped at the idea."

"Your playing together was both intimate and sublime." She glanced behind him. "Quite a crowd you brought with you."

"They're playing with me tomorrow night."

"I thought as much. Who's the lovely lady?"

"Kariel. The artist."

She stepped forward, far enough to study the lady. "So that's really her."

"Come to the gala. I'll introduce you."

"Of course I'm coming." Her gaze tightened. "Are you two an item?"

"No comment."

"This night is just full of surprises."

Ian asked, "Would you do me a favor?"

"You've caught me in the disadvantage of a rare good mood. Ask away."

"Make a fuss over Connor at the gala. He's nervous. I want him to feel like he's really the star attraction tomorrow."

"You want me to charm a movie star. What a hard gig."

"Is that a yes?"

* * *

Three limos were waiting outside the main entrance, the drivers all holding illuminated signs bearing Kari's name, ready to sweep them off to the gala. The night carried an exquisite feel; Ian assumed Kari felt it as well from how she refused to stop smiling. Ian had so much he wanted to say, about the music and the performance and what it meant to have her there. But in the end it was enough to ride in silence, smiling at comments by Rafi and Graham, and hold her hand.

The Miami Beach Convention Center's second floor was home to the largest ballroom in Florida. The downstairs lobby and bar were all packed. The band played a good version of Latin salsa. The grand staircase leading up to the ballroom formed a curving velvet entry to the gala.

Ian's first conscious hint of something being seriously wrong was when an unseen man up ahead barked.

Instantly, Kari jerked her hand away from his and froze.

When Ian turned, he faced a frightened child. "What is it?"

The man's bark was clearer now. And his fury. "Get out of my way!"

Ian did not need to see Kari retreat down another step to understand. The description she had shared of her awful childhood, the terror she had felt toward that man and his rages . . .

He told a wide-eyed Rafi, "You and Graham take Kari back to the bar." He then turned to Connor and added, "Don't let anyone near her until you see me signal."

Connor nodded. "On it."

Ian turned to Megan and Danny and Arthur, but before he could speak, the attorney said, "Go, Ian. We'll keep Kari safe."

He nodded and faced the three ladies and the band. "I need your help."

"Honey, you just name it." Maxine.

Trish demanded, "Who's up there making all that racket?"

Ian waited until Kari was back down at the base of the stairs to reply, "Her father."

"Humph." Maxine again. "That man needs a lesson in how to shut up."

Ian started up the stairs. "I couldn't agree more."

As they neared the landing, Ian heard a woman say, "Sir, Mr. Langham, this event has been sold out for months—"

"I am *ordering* you to bring my *daughter* out here *right now.*"

"Sir, I'm trying to tell you, Ms. Langham hasn't arrived—"

"That's *absurd*. This is *her show.*"

"Even if she was here, we couldn't possibly allow—"

"Enough of that. Now get out of my way!"

Ian reached the landing as a middle-aged woman in a yellow-gold sheath turned to a younger aide and said, "Call security."

"That won't be necessary." Ian moved in tight, invading the man's space. "Come with me, please."

"I'm going nowhere but through those doors and into that—" His words were chopped short by two massive ladies grabbing his upper arms and lifting him partway off his feet.

Maxine asked, "Where do you want this garbage?"

Ian pointed to a single pair of double doors opposite the ballroom. "In there."

Maxine and Trish kept Maxwell Langham up just high enough for his tiptoes to touch the carpet. The band members formed a human wedge and shooed people out of their way. The foyer was jammed with gawking guests, many with phones raised.

Behind him, Lucinda demanded, "What should I do with this one?"

Ian shot a glance back to where a wide-eyed Justin hovered out of reach. Ian could see traces of Kari in the handsome middle-aged man. But his crystal gaze was blunted by an avaricious gleam. Traces of the rich life were already blurring the lines of his face and frame.

Ian said, "He can come, long as he behaves."

Kari was still recovering from the shock of hearing her father's almost incoherent rage as they approached the lobby bar.

"Wait."

Graham had a firm hold on her arm. Connor was keeping such a tight step behind her, he collided with her when she stopped. Rafi was almost at the bar when he realized they were not following him. Graham tugged. She tugged back. Harder. Freeing herself.

"I said *wait*, Graham."

Megan was the one who asked, "What is it?"

Kari's heart was racing so fast, she could take them all in with a single glance. Rafi scurrying back, Graham worried, Connor and Megan and Danny all ready to take on whomever she asked. Her thoughts and emotions made for a tumbling mix. Just the same, two thoughts formed with crystalline clarity.

The first was, *I am surrounded by friends. Connor, Megan, Danny, Arthur, Graham, Rafi.* All sharing the same stalwart concern.

The second thought she spoke aloud. "I need to go help Ian."

Megan served as their spokesperson. "Are you sure?"

"Yes." And she was. Scared, of course. Petrified, really. But certain just the same.

The velvet-clad stairs with their brass railings made a sweeping curve before arriving at the ballroom's foyer. This antechamber was huge, and over a hundred people milled about, chattering quietly. Music and laughter drifted through the doors leading to the ballroom. The way people kept shooting glances at the closed doors opposite told Kari where she would find them.

As she started across the foyer, a woman standing by the ballroom's entrance called, "Ms. Langham! Kariel!"

She spoke without breaking stride. "Graham, Rafi. Please."

Rafi told Kari, "We have this, dear. You go ahead."

As Kari moved away, the hostess called more loudly, "Please, you really must— "

Graham stepped directly in front of the hostess and snapped, "Not now."

As she approached the closed doors, Kari felt utterly split in two. Part of her, the old part, the hurting hidden child, was frantic to escape. Go back to playing the ghost. Find safety in remaining unseen.

The other part felt something else entirely. An overlay of calm rested upon her, so strong it muffled her nerves, as well-fitted as her Fendi. An invisible suit designed just for her, fashioned for this very moment.

The double doors were open just a crack, enough for Lucinda, one of the backup singers, to notice Kari's approach. The lady pushed the doors open farther, allowing them entry. The room held a vast oval table set for a formal dinner, encircled by two dozen chairs. Between the table and the doors, the other two backup singers held Kari's father.

The affray had rendered Max Langham almost incoherent with rage. He snarled at Ian, "You think you're in trouble now? I'll flay you alive. Your career is ruined— "

"That's enough." Hearing her father threaten Ian was precisely why Kari had come. Why the calm now felt like a sheath of crystalline ice. "Be quiet, Daddy."

Max Langham was a precisely elegant man, perfectly tanned, every hair in place, hand-tailored suit, twenty-thousand-dollar watch. Gaze like a gray blade. His nickname inside the agency was the Lion King, a title he bore with pride. He was not a tall man, standing only an inch or so higher than his daughter. Always in the past, his rage had seemed to magnify his presence, building him up to immense, mountainous proportions. Just like now. "*You*! How *dare*—"

The two ladies exchanged a nod over his head. They lifted Kari's father off his feet and shook him. Hard.

"Best hush up now," Maxine told him. "Else we'll dump you on the street, where you belong."

"Sis, you've got to—" Justin was halted by Lucinda, who showed him a pale palm, ready to strike.

In his rattled state Max Langham tried to push his spectacles back up his nose, but his hand trembled, so he only dumped them on the carpet.

Kari heard herself calmly say, "Listen to what Ian tells you, Daddy. He speaks for me."

"It seems pretty clear what's brought us to this point." Ian's voice sounded as calmly detached as her own. "You heard about this event through your son. Who agreed to let her managers display the painting Kari gave him. But only if he could attend tonight's gala."

"Get your hands *off*—"

The ladies shook him again. Not too hard or for very long. Just enough to shut him up.

Ian continued, as if the interruption had not happened. "You probably heard some of your LA biggies were coming. So you decided to show up. Play the kingmaker. Shake a few hands. Claim the spotlight. Like it belonged to you. Like you mattered."

Ian bent down, picked up Max's spectacles, slipped them into his jacket pocket. Ian patted the spot on Max's chest in time to his words. "That. Is. Not. Happening."

Ian gave it a long beat, then continued, "This is Kari's event. Not yours. She's the star. And she's not sharing the limelight with you. So now you and your son have two choices. You can apologize to your daughter, then join her entourage and follow her inside. Where you'll play the silent, happy father for as long as you care to stay." Ian glanced at her brother. "The same goes for you. Apologize. Behave."

He turned back to Max. "Either that or these ladies will escort the pair of you outside and inform security you are not welcome." He stepped back. Crossed his arms. "Which is it going to be?"

CHAPTER 42

Kari reentered the ballroom's foyer with all her friends. The hostess greeted her as warmly as she could manage, while shooting nervous glances back to where her father and brother stood between three ladies dressed in matching gowns and bolero jackets of midnight silk. Their sheer presence was enough to maintain a semblance of control over the pair.

Kari said, "My entourage has been expanded to include two more. Do I need to ask Ms. Kerkorian's help with this?"

The hostess did her best to offer the star a welcoming smile. "I'm sure that won't be necessary."

As Kari entered the ballroom, Ian slipped his hand into hers and murmured, "You're the star. Stars shine."

It was the right thing to say at precisely the moment she needed to hear it.

Kari faced the swirling throng, the flashing cameras, the applauding crowd. And did her very best to shine.

"Slow and easy does it," Ian said, and released her hand.

She began a slow forward procession, keeping abreast of

Ian, holding to a pace that brought one excited, smiling, chattering individual after another into her field of vision.

Danny and Megan and Arthur were loudly greeted by someone Kari did not need to see and were pulled away. The band drifted toward the trio playing excellent samba, while maintaining close tabs on Kari's relatives.

Then Kari realized Connor was keeping a discreet distance, two steps behind Ian. She decided that simply would not do. She reached out, grabbed his arm, and pulled him closer. From that point on, it was the three of them, Connor and Ian and her.

Kari handled the event with an impossible ease. Every now and then she became caught up in observing herself, this remarkable woman who flowed through the swirling clamor with something akin to grace.

She did not enjoy herself. Certainly not. This wasn't her world and never would be. At the same time, for the *first* time, she handled the stress and attention with ease.

As a result, she remained the calm center of a colorful, elegant, chattering whirlwind.

Camera flashes formed a constant backdrop to her slow procession. She was glad now for that afternoon's interviews, because the journalists had *wanted* her to stop and visit with her former works. They had asked question after question, eager to hear how she had come up with the idea, what it meant to her now. So many of the paintings on display had framed her development, helped her become who she was artistically. Some were famous because of the posters and cards. Others she had not seen in years. Having the opportunity to examine these old friends had made the interviews almost pleasant.

The gala could not have been more different. The noise was deafening. The people talked and laughed so loudly, the jazz band in the far corner was completely overwhelmed. One person after another came rushing up, shouting at Kari.

The words were almost always the same, at least, those she managed to hear. How thrilled they were to meet her. How exciting. Then came the story of how they first saw her work and were enraptured, or how they came to own one of her pieces, something. Time after time she was drawn over to stand with the owners in front of one painting after another while camera flashes illuminated the ballroom.

All the while, Kari remained shadowed by Ian and Connor.

Somewhere in the distance, her father and brother drifted. She couldn't actually tell whether they remained attached to her progress or if they had established a minor orbit of their own. But Ian knew. Every now and then he would step a bit farther away and exchange a silent communication with the ladies. His tight focus, the nods and waves in their direction, were enough to assure Kari that the two men continued to behave.

After what seemed like days, Ian leaned in close and said, "Anytime you're ready."

It was only then Kari realized how tired she had become. As if she had somehow managed to forcibly remove the rising tide of exhaustion from her mind. Now, though, she wanted nothing more than to find a quiet space. She said, "Let's leave."

Progress across the room was slow, but the trio of ladies joined them, and together they maintained a steady momentum toward the exit. As they were finally about to leave—the hosts had been thanked and the last two owners had been almost forcibly backed away—Kari realized there was one more task. One more item to make the night complete.

She patted Ian's arm, smiled at the two beaming hostesses, and walked back to where her father and brother tried as hard as possible to smile at something a gray-haired couple were saying.

Kari excused herself for interrupting, kissed her father's and brother's cheeks, ignored their astonishment, and said, "Thank you for coming."

Chapter 43

Kari woke to the sound of laughter.

She sat up in bed, dislodging Sienna from her covers. The kitten rolled upright, mewed, and waited for attention.

Kari smelled food. Then heard voices. Several of them.

She used the bathroom, dressed, slid open her bedroom doors, and demanded, "Why wasn't I invited to the party?"

"It just sort of happened." Ian was up and holding a chair. "Coffee?"

"I can get it." She padded barefoot to the bar, coming to terms with all the smiling faces. Graham and Rafi and Danny and Arthur and Megan and Connor and Maxine. Beside the coffee maker stretched an array of breakfast items in chafing dishes. "What time is it?"

"Almost ten." Ian waited until she had poured a mug and seated herself at the table to say, "We can move this crowd elsewhere if you like."

"No. Stay." The balcony doors were open, and the large parlor was awash in a tropical sea breeze. She was surprised by her own ease with these people. Crowds of any size normally sent her scurrying to another room. But here she was, not just seated at the table but now the center of attention. And comfortable with the fact.

"Would you like something to eat?" Ian asked her.

"Not just yet." She patted the empty seat next to hers. When Ian retook his place, she said, "Thank you for helping me with the gala. So much."

The smile diminished to just the faintest spark in his eyes. "I liked being there for you. So much."

Despite the crowd, despite everything, she took his hand. "I mean it."

"I know you do. And so do I. I like helping you. A lot."

"I could never have spoken to Daddy like you did. Never, never, never."

"You didn't need to. That was my job." He smiled across the table. "And only after the ladies made him listen."

Kari set down her mug, reached across the table. Maxine's hand was warm, strong, massive. "If there's anything I can ever do for you, all you need is to just ask."

"Well now." Maxine pointed to the multitude of sketches adorning both side walls. "I wouldn't mind one of these."

"Take whichever you want," Kari told her.

Rafi made round eyes. "Really?"

"Yes, really. Else I wouldn't have said."

"It's just . . . you never show your sketches. Much less give them away."

"Or let us sell them," Graham added. "Which we could."

Kari told Maxine, "Choose whichever you like. I'll sign it for you and have it framed."

"And here I thought this day couldn't get any better." Maxine rose to her feet and padded across the room. "As if singing in front of a thousand people doesn't already have me floating."

Connor groaned softly.

"More like double that number," Arthur said. "According to the dragon lady."

Connor groaned again.

"He means Kiki," Ian said.

"Kiki is nice," Kari said. "I like her."

That silenced the table.

Megan said, "Obviously, we're talking about two different people. Because the one I negotiated with breathed fire over the phone. My ear has blisters to prove it."

"This is also the lady whose lawyers barred me from my own house," Ian pointed out.

Kari shrugged. "I thought she was delightful."

"In that case," Megan said, "you can handle Ian's next contract."

"No thank you very much." To Ian, she said, "What contract is this?"

"Kiki wants me back next year." He shrugged. "I told her we needed to wait and see."

"Which she took as a negotiating ploy," Megan said. "Enter the fire and brimstone."

Danny asked Maxine, "Where are your friends?"

"They decided to hang around the hall. Supposedly they're helping Arthur's team do the mike check. But really they're just jazzing over where we'll be playing." She gently peeled a sketch off the wall. "Those girls, you wouldn't believe how much complaining I had to put up with. Getting them up before noon, I needed sirens and a forklift. Then they walk into that concert hall and just go crazy. If I wanted crazy, I could have stayed in California." She walked back over, holding one of Kari's pages. "Can I have this one?"

"Of course. It's my favorite."

"You're just saying that."

"Not at all. These are going to become my next paintings. That sketch you hold is the key to the first one I'll work on."

Maxine held it out. "Take it. Mail it to me when you're done."

"No need." Kari tapped her head. "The idea is already fixed in here."

Ian asked Danny, "Are you sure a half hour is enough for the sound check?"

Arthur was the one who responded. "Danny's guys are the best. Let them handle the preliminaries."

Danny told Connor, "So is your band, by the way. Working with pros makes our jobs so much easier."

Arthur went on, "Larry is setting up the piano for you, and Vanessa has a dab hand on the guitar. This afternoon we just need time to run through a couple of songs, check the voices, make sure it's all in balance."

Connor's response was cut off by a plaintive mewling from the other room.

Ian told Kari, "I'll get her. Have some breakfast."

"She won't come." Kari rose and stepped to the bar. "This smells wonderful."

Ian returned with a kitten purring in his arms. "Can she have a piece of bacon?"

"I don't believe this." Kari walked over, put her face within inches of the kitten. "You complain like a banshee when somebody comes to see me, but Ian can bring you into a crowd?"

"She's a girl kitten," Maxine said, smiling at Ian. "I'd let that man carry me anywhere."

Connor remained as he was, elbow planted on the table, forehead in his hand. "Why did I agree to let you move us to the main hall?"

"You didn't," Ian replied. "It sort of happened."

When Kari returned to her seat, the kitten padded her way across Ian's thigh and settled into Kari's lap. Ready to be fed.

It was only then Kari realized how tense Ian had become. He pretended calm. But his focus was so intent, Kari doubted he had even noticed the kitten's departure. He looked across the table at Connor and said, "I think we're facing a choice here. A decision. We can spend the next hour or so hashing over your worries. And we will all do just that, if you really think it will help."

"That's pretty cold," Connor said, lifting his head, staring across the table at Ian. "Hash through my worries."

"I have a different suggestion. Because I think we should spend this time talking about a very big what-if. But to do that, you have to be willing to stop seeing tonight's concert as this dark shadow looming over your world. Because it's not. And I think maybe you're ready to accept this. Hard as it may be."

The room was so silent, Kari could hear the laughter and the crashing waves from far below. The only motion around the table was the kitten's nuzzling her hand for another bite.

Ian went on, "Say we have a total smash hit tonight."

Connor shook his head. "What a terrifying thought."

"Say it happens. Say they bring us out after our encore. We can't just stand there empty handed."

Arthur said, "I've been wondering about that myself."

Danny said, "Why are we hearing about this only now?"

"It's not the place of the resident grump burger to go adding songs at the last minute."

"Say they call us back," Ian said, pressing. "The audience is on their feet. Shouting for us to give them something more."

"A farewell fling," Arthur said. "A tune designed to send them dancing out the exits."

Danny asked, "You have something in mind?"

"Yes." Ian named the song. And waited.

CHAPTER 44

In order to include this new song, they needed to head straight to the Knight Concert Hall. Work on it while the band were still there. Use it as an early sound check. Which meant Ian would miss the start of Kari's interview, maybe all of it. Which he hated. But when he told her, she simply smiled and handed him the kitten and left the room.

Ian asked Danny, "Did I say something wrong?"

Danny grinned. "Ask my attorney how high I am on the sensitivity scale."

"Sub-basement," Megan replied. "And to be clear, I can't be your attorney and your . . . you know."

"Sweetie pie, love of my life, stuff like that."

Megan smiled, "Okay, so maybe you can move one notch up from basement level."

Kari returned, carrying her sketch pad and case of pencils. "Everything's fine."

"I wanted to be there," Ian told her.

"Put a little more sorrow in that final note," Arthur said. "Whine it up a notch."

Kari opened the pencil case, told Arthur, "Hold still."

"You're talking to me?" The old man showed genuine horror. "Why on earth would you go wasting a perfectly good piece of paper?"

"Quiet now."

Kari sketched swiftly and twelve minutes later declared herself satisfied. She refused to let anyone see her work.

Ian hated leaving. But Danny and Arthur and Maxine were already on their feet. He nudged Connor, rose, set the kitten on his empty chair, and said, "Back to the salt mines."

The practice session went well. No fireworks, no great moment of delight for Ian or the band. Just the same, Connor did not overlay the sound check with his own shadows. Instead, he played the pro. Showed up, hit his lines, gave each note his best. Ian was fairly certain the others knew it was an act. But at least Connor was trying. At least the performer was there for them.

Still, everyone had their own nerves. It was actually Leo, the drummer, who pointed out, "We're never going to get this as tight as the others."

"We don't need to," Maxine replied. "Isn't that right, boss?"

Ian pretended the words were directed at Connor. When Connor remained silent, Ian pressed, "Tell them why the lady is right, *boss*."

Connor gave him a long look, then replied, "If they bring us back for a second encore, they won't be after perfection."

Arthur's soundboard was positioned on the middle balcony, near where Kari had sat. He called down, "They'll be wanting a reason to dance."

"They want fire, and that's exactly what the song delivers," Maxine said.

"Like the lady says," Arthur agreed.

Maxine gave him her full-wattage smile. "Come on down here, where I can hug you."

"I'm quite happy where I am, thank you very much," Arthur replied. "These old bones can't take much in the hug department anymore."

They broke up soon after. Ian shifted over to stand beside the piano, waited for the others to drift away, said, "You played really, really well."

Connor gave the massive arena a sweeping glance. "Long as I don't think about where we are, I'm able to keep my breakfast where it belongs."

Ian pretended to inspect the stage. "Wait until the lights go down and the sold-out crowd is applauding. Our little ensemble is going to feel like a tiny little morsel stuck on this huge wooden plate. Ready for the crowd to reach out and devour."

Connor looked pained. "You really want to watch me barf?"

"No barfing!" Arthur's voice drifted down. "Barfing on the instruments is verboten!"

"What I want," Ian said, "is for you to accept you're taking your own steps in the right direction."

"You're talking about what that lady said to you. Am I right?"

"Indrid. Yes. I am. We're also going back to what you told me in the studio. How I needed to understand the core issue." Ian rapped his knuckles on the piano's slanted top. "You are a great artist. Actor, singer, pianist. All of them. And this is your time. It's not about one performance. This is not a moment in the sun, and then you go back to Castaways and your life. You can do that—of course you can—if you want."

Connor was quiet so long, Ian feared the man would not respond. But in the end, he ran his hands lightly, soundlessly, over the keys and asked, "And if I want more?"

"Danny already has gold on tape from our performance at Castaways. Arthur said that, and I believe him. So should you. Now we're giving them more, and all this is going out as a parallel release to Danny's film. Which you and I also play on. This has the potential of relaunching your musical career. If you want."

Connor nodded slowly, with a creasing of his body at waist level. He closed the keyboard, tapped the cover, rose to his feet. "You sure have a way with a point."

"There's more. Danny's starting a new film. He's offered me the chance to do the score. I want you to partner with me." Ian smiled at the man's response. "It's a pleasure to rock your world. Now come on. Let's go watch Kari perform."

The Miami Beach Convention Center was two blocks off Dade Boulevard, the island extension of the Fifteenth Street Bridge. The traffic congealed three blocks away, so Ian texted Rafi and had the Uber drop them off. Before alighting, he made the same offer to Connor he had made back at the concert hall: return to the hotel, kick back, get his head ready for tonight. At the hall, Connor had said kicking back held no appeal whatsoever. This time, he simply started down the sidewalk, moving with the crowds.

The convention center was a massive beast of a structure, with over a million square feet of exhibition space. The line of cars waiting to enter the multistory car park was backed up almost to where the Uber had left them off. The huge front plaza held a dozen or so mobile food vans and a large band playing Caribbean calypso. Ian texted on their approach, and Rafi popped out of a side entrance and waved two VIP badges over his head. The man's grin literally split his face in two.

The noise was only slightly muted inside. The foyer was marble tiled and high ceilinged and so crammed with people Rafi had to move sideways through the milling crowd. A pair of beefy security were stationed at either side of a roped-off entrance marked EXHIBITORS. The guards carefully inspected the badges before they were granted entry.

The people surrounding Graham and Rafi's booth formed a solid, unmoving wall. Far up ahead, brilliant lights shone on Kari and a pair of interviewers. Ian caught a few words, but mostly just the flavor of Kari's voice. Rafi signaled for them to stay where they were, departed, and swiftly returned with a beefy woman in a red security jacket. She stepped forward and began firmly nudging viewers aside, making room for them to enter the fray.

It was easy enough to identify the major art critics. Better dressed, arms crossed, the only people in the front row not hanging on Kari's every word. Instead, they glowered in unison at the woman who was upending their authority. And their world.

Ian stood beside Graham as Kari and the interviewers stepped to the next canvas. The guitarist in the tempest of cinders and smoke. She smiled in Ian's direction, pointed, and said, "It's a portrait of that man."

The cameras and the journalists turned together, a movement that would have suited a chorus line. The interviewer to Kari's right squinted against the television lights and said, "That's Ian Hart."

"It is. Yes." Kari motioned for him to join them. When he didn't move, Rafi gently shoved him. Or maybe it was Connor.

As Ian stepped forward, Kari said, "The entertainment blogs have been feasting on his recent troubles. There's no need to go over all that again." She took a firm hold of his hand. "Is there?"

"No," Ian replied. "Definitely not."

Kari continued. "What impressed me so deeply is how Ian managed to hold on to what was most important in his life. Despite the fact that the world was doing its best to tear him apart. Separate the man from his music. That made a huge impact on me."

One of the journalists asked him something inane. He offered what he could, and after a few moments, their attention and the cameras' focus shifted away. Kari and the interviewers stepped to the next canvas, and Ian managed to return to where Rafi and Connor and Graham all greeted him with grins.

Ian waited until the audience's attention returned to Kari, then muttered, "I'd murder somebody if I could figure out who pushed me forward."

Rafi made a process of inspecting him. "I don't see any gaping wounds."

Ian stood between Kari's two managers and watched her step up to yet another painting, describe the process that had brought her to this point.

Graham said softly, "I'm truly glad you two found each other."

"As am I. Truly."

"Kari has discovered things through you I never thought she'd manage." A pause. Then, "I worry about her, you know. So much."

Ian glanced over. Saw the man struggled for control. "She is beyond lucky to have you two as friends."

Graham's swallow was audible. "She's the sister I never had. And Rafi's."

Kari stepped to the next and final painting. The relief was clear on her face as she launched into yet another quietly spoken description.

Ian said, "When she's done here, why don't we see if she'd like to stroll around the place?"

Graham glanced over. "The four of us? Together?"

Ian pointed to where Connor stood whispering with Rafi. "Five."

"Ian Hart. Connor Larkin. Kariel. Touring the exhibition hall."

"With her pals."

Graham chuckled. "Prepare to be mobbed."

CHAPTER 45

Ninety minutes before they were due to go on, they gathered in the orchestral ready room, the only chamber large enough to hold them all. Everyone came. Kari and Rafi and Graham, the gentlemen in tuxes tonight, Kari in another amazing Fendi design of russet and gold and gray. Danny and Megan and Arthur. The three ladies. Connor's band.

They gathered by a long table holding food and drink and sang their way through the second encore. A straight run-through, pushing each other, the ladies marking time with the band. Ian on guitar, Connor thumping out the melody on the battered upright they had pulled from the far corner. Danny and Megan and Kari and Rafi and Graham clapping time. And Arthur. The old man's features stretched in a smile he seemed unable to let go of, hard as he tried.

When they were done, Maxine said, "Well, all right."

"If that doesn't get them on their feet, they're ready for the cemetery," Arthur said. "Given as how this is Miami, that might actually be the case."

"It's still rough around the edges," Connor said. "But good."

"Better than that," Danny said. "A lot better."

Arthur pretended to inspect the backup trio. They were decked out in tuxedo-style full-length dresses and sparkled from wrist to neckline to ankles. "I didn't know there were that many sequins on the entire globe."

"That does it," Maxine said, extending her arms. "Come here, old man."

"No."

But Trish moved in behind him and sort of bounced him in Maxine's direction. She embraced him hard enough to earn a soft *whoof*.

Arthur adjusted his spectacles and groused, "Careful with the antiques."

Maxine made a show of dusting him off. "If you were only ten years younger."

Arthur actually laughed. A rusty sound. "Try seventy."

Danny said, "Say we have a hit tonight. The audience likes you—"

"Correction." This from Maxine. "They're gonna *love* us."

Danny nodded. "Say it happens. What are we going to read tomorrow?"

Ian had been hoping for something like this. A reason to tell them, "At least some critics will come out against us. They've been looking for another reason to put me down, and they'll see this as a perfect excuse. They'll call it mediocre renditions of tired music that has been done better by more talented groups. They'll claim some of our songs should have been shelved long ago."

"Stop holding back," Connor said. "Tell us what you really think."

"You need to understand, what they say here isn't the issue," Ian noted.

"It isn't?"

"No, Connor. It's not." Ian pointed to the door leading to the main hall. "The public has the final say. That's what matters most. And with the public, we have two opportunities. The first is the concert. And it's important, don't get me wrong. But even more important is what happens with Danny's documentary. If it and the film are hits . . ."

"What?"

Ian reached for Kari's hand. "This afternoon, watching Kari perform, I saw something big happening."

Graham told her, "You were wonderful, by the way."

Ian pressed on. "What I mean is, I watched the critics. Their bitter disapproval. Kari represents a direction the audience is happily willing to take. Their enthusiasm relegates the critics and their dark ways to the past. It's happened before, and it will happen again. Who knows? It might even be happening with us. Our job is to wow the audience, go home, and get ready for tomorrow."

Connor said, "I think you should tell them what you told me about tomorrow's new opportunity."

"Really?"

He nodded. "Invite them along for the ride. But that's your call. You're the boss."

Arthur laughed a second time.

Connor smiled at the old man. "Somebody has to be. Right, neighbor?"

Ian asked Danny, "Are you okay with this?"

"That's the sort of decision I leave to my music producer."

Arthur added, "He means you, mate."

So Ian told them. About the new film's soundtrack. Inviting them all along for the ride.

While they were still recovering, there was a knock on the door. "Five minutes."

Ian reached for his guitar. "Okay. Everybody gather round. It's fever time."

And it was just that.

CHAPTER 46

The first two songs, Ian thought the group played almost mechanically. Which was hardly a surprise. None of them had ever performed before an audience of this size. The concert hall was jammed. He thought he saw people standing behind the back row. Certainly the balcony's upper tiers held more people than they should. It was a well-heeled older crowd, which, given their music, was to be expected. But the audience responded warmly to both songs, applauding far longer than was simply polite. People whistling. People shouting and calling between the songs. People with them.

On the third song, Winwood's "Higher Love," the band started to fire in sync.

On the fourth song, it all came together. The night, the band, the music, the audience.

Their rendition started with Ian playing by himself. Which was Danny's idea. The lighting was dimmed to where there was one single spot tight upon his guitar's heart. He found himself thinking about Kari's painting as he played.

He could see nothing of the audience at this point, which helped him fly. He thought back to other concerts. The heady electric rush of performing live, the sense that here was the point where his life came together. He had not felt that way in over a year.

Now he tasted something new. The old flame was dampened, but quietly potent just the same. He played and felt his music becoming a tapestry. Drawing the band together. Lifting them all up. Giving them the chance to become something more than they ever would be alone.

He had no idea how long he played, riffing on one concept after another. But they all seemed to sense when it was time. Which was the only sign he needed to know the others felt it, as well.

Leo brushed the snare, a quick rush of intro, and then Larry came in on the alto sax. A drifting hint of melody, a silken cord tying Ian's riffs together. Getting them ready for when Connor began singing . . .

Round like a circle in a spiral, like a wheel within a wheel . . .

"The Windmills of Your Mind" was originally written by French composer Michel Legrand. The English translation was introduced in the original version of the film *The Thomas Crown Affair*, which won the Academy Award for best original song. It was revised and sung by many others, including Andy Williams, Jose Feliciano, Dusty Springfield, and Sting.

Slowly, slowly, the single spot expanded to include a second light on Connor, another on Larry, and then . . .

Connor began playing, alternating with Ian, a dance almost classical in its alternating melody.

The ladies took up the lyrics then. Three voices almost weeping with the labor of sharing the song's message. *Like a door that keeps revolving in a half-forgotten dream.*

Connor joined in, for two lines only. Then they began alternating. One line by each singer. On and on, building in power and volume until . . .

The lights cut off entirely. Then four spots. Four faces. Singing together, repeating those first amazing lines.

Back to the single spot on Ian's guitar. A quick riff, a melodic farewell.

The applause was thunderous.

From that point on, they remained a single tight unit. Bonded at the level of heart and bone and sinew. Communicating with each breath. A single glance, a lifting of his guitar, a subtle shift in Connor's voice. They all heard and understood and responded.

What was more, the audience was with them, as well. Their response to each song became increasingly potent, a rising crescendo of applause and cheers.

They finished the set, returned, played their encore. Stepped to stage right. Stood as a unit. Accepted towels from the stage attendants. Wiped the sweat. Listened to the audience. No smiles. Not a single word between them. It was too intense a moment for words.

Connor and Ian walked back onstage to rapturous applause. They took their places and waited until the crowd went quiet. Connor ran through a bluesy riff. A quick punctuation, no real suggestion of where they might wind up. Only while he was still playing, Ian repeated it back to him. Connor launched into another, different riff while Ian was still playing. Ian shot it back. Connor picked up the pace and gave him another. Ian met him stride for stride. On and on they went, pushing each other to furious levels. Fire and tempo, but controlled.

To the audience, it probably looked like Ian simply lifted his guitar in punctuation to another riff. But the band was ready and walked onstage and took up positions and waited while the audience roared their version of a "Welcome back."

When the hall went quiet, the women sang a soft dirge. Slow and full of knowing remorse.

Feelin' better now that we're through, feelin' better 'cause I'm over you.

"You're No Good" was written by Clint Ballard Jr. and first recorded by Dee Dee Warwick in 1963. In the early seventies, Linda Ronstadt began performing the song live while she was the opening act for Neil Young. Then in 1974 Ronstadt was working on tunes that eventually became her *Heart Like a Wheel* album, and at the last minute they decided to record a studio version of "You're No Good." It was a throwaway song, a last-minute choice meant to complete the album, just fill an empty space. Seven months after the album's release, the song hit number one on the Billboard charts. It remained there so long, *Rolling Stone* magazine complained it had been nailed in place.

The ladies completed their mournful first stanza, and Connor took up the vocals. Ian and the sax and the brushes on the drums were soft little punctuations to his almost conversational rendition of that amazing verse.

I learned my lesson, it left a scar, now I see how you really are . . .

When they arrived at the chorus, they went from soft and slow and melodic to . . .

Fire.

What attracted Ian most to Ronstadt's version of the song was how the lady could go from sweetly gentle and intensely feminine to full-on rage. And all without losing control of her vocals.

In his late-night reflection, it had struck Ian that Connor had the same ability. If only they could find a song that released his full potential.

Baby, you're no good.

Connor did not sing the words. He roared. The force of his accusation literally propelled him from the piano stool.

The audience did what they had all hoped. The aisles and the open space surrounding the stage became filled with people, most of whom had probably not danced at a live performance in years. Decades even. Ian and Vanessa exchanged a goofy smile, watching the spectacle of blue-haired aristos on their feet and shrieking the next refrain back at them. *You're no good.*

The next verse was remarkable in terms of how Connor resumed his conversational tone, which was necessary, because he confessed that he himself had dumped a good and gentle woman. So he could take up with the bad lady. And he himself was no good. And maybe he deserved what he had been given. Only now the three ladies were shrieking with the audience. Pointing at Connor and singing their accusations at full volume, musically beside themselves with rage over his behavior. *You're no good.*

Then they were sharing the blame. Four voices that alternated here, joined there, all of them filled with remorse over all the terrible mistakes that had brought them to this point. Where they could arrive at the last refrain. The instruments silent except for Ian's furious final solo, while the four singers pointed at each other. All of them guilty of the worst crime of all. Breaking a good person's heart. *You're no good.*

They hit the final note. The lights came on full.

Bedlam.

They stepped around the instruments. Walked to the front of the stage and linked arms together. The audience was all around them here. The applause a human thunderstorm.

Ian looked up, found Kari standing by the balcony's railing. And suddenly it was just them. The two of them joined by something more powerful than the finale. A moment that was uniquely theirs. A promise that did not need to be spoken, because they both knew it was there and true. A tomorrow defined by what they now shared.